WRECKER OF ENGINES

Cobalt City Universe Stories

by DAWN VOGEL

Sparx and Arrows
2016, DefCon One Publishing

Coast to Coast Stars
2020, DefCon One Publishing

Sure Shot in Las Capas: The Case of the Absent Star
2021, DefCon One Publishing

Avatar of Freya
2022, DefCon One Publishing

Brother's Keeper
2023, DefCon One Publishing

by JEREMY ZIMMERMAN

Kensei
originally published as a part of *Cobalt City Rookies*, 2012, Timid Pirate Publishing; reprinted 2014, DefCon One Publishing

The Love of Danger
2015, DefCon One Publishing

The Devil, You Say
2015, DefCon One Publishing

Snowflake War Journal
2016, DefCon One Publishing

Kensei Tales: Offensive Driving
2016, DefCon One Publishing

Kensei Tales: It's the Great Yule Cat, Jamie Hattori
2016, DefCon One Publishing

Kensei Tales: Live and In Concert
2017, DefCon One Publishing

Kensei Tales: Unorthodoxy
2017, DefCon One Publishing

Cobalt City Anthologies

Cobalt City Christmas
2009, Timid Pirate Publishing

Cobalt City Timeslip
2010, Timid Pirate Publishing

Cobalt City Dark Carnival
2011, Timid Pirate Publishing

Cobalt City Double Feature
2012, Timid Pirate Publishing, featuring *Eye for an Eye* by Erik Scott de Bie and *The Place Between* by Minerva Zimmerman

Cobalt City Rookies
2012, Timid Pirate Publishing, featuring *Tatterdemalion* by Nikki Burns, *Wrecker of Engines* by Rosemary Jones, and *Kensei* by Jeremy Zimmerman

Cobalt City Christmas: Christmas Harder
2016, DefCon One Publishing

Cobalt City Dragonstorm
2021, DefCon One Publishing

WRECKER OF ENGINES

TALES OF COBALT CITY'S ADVENTURERS CLUB

BY ROSEMARY JONES

For Dawn, Janay, and Rosie:
You made this book beautiful in so many ways.

CONTENTS

COBALT CITY 1898

.---- ---.. ----. ---..

EXTRA! EXTRA!
ELECTRIC GIRL DISAPPEARS!

THE LIGHTNING-POWERED BATTERY OF HER TWO-WHEELER buzzed with the urgency of a thousand bees. Lizzie Blythe leaned over her iron handlebars and shot the bike under the startled nose of a dray horse. The shouts of the carter followed her down the street.

The rising sun tinted the windowpanes pale pink as she sped past the Parkside mansions. Luckily, the streets were empty except for the iceman, the dairy cart, and a few other odd tradesmen making their way to the back entrances of Cobalt City's great mansions.

Heaving on the stiff handlebars, Lizzie rounded the corner. Behind her, she heard the startled squeak of a housemaid who had opened a casement window to shake out her feather duster.

"My stars! It's one of those science heroes," the maid exclaimed.

Onward Lizzie raced, ignoring the shouts and cries behind her, desperate to reach her destination. Already the wood and leather grips beneath her clutching fingers felt more insubstantial. The clack of her wheels sounded a litany of "if only... if only ..." If only she was rushing to the office with a scoop, ready to pound her typewriting machine with the headlines of the day.

In her head, she could see her friend Charlie ripping the copy from her hand and running for the door, yelling as he went. Then the page falling into shape as the nimble-fingered pressmen slung the metal letters into place. Almost, she could hear the comforting roar of the giant presses as the ink rained onto the paper and the news went out into the world.

But the headlines rattling through her head broke her heart. Cobalt City's mighty heroes conquered. The Six-Shooter, Appleseed Angus, the Lady Detective, the Steel Suffragette, and more. All vanished into the villain's calculating engine.

Even Pharaoh's Ghost had disappeared during the last conflagration. Lizzie wondered if the mysterious magician still lived. She had thought him indestructible. But then, she once considered herself a fair match for any evil that rose in Cobalt City. And she had lost that bet at dawn.

With the same grim determination that drove her across the rooftop of the madhouse in pursuit of Burning Bertha, she gritted her teeth and rode on. She snagged that story. She captured the villainess and proved herself to the others. Now she must survive, if only to honor their friendship and trust in her. There was still time, a few precious minutes. She was almost there. The place where the Steel Suffragette had promised her safety.

The enormous oak door already stood open at the top of the steps. The butler waved her forward. "Hurry, miss, hurry!"

Lizzie leaped from her bike and ran. Even as she sprinted forward, each footstep sounded fainter and fainter as she faded from the world.

THE ADVENTURERS CLUB
OPENS ITS DOORS

THE RIBBONS HAD BEEN CUT, THE CHAMPAGNE DRUNK, AND
the reporters sated by a truly sumptuous feast. Joanne Morrison
Quincy DeCamp even descended via her electric elevator car to
say a few words of welcome to the assembled throng. She promised them that long after she was gone, her home would remain
a place where adventurers of all types would be welcome. The
explorers of lost cities, the climbers of mountains, the hunters of
big game, the raiders of ancient tombs, and those who sought to
build steam-powered rockets to take them to the moon would find
sanctuary in her stately mansion. "My libraries are your libraries.
My laboratories and electrical marvels are yours," she said, in a
voice remarkably strong for a woman nearing the century mark.
"Use them well. The world is at peace. The time has come for us
to explore the limits of our abilities and beyond. Let us usher in
a new age of heroes for the twentieth century in honor of the science heroes and the wonders lost to us. Let this be an age when
ordinary men and women prove themselves to be adventurers in
the best sense of the word. Make this home, this club, be a place
of meeting, of inspiration, and of rest when needed."

After the rounds of applause, remarkably strong given the
amount of drink and food already consumed and longing glances
that some gave the overstuffed couches filling the library on the

first floor, DeCamp left the room, leaning heavily on the arm of her butler Tidwell.

In her own chambers, once more settled in her favorite armchair, DeCamp viewed the single glass of port placed at her elbow with a look of heavy disfavor. "There was a time when you would have brought me the entire bottle and a beef steak to go with it."

"Yes, ma'am." Tidwell moved silently around the room, tidying an already overly tidy space. A spare, dark-haired man with a somewhat cadaverous cast to his face, he had been in service to DeCamp for many decades.

"Tidwell," said DeCamp, "I must tell you that of all the many injustices I have encountered in a long and adventurous life, the greatest of all is growing old. It is simply salt in the wound that you do not change."

"Understood, ma'am." Tidwell came to a full halt in front of DeCamp's chair. "Should I age?"

"Why bother? I will be gone soon. There must be someone to look after our guests. You appear exactly the right age to assert some authority over the younger ones while failing to offend the older. I predict in time they will simply accept you as a fixture, much like the elevator or the telegraph machine in the basement."

"Very good, ma'am. I will try to be as unobtrusive and as helpful a fixture as possible."

DeCamp nodded and sipped her port. Above the mantel, the portrait of a woman, the woman she once loved, looked down on her. The actress Sybil Campbell, dressed in silver armor and mounted on a white charger. The painter had portrayed her in her greatest role, as the young Joan of Arc leading the armies of France. DeCamp wondered if any remembered that the Steel Suffragette had worn the same armor when combatting villains in the city's streets. She had given her considerable resources to support the Steel Suffragette's campaigns against the injustices of inequality and servitude suffered by so many. But her wealth had not been enough to save Sybil. Still, she would do what she could to preserve the Steel Suffragette's legacy and guard the last slender hope that her greatest protégé, the Electric Girl, would return to Cobalt City.

"You know what you must do, Tidwell," she reminded her servant.

"Certainly, ma'am."

After DeCamp fell asleep in her chair, Tidwell placed a well-worn wool blanket across the old woman's knees. "Do not worry," he said softly, so as not to disturb but only guide whatever dream caused the restless stirring of DeCamp's hands. "I will protect this house. I will protect her. I will guard as I was meant to guard all who dwell within, even as the century advances."

In the basement, a calculating machine ticked away the hours, quietly humming to itself. A small ribbon of paper spooled out the headlines of the day, and the most recent headline read "THE ADVENTURERS CLUB OPENS ITS DOORS."

CALCULATIONS OF DESTRUCTION

KIMBALL WILDE EYED THE GIANT GLOBE IN THE CORNER OF the library. Sitting on a large leather chair that left his five-year-old legs dangling above a multicolored carpet of *Arabian Nights* splendor, he calculated how he could traverse over the back of the chair, slither under the oak table, and, crawling on his belly, rise to spin the globe like the heroes of his favorite stories. A wiggle put one toe upon the leather cushion, ready to begin his adventure.

"Kimball, be still," said his father without turning around.

Kimball restrained a sigh. The great adventure of crossing an ocean with his father and a seasick nanny had lost some luster since they had landed in Cobalt City. Despite all the reported dangers, they had not even sighted a single U-Boat in the days on the water. Then, after one or two experiments in the hotel's fascinating boiler room, Kimball had either been confined to quarters or escorted under fatherly guard on all excursions. Worse, with Nanny Singh still incapacitated, his austere parent had developed the ability to know exactly what Kimball was planning at any minute.

The butler returned to the library. "All the guests are assembled, Mr. Wilde."

"Thank you, Tidwell," said Kimball's father. "This should

not take long. We greatly appreciate the use of the Adventurers Club."

"Anything to help bring this war to an end."

"Quite." His father turned his attention to Kimball once more. "No running like Akeela, no jumping like Mowgli, no slithering like Ka, no stalking like Bagheera, nor removal of books from the shelves to climb the shelves like a bandar log."

"Yes, sir." Kimball sighed, but then brightened when he realized that the spinning of globes had not been included on his father's list. Nor anything that would prevent him from delving into the mantle clock's fascinating cogs and wheels. A quick perusal of the mantle clock and he began calculations on how swiftly he could climb the mantle, remove the clock's gears, and construct a mechanical man to march across the library and spin the globe so large and temptingly still in the corner.

"Also, no spinning of globes and no dismantling of anything," added his father.

"Yes, sir," Kimball repeated, now thoroughly crushed.

"Perhaps I could take the boy," offered the butler. "We have a very unusual calculating machine in the basement. He may find it of interest."

Mr. Wilde glanced at the butler. Kimball saw a rare look of uncertainty cross his father's narrow face. "Were you with Mrs. DeCamp? I seem to remember seeing you here when my wife and I visited."

"The year before the Adventurers Club was established. I had the pleasure of serving Mrs. DeCamp then and staying on," answered the butler. "She always enjoyed her niece's company."

"But not the English adventurer who her niece married?" A brief grin lightened his father's face. Unusual for any discussion regarding his much-mourned mother, and enough to distract Kimball.

"Mrs. DeCamp had very strong views concerning men, especially her husbands," said the butler.

"I do recall that amused my wife considerably," said his father. "Very well, take Kimball to see the calculating machine. And Kimball, remember, no dismantling of any engine, no matter how great or how small."

"Certainly, father," answered Kimball, as he slid off the chair and onto the carpet that gave an unexpected ripple under his feet. "I will be careful and promise not to wreck anything."

He followed the butler down the long hallway. When they entered the elevator and pulled the cage door shut with a satisfying bang, the butler said the most thrilling thing Kimball had heard in a very long time. "Would you like to pull the handle?"

With complete concentration, Kimball manipulated the handle to the down position and felt the elevator respond with a satisfying bump. Their descent took only seconds, but a little more manipulation of the handle was needed to level the elevator with the outer floor.

"Quite good, Master Kimball," said the butler.

Kimball smiled as they moved down another long hallway toward the fascinating sounds of clicks, clangs, and the faint ringing of a bell. When they entered the room from which the noise emitted, the butler moved around the perimeter, switching on electric lights. Fascinated by all he saw, Kimball stood, finally still, in the center of a room filled with more machinery than even the hotel's boiler room.

Brass levers and scrollwork decorated gleaming wooden boxes topped with mysterious tubes made of molded glass. A faint buzzing sound came from the flickering electric bulbs. Cloth-covered cords crisscrossed the walls, while glass pneumatic tubes disappeared into the ceiling. A great row of metal boxes filled the far wall. Adorned with dials, gauges, and interesting slits in the front, the very air crackled with electricity. With a thrill, Kimball observed an arc of blue light transfer from one metal globe to another located on top of the machine.

"What is it?" he asked.

"A telegraph receiver, for starters. But much modified by its inventor. It was built along the principles of Babbage's Analytical Engine."

"But it has been electrified." Kimball walked closer for a look.

"Oh, yes. The gentleman who invented it was convinced electricity would allow him to gain control over the entire city. This invention helped him stay informed and communicate his plans to his minions. Today, it allows us to speak to the entire city." Tidwell pointed at the telegraph key and other items gathered in front of the machine. "To the world. To learn of new heroes as they rise…and as they fall. It is an oracle of sorts. One designed for the coming years."

"It's wonderful." Kimball paced the length of the machine and back. It was the most beautiful thing Kimball had ever seen, a machine of such gorgeous complexity that it should last forever, to amaze others as it bewitched him. "Although given the electrification, it is more like Babbage's designs for the Difference Engine."

Tidwell blinked. "You seem very well informed."

"I am nearly six, and I learned to read from Nanny when I was four. Since then, I have studied machines." Largely he read so he could understand the easiest way to dismantle mechanical devices. Looking at this machine, his fingers fairly itched for a wrench and a screwdriver.

The machine made a clicking and whirring noise. A small white card dropped out of a slot in the front, falling into a wire basket placed to catch it before the card hit the floor.

Tidwell reached into the basket and examined the card. "For you, sir," he said with a slight bow, handing the slip of paper to the mystified Kimball.

"**WELCOME TO THE ADVENTURERS CLUB,**" Kimball read aloud and added with some delight, "**MR. KIMBALL WILDE.**" With wide eyes, he looked up at Tidwell. "How did the machine know my name?"

Tidwell smiled. "I sent a message just before I invited you to tour this room."

"A message?"

"We have a telegraph key in the hallway. As well as a telephone. In fact, we recently installed phones in all the guest rooms. There is a full switchboard on the ground floor. I informed her I was bringing a guest."

Kimball had noticed the switchboard at their hotel in Cobalt City but had been firmly forbidden by his father from even asking for a demonstration from the friendly switchboard ladies. The laughing women had expressed some disappointment, as Kimball had made a point of being on his "best behavior," as Nanny called it, prior to being apprehended by his father in the switchboard room.

"May I see the switchboard?" Kimball asked, wondering if Tidwell would let him connect a call or two.

"Certainly. But would you like to ask her any questions before we return upstairs?" Tidwell waved at the calculating machine and a few lights flashed in a friendly fashion on its top.

"What type of questions? Mathematical equations?" Kimball knew Babbage's various engines had been designed for complex calculations.

"You may ask anything you wish." Tidwell indicated a tele-graph key on a small box in the center of the room. "We use that to communicate with her, although I am working on adapting a phone so we can speak directly with each other."

Kimball was glad the machine could do more than mathe-matical equations. There was so much he wanted to know, so much that could not be answered by the simple addition or sub-traction of numbers. When contemplating these questions, he found himself unusually at a loss for words. Then, quite clearly, a question came to him.

Kimball stepped forward and, without waiting for Tidwell, began tapping out his question on the telegraph key. While on the ship crossing the Atlantic, he had spent many hours in the communications room, watching, listening, and learning how to manipulate such a key. With a delicate precision that would have astounded his father, he tapped out his question.

The machine's electric bulbs brightened. Various chimes rang and the arrows on a few meters quivered, then shifted from side to side. A whirring sound and click preceded the dropping of a white card into a small brass tray.

Tidwell stepped forward, retrieved the card, and handed it to Kimball.

The boy read it and then looked puzzled at the butler. "'BEWARE THE MECHANICAL MAN.' I don't understand."

"What question did you ask?"

Kimball blushed slightly. "How I could help my father win the war. It's so important to him."

"Then this advice should help you do that," said Tidwell. But how or why that particular answer had been dropped into the tray, he could not explain. "She has her informants, but the energy to speak more fully eludes her. We are working on improvements."

Kimball, however, found this information even more mysti-
fying than the white card he had slipped into his pocket. "Who
is she?"

"The electric soul in the heart of the machine." A bell chimed
higher on the wall and Tidwell extracted yet a third card, this
one from a slot in the side of the fascinating construction. "Ah.
More guests have arrived. I am sorry to cut this visit short, but
I must return to the main floor. Perhaps you will help me with
the elevator again?"

Distracted by the running of the elevator, Kimball asked no
more questions about the machine in the basement. Upon returning to the library, he found the room was now occupied by two
new guests, as well as his father.

Kimball's father stood at the edge of the room looking over
a series of maps and diagrams with a white-haired woman clad
in black.

Kimball retrieved the leatherbound atlas and seated himself on
an ottoman near his father. He turned the pages slowly, wondering at the twisting rivers and outlines of rugged coasts, dreaming
of setting sail in a pirate ship to the other side of the world.

"I cannot like it, Isabelle," Kimball's father said to the woman.
"This attempt to take an airship over the pole. It has never been
done before, except in the wildest of fiction."

"Some may call it fictional." She gestured at the papers lying
before them. "But flight over the pole can be cast in the light of
a scientific expedition, disguising that this is a mission of mercy
to extract the Romanov family. With them, we can rally the
White Russian cause. Perhaps even ease some of the German
hostilities."

"I doubt that will make much difference to the Kaiser,"
answered his father. "He has been able to go to war against his

British cousin without much heart searching. Why would a refugee Russian cousin cause him to doubt his course?"

"Certainly, your king has done nothing to help his Russian cousins," said Isabelle.

"To the majority of the British public, the Tsar and his wife are no more than relics of a time past," replied Kimball's father. "And the Empress is far too fond of her German relations to fit comfortably into a London life. At least for now. No, Isabelle, my government cannot support this wild plan. If you fly, you must fly under another country's flag."

The third guest spoke. From Kimball's seat on a padded ottoman near them, this man was remarkably tall. Long and lean, with unusually pale features, he resembled the stick insects found in hedges near their home in the English countryside. There was a certain stiffness in how he moved his legs and arms that also reminded Kimball of an insect's hesitant walk from one end of a leaf to another.

"The British's cowardly abandonment of the royal family will not be forgotten," the man lisped. "Had you extended asylum when it was sought, they would not be in such mortal peril now."

"We do not know that they are in mortal peril, Pavel. We must assume they are being held under house arrest for their own safety," argued Kimball's father.

"Of course, they are in danger," said Isabelle. "The telegraphs we intercepted with the help of the marvelous calculating machine downstairs make that clear."

The man named Pavel shifted his position, and Kimball heard a strange click-click sound that reminded him of a clock ticking.

"It is clear to us that the Americans will do nothing to aid our royal family and the British have abandoned us," Pavel said. "This trip to New York is a waste of my time. We have received overtures from other parties. In exchange for our assistance, they will ensure the Romanovs have safe passage to the Port of Tanggu."

Kimball's father looked troubled. "Are you suggesting a treaty with the Dragon Queen?"

"She prefers to be called the Empress of All China," said Pavel, "now that the young Emperor has abdicated his throne."

"Her antecedents are nebulous," replied his father. "At best, she is a queen of bandits located in the Wei River Basin."

"For a minor bandit, it sounds like British intelligence has made a study of her," Isabelle said.

"I never said she was a minor bandit," said Kimball's father. "She is said to be a descendant of Jiang Yuan, the founding mother of the Zhou Dynasty, and her territory encompasses the traditional lands of those emperors. Naturally, there are a number of warlords and what's left of the current government disputing her claims. Nevertheless, she is a woman of great power in an unstable region. So of course we are interested in her plans and allies."

Pavel shrugged with another tick-tock sound. "We think her plans have great merit."

"And yet, I doubt her alliance comes for free," said his father.

Kimball slid closer to the trio, fascinated by this talk of a Dragon Queen. He wondered if the lady in question had scales and talons.

"We find her price acceptable." Pavel reached across the library table, sweeping up the maps and plans laid out by Isabelle. "With these as our currency, I will free our beloved royal family."

Isabelle gave a cry and sprang forward to grab the papers from Pavel.

With an increased clicking sound, Pavel picked the woman up and threw her across the room, knocking down Kimball's father.

As he threw her, his shirt ripped, revealing gleaming armor constructed wholly of springs and cogs.

"I am sorry to cut this visit short," he said to the pair now sprawled on the floor, "but I have transportation waiting for me in the harbor." With a twist of his wrist, a small gun sprang from under his cuff and settled into his left hand. "Do not try to stop me. Not if you value the boy's life." He gestured with the gun at Kimball, sitting frozen on the ottoman. "Come to me. We will leave now, very quietly and quickly."

With a roar, Kimball's father staggered to his feet, but Isabelle grabbed at him. "Don't! He'll shoot your son before you reach him."

"Clever woman," said Pavel. "Boy, come to me now!"

Kimball rose from the ottoman. As he passed the globe, he twisted suddenly and grabbed it, sending the world spinning off its pedestal into Pavel's left hand. The Russian's shot went into the ceiling of the library as Kimball dived behind one of the leather chairs.

Kimball's father vaulted across the room. He punched Pavel in the nose, causing the man to trip backward. Another flying punch caught Pavel on the chin, lifting the Russian into the air and depositing him with a clatter of clockwork on the carpet.

Isabelle grabbed the ropes tying back the curtains at the window and hurried forward to lash Pavel's hands and feet together. She snatched up the Russian's gun and tucked it into her waistband, just as Tidwell appeared in the doorway.

"Ah," said Tidwell. "I see we have discovered the clockwork man."

"Kimball!" cried his father. "Are you unhurt?"

"Of course, father." Kimball rose from behind the chair where he had taken shelter. He looked at the clockwork man with some fascination. Such an armament would be an interesting challenge to build. He wondered if he could ask his father for a closer look.

Isabelle gave a strangled cry as the copper wires encircling Pavel's legs and arms began to glow. The curtain ropes she'd used to secure the Russian spy burst into flames and fell into ashes on the rug.

"You'll never get away," said Kimball's father, as the clockwork man struggled to his feet. "Let us help you. There will be a way to aid the Tsar and his family. We just need to take the time to find the right answer."

"No!" cried Pavel, once again snatching up the maps that had fallen to the floor. "We are out of time! I must go to the Dragon Queen."

Isabelle pulled out Pavel's gun and aimed it at the clockwork man.

"Stop!" shouted Kimball's father, pulling Kimball behind his back. "Don't shoot. It's too dangerous."

But Isabelle fired at the clockwork man. Pavel twisted and the bullet pinged off his breastplate and crashed through the glass window. With one last wild look around the room, Pavel leaped to the window and out through the shattered glass.

Isabelle, his father, and Kimball rushed to the window, staring at the street below. Broken glass was spread across the pavement, but there was no sign of the clockwork man.

"Springs in his boots," murmured Tidwell behind them. "You can see him just at the end of the street."

Looking up, Kimball did catch a glimpse of Pavel bouncing out of sight, the sun winking off the copper armature that encased him.

"Well, that's torn it." Isabelle turned away from the window.

"Without those maps, I have no hope of making the crossing safely."

"Surely you can contact your Norwegian friend for another copy?" said Kimball's father.

Isabelle shook her head. "He's off to the South Pole. By the time I tracked him down, it may very well be too late. I fear Pavel is right, and the Romanovs are running out of time."

"I'll do what I can," said Kimball's father with a sigh. "We had a man in Moscow, but his position was compromised. I doubt my government will do more." He turned to Kimball, patting him down in that awkward way of fathers unused to hugging. Kimball leaned forward and hugged his father fiercely, suddenly glad the clockwork man was gone and his father safe.

Tidwell had pulled the brush and pan from the fireplace set to sweep up the ash left behind by the burned carpet ropes. "Ingenious device," Tidwell murmured, as he tipped the ash into the fireplace.

"Indeed," said Kimball's father. "I didn't know the Russians had advanced so far in their spycraft. We may need to expand our own research."

Isabelle shook her head. "Just what we need, another generation of science heroes."

"Oh, I don't know," said Kimball's father. "Perhaps a new generation of heroes is exactly what we need. What do you think, Kimball?"

Distracted by a copper cog left lying on the floor by the window, Kimball barely heard his father's question. Instead, he responded with one of his own. "May I please try the switchboard now?"

CLAWS OF
THE DRAGON QUEEN

BANG! BANG!

The watcher on the opposite roof leaped up and raced toward the fire escape.

Two shots, barely a heartbeat between them, two flashes of light in the darkened apartment across the street. Sammy Mongo must be home. And somebody else had already intercepted him.

The Wrecker of Engines cursed softly behind his porcelain mask as he lunged down the fire escape, not bothering with the final ladder. He leapt out from the landing, his training dropping him cat-soft upon the sidewalk below.

That night, his careful detective work looked to end in murder. He knew the sounds of those shots: two Colt 45s, the guns favored by Sammy Mongo.

Fast-draw Sammy would have hit whoever was hidden in his apartment and then be out the door, taking such secrets with him as the current whereabouts of Dr. Caesar.

The Wrecker of Engines raced to the back of the building, guessing Sammy probably would take the alley exit. He still had time to catch the gangster before Sammy disappeared into Cobalt City's darker neighborhoods. But the alley was empty. For once, he was wrong. The crook must have gone out the front.

He put his hand on the back door of the little apartment building. Already, in the apartments above, he could hear lights being switched on, anxious questions shouted. Two shots, well after midnight, even in this part of town, somebody would be dialing the operator and asking for the police.

No time for hesitation. Once the flatfoots arrived, no hope to find any evidence of where the elusive Sammy had fled. He took the stairs two at a time, cracking the door open on the landing of the third floor, the floor where Sammy lived.

No one moved in the dimly lit hallway. The neighbors might be calling the cops, but nobody was coming to investigate on their own.

The Wrecker of Engines slipped down the hall to Sammy's door, unlocked and slightly open. The apartment beyond was dark.

Pulling a flashlight out of his pocket, the Wrecker of Engines cautiously rolled the beam around the room. A pair of polished men's shoes, black silk socks encasing the heavy ankles, good wool trousers. The Wrecker played the light up the man's body even as he crossed the room for a closer look.

It was Sammy Mongo. And, given that his body was the only one cooling rapidly on the apartment's cheap rag rug, for once Sammy Mongo had missed his target.

Two Colts lay on the floor, just inches from the gangster's outstretched hands. A quick sniff of the barrels confirmed both guns had been shot just minutes before.

The Wrecker did a fast visual search of the room, moving the flashlight with a steady hand to illuminate each corner and then pass beyond. The place was as neat as might be expected for a bachelor gangster with no steady doll to keep him in order.

Two bullets had punched holes in the plaster of the wall opposite where Sammy lay. No blood splatters. He had definitely missed his target; surprising for a man feared throughout the tongs for his deadly accuracy.

The Wrecker of Engines turned the light back on the corpse for one last look. Already he could hear sirens wailing up the street. The cops were on their way.

Sammy was sprawled flat, face down. No visible wound. He rolled him over. The suit was clean, no bullet holes from head to heel. Well, he hadn't heard a third shot, so that made sense, although he could see no sign of what had actually killed the killer.

Then the Wrecker of Engines noticed one of Sammy's hands was clenched in a fist. He pried the dead man's fingers open. A white jade hairpin carved in the shape of a clawing dragon dropped onto the carpet. This was no bauble from Woolworths—such ornaments once decorated the heads of Chinese noblewomen.

He heard voices, the elevator cage creaking up the front of the building. The police had arrived, and it was time for him to go.

The Wrecker of Engines hesitated for a moment. He disliked making the job more difficult for the boys in blue who fought crime in Cobalt City. But his instincts had kept him alive and the scourge of evil scientists. He swooped down and grabbed the hairpin, pocketing that one piece of evidence before slipping noiselessly out of the apartment and down the back stairs.

On the street, he pulled his porcelain mask off, rotating it in his hand to stare into the hexagram painted across its smooth surface. Shih Ho: hexagram 21 of the I Ching, his reminder to all that without justice, balance was unattainable. He slipped the mask inside his suit jacket and shoved his black fedora higher on his forehead, then buttoned up his trench coat to hide his own handguns. Satisfied his Webleys were well concealed, he ambled to the front door.

The cop standing next to the car was a guy he knew.

"Hey, Johnny," he said, as he pulled a notebook and pencil from his coat pocket, "what's with the midnight house call?"

"Wilde," the young patrolman replied with a start. "Where did you come from?"

"Ah, you know how it is, slow news night, thought I might as well take a walk around, see if there's any action."

Johnny Maguire shook his honest, red head. "You reporters, you must have a sixth sense or something. There was a murder up there, less than a half hour ago. Detectives just went up to take a look."

"Heard who the body is?" Kimball Wilde asked. For this character, his flat American accent overrode the Anglo-Indian lilt of his childhood.

"Some Chinese gangster. Guy named Sammy Mongo. Chief's been after him for years for people smuggling, but he's slick. Every time we'd get close, he'd disappear, wait for the heat to die down, then come back to Cobalt City."

The coroner's truck pulled up behind Johnny's patrol car.

"Looks like he's going on his last trip now," said Wilde.

"Sure does," replied Johnny. "I wonder who got him."

"So do I, so do I," murmured Wilde, dropping one hand into his pocket and tracing the white jade dragon hairpin with his fingertips.

Once the club had been a celebrated hotspot, infamous in the early 1930s for the mysterious disappearance of a jazz pianist. Almost twenty years later, the place was just another dive, full of sailors, dollar-a-dance girls, and the other flotsam of Cobalt City's docks. But a hot tip from a cool dame at the teashop down the block led Wilde to his current seat at the bar. According to

Lady Pekoe, Sammy Mongo came here regularly, working with the tongs to provide safe passage for certain criminals looking to leave Cobalt City for less hero-ridden climes.

Wilde suspected Mongo's latest client was Dr. Caesar. The nasty Italian had struck a deal with the OSS to skip his master Mussolini's fate by bringing his Project Pompeii to the Allies. But for months, Wilde had been hearing rumors that Dr. Caesar was trying to peddle his lava bomb elsewhere. He'd slipped the OSS boys back in London, hopped the Atlantic, and then scampered to Cobalt City faster than a man could say "Spaghetti Bolognese."

The less-than-good doctor did an excellent job of hiding. None of Wilde's usual sources could turn up a lead. A solid month of hunting only yielded one clue. A frightened little man in a shiny suit whispered "Marco Polo" at an exhibition of Italian Renaissance paintings.

If his source was right, Dr. Caesar meant to follow another famous Italian to fame and fortune in the Far East. It fit the man's pattern—basing his crimes on the exploits of Italian heroes. Previously, he'd tried to take over the world from Alexandria before being sunk at Actium. Lucky for the Allies that the Queen of the Nile refused to play Cleopatra to his Mark Antony. The Egyptian superheroine used her asps to good effect then.

Wilde slid a quarter from finger to finger, making it disappear and reappear. Anyone looking at the bar would see just a tired hack, grabbing a highball before heading back to the night desk. The roving reporter disguise let him wander where he wanted, even into the laboratories of industrial magnates, government geniuses, and mad scientists, not that he ever saw a difference. It was all matters of degree, and every degree dealt death to the innocent, as far as he was concerned. Let them build their engines of destruction; he would find them and destroy them.

But first he had to unearth Dr. Caesar from his current hidey-hole. With luck, the lunatic Latin hadn't heard about Sammy's sudden demise and would still come here to arrange his passage.

He flipped the quarter one last time, making it vanish in midair.

"You make magic. I make magic too." A Chinese woman slid onto the barstool next to him. She wore a crimson cheongsam dress, the embroidered silk caressing every curve like a lover, from the high collar to the long slit up her left thigh. Her dark hair was piled high and secured with a green jade ornament carved in the shape of a dragon. With a quick glance, he knew immediately that she was no working girl.

The lady pulled a cigarette from the tiny black satin handbag dangling from one wrist.

With a practiced flip of the fingers, Wilde made a lit match appear and held it to the tip.

She drew in her breath and then blew it out, pursing her scarlet-painted lips to create one perfect smoke ring to float as fragile as a soap bubble before them.

"Magic," she whispered.

He laughed. He rarely did, not like that, a true rolling laugh that made heads turn in the bar, seeking the sound of a man's delight.

"The name's Wilde," he said.

She smiled but said nothing more.

"Can I buy you a drink?"

She shook her head and gave a tiny shrug, barely a ripple of silk. Her eyes never left the room, her glance lightly grazing and then discarding every man.

"Can I help you find someone?" A true shot in the smoky dark, but there was something about the way she sat, so still, so calm, and so very conscious of everyone around them. He knew that pose, knew it like he knew his own skin, for once he'd trained with the masters who taught that perfect stillness of utter awareness. The tranquility of the tiger, one old woman called it, long ago in a temple at the top of a wind-racked mountain.

She shook her head, a regretful moue of those faultless lips.

In the back of the club, somebody plunked a nickel into the jukebox and punched the latest romantic hit by Perry Como. The dollar-a-dance girls shrugged themselves off the wall and began to circulate the room, sliding with tired sensuality around the tables to trail their fingertips along one masculine shoulder or another.

At the doorway, a group of men entered, chatting amongst themselves, pulling off hats and scarves, waving at the cigarette girl to come closer.

Beside him, the mysterious beauty in red focused suddenly on one man hanging slightly behind the others. It was just the slightest twitch, a heel planted more firmly on the floor, the fingers loosening just slightly on the cigarette, ready to discard it.

He looked beyond her, letting his senses open, seeing exactly what she was seeing. The man by the door, the hat pulled low and the white velvet muffler swathed around his chin to disguise a distinctive jaw line. But nothing could hide that grand Roman nose.

"Dr. Caesar!" He barely breathed the name as he left his barstool. But as quickly as he moved, the scarlet cheongsam was first to reach Mussolini's favorite scientist. Her long fingers reached up, and a blur of red nails raked Dr. Caesar's cheek. The irritated Italian whirled away, staggered, and fell in a crumpled heap across the entrance.

Wilde barely paused to check for a pulse. Even as his fingers touched the corpse, he knew Dr. Caesar would never reach the Far East.

On the jukebox, Como crooned about an enchanted evening. But Wilde saw that his beautiful stranger had already left the room. He followed her into the night, leaving behind the gathering storm of exclamations as the others in the club realized a dead man blocked the doorway.

The mask was cool against his face as he trailed the slender shadow down the alley. Somewhere, a cat hissed in warning as one of Cobalt City's mutant rats scampered over the garbage cans and up a wall. From an open window high above, the crackle of the radio nearly drowned out the fight between a woman and her husband over his disappearing paycheck.

All these sounds registered and were ignored. "Be always aware, never overwhelmed, concentrate on the one shadow among the many," the mask maker had said, as he poured a thin stream of steaming green tea into the translucent porcelain cups. It was a lesson he never forgot.

The Wrecker of Engines continued down the alley, past the rundown apartment buildings, letting the noises of the night fall behind him as he followed the mysterious woman in scarlet.

Now his particular shadow slipped into a doorway. The flickering lightbulb barely illuminated her lovely face as she knocked twice, paused, and then knocked twice more.

An eyehole in the door slid open. A muted exchange ensued. Too far away to make out the actual words, the Wrecker of Engines still recognized the fluting cadences as Mandarin, the preferred dialect of Northern China.

All his life, he had been fascinated by tales of the empire so much older than the one that had spawned him. At various times, he had traveled to China, wanting to understand the culture, philosophy, and history, which seemed so much more vast than anything held in Europe. As Lawrence had fallen in love with Arabia, so Wilde had wanted to immerse himself in the region so devastated by the beginning of the century and discover the beauty slowly being regained.

As soon as she finished speaking, the door opened. His mysterious lady hurried inside. As she passed directly under the light, he caught another glimpse of the intricate jade hair ornament securing her chignon.

Wilde waited a few minutes. Then he scanned the side of the building. Against all city regulations, there was no fire escape to allow easy egress or entry to the upper floors. More telling, all the windows to the roof were barred. The steel bars looked suspiciously new and secure. The large moon overhead revealed a telltale glitter along the roofline: broken glass to cut any rope thrown up there with a grappling hook. Whoever defended this building knew the peculiar talents of Cobalt City's villains and heroes.

Now which, he wondered, as he made his own quiet exit from the alley, did they fear?

A quick reconnaissance at the front of the building showed an equal amount of fortification. The ground floor business was an importer of Chinese antiquities, with heavy lacquered red and gold doors ornamentally bolted and barred against night intruders.

Disguised under the curlicues of black iron, the Wrecker of Engines spotted a Springhold triple-action lock, the type favored by banks and government offices, nearly impossible to pick without the right tools. He fingered the black leather case in his trench coat pocket. He carried the right tools, of course, but the streetlamps in this section seemed unnaturally bright. Directly across the street from his intended target was an all-night diner with large, plate-glass windows. Even from his shadowed corner at the mouth of the alley, he could easily pick out the white-jacketed counterman and his late-night customers slumped over their coffee cups.

Any man attempting the front of the building would be spotted immediately. It would be easier and less conspicuous to come back during daylight hours.

Slipping off the mask, Wilde turned on his heel, intent on some research. The green jade hairpin that she wore so carefully inserted into her ebony braids—he was certain the design was the same as the white jade hairpin found clutched in Sammy Mongo's dead hand.

When his own library proved unusually inadequate, Wilde sought out the only man in Cobalt City with an even greater collection of esoteric history books.

Professor Norman Chandler had returned from his mysterious explorations with an ailment that left his body crippled but his mind intact. Through a large endowment, paid in gold coins, according to certain gossips, he persuaded the Adventurers Club to let him turn the top floor of their brownstone building into his own private residence. He had his meals sent up from the Club's kitchens, had his rooms cleaned and his errands run by the Club's staff, and his visitors vetted and announced by the Club's doorman.

With a nod at Tidwell, the doorman, Wilde went straight to the professor's private elevator. A push of the button whisked him to the entry hall of Chandler's apartment.

"In the library," called out the professor, as Wilde paused to hang his hat and coat on the oak hallstand.

There, Wilde found Chandler settled in his favorite leather chair, a cigar and a brandy on the little brass table at his elbow, and a pulp magazine resting in his lap. His ivory canes were propped neatly against the wall, within easy reach if needed.

"You'll forgive me if I don't rise?" Chandler gave his usual greeting. "Help yourself to a drink, you know where."

Wilde smiled and strode to the sidebar, with its ornate cut-glass decanters all clearly labeled in sterling silver. Ice from the leather bucket, a splash of soda water, and a healthy shot of the professor's excellent Scotch were quickly mixed. He pulled a chair next to Chandler.

"Cigarette?" asked his host, indicating the cloisonné box on his table.

Wilde shook his head. "I never smoke."

"Really?" said Chandler. "I thought all you detective types smoked hard, drank harder, and chased anything wearing a skirt."

Wilde chuckled. "You should never believe what you read in those magazines."

"Oh, this?" asked the professor. He held up the magazine so Wilde could see the cover. A giant with brilliant green skin straddled a shrieking blonde while a man with two smoking guns lunged through a door at the pair. "I read these as part of my research into the current Western attitude toward the other half of the world. Fascinating bits of truth mangled by the jaws of the commercial hyenas who publish this debased entertainment for the masses. And a disturbing amount of xenophobia. As long as we feed the public such stories, I fear for this nation."

"I thought you had a story in this issue."

"I do," said Chandler. "But they gave the cover to some Dutchman writing about an Asian mastermind with fiendish minions. And buried my serial of lost civilizations high in the Himalayas in the back. According to the bloodsucking sensationalist who I laughingly call an editor, shrieking blondes in red lace tops and torn skirts sell better than sturdy explorers in khaki."

"So add a blonde to your next chapter," suggested Wilde.

"And defile the purity of my tale!" Chandler snorted. "I'm outraged!" He sipped his brandy and took a couple of puffs on his cigar before replacing it in the bronze holder shaped like a miniature sacrificial cauldron of the late Han Dynasty. "Of course, she could be an immortal Viking princess, imprisoned in the temple."

"Wasn't there a Sultana infatuated with your explorer earlier?"

Chandler beamed at him. "You do read my work! But she died on the sacrificial altar, taking a knife to the heart intended for my hero. That month I did get the cover." Chandler took another sip of brandy. "A Viking princess, her fur robes slipping down to reveal...hmmm...yes, I can see that appealing to the hyena. Very good, Wilde, very good. Now that we've solved my little literary problem, what can I do for you?"

Wilde pulled the white jade hairpin from his breast pocket and handed it to Chandler. At once, his chuckling host became the serious scholar, dropping the magazine into a basket by his chair and pulling out a small magnifying glass from his own pocket.

"Quite fine," he said. "No flaws or discoloration in the jade. Exquisite detail. And a ruby...no...a pink diamond, quite rare, for the eye. It's an imperial dragon, of course."

"Yes," said Wilde. "Five claws."

"But a woman's hair ornament." Chandler tapped his magnifying glass against his lower lip. "Where have I seen this beauty before?"

"I could find no reference in my collection."

"Most likely not, if this is what I think it is. Third shelf from the top, the fourth volume from the left."

Wilde went to the bookcase Chandler indicated. He pulled the slim blue book from the shelf and handed it to his friend.

Chandler flicked through the pages. "Ah, there you are." He flipped the book around so Wilde could see the sketch of five hairpins, each one exactly like the one now resting on the professor's gray flannel-covered knee.

"So what are they?" Wilde asked.

"Loosely translated, the Empress's Claws. Five hairpins, each made from a different shade of jade, each containing a deadly secret." Chandler set down the book and his magnifying glass to pick up the white jade hairpin. His thin, clever fingers ran the length of the long, jade spike that formed the dragon's tail and up again to the head. "Ah, here, the eye, of course." He pressed the pink diamond eye of the dragon, and a steel needle sprang out of the dragon's tail. He tested it lightly with one fingertip, drawing a droplet of blood. "Razor sharp. Driven with the proper force and placement into the base of the skull—"

"It could kill a man instantly." Wilde nodded. "But this one was found in a dead man's fist."

"Then it isn't what killed him," Chandler said. "But remember, there is more than one claw. According to reports filed by one rather questionable eyewitness during the Opium Wars, the man who made those sketches, the five hairpins were doled out by the Empress to her favorite assassins. All ladies, by the way, and all trained to kill with a variety of innocent objects that might be found in any lady's possession: a silk scarf, an ivory chopstick, a paper fan, or a jade hairpin."

"The scratch of a painted fingernail?"

"Certainly. I've seen that done with certain poisons in Singapore, which could be painted on the nails with no harm to the wearer but proved deadly when entering a man's bloodstream."

Wilde grunted, sipping the remains of his Scotch. "But there is no Empress of China. The entire royal family either fled to the West or was captured by the Japanese. They say the last Emperor is a prisoner now."

"Poor old chap, he was never all that keen to be Emperor in the first place. I met him once, a little boy bicycling about the Forbidden City. But there were rumors at the end of the war, odd things stirring out in the hinterlands. Have you ever heard of a city called Xian?" the professor asked.

"The tomb of the First Emperor?" Wilde recalled a few books that had enchanted him as a boy.

The professor nodded. "So legend says. A large grassy knoll. The locals grazed their animals across it when I was there. Supposedly an entire city is buried beneath it."

"With rivers of mercury and palaces of silver and jade. And an entire army of living clay soldiers to defend it," Wilde recalled.

Chandler nodded. "Quite the fairy tale. But, after the war, a number of imperial treasures were discovered to be missing from the Forbidden City. The Communists blamed the Japanese, the Japanese blamed the General, and the General issued edicts from his island that he took nothing. The most notable loss was the jewels of the Empress, a collection that included this white jade hairpin."

"And what does this have to do with Xian?" Wade asked.

"The Communists have closed all roads going there. All trains. All air transport. There was talk of a natural disaster, an earthquake or a flood, devastating the region. And, of course, with China's borders sealed tight, reports these days are sketchy and unreliable." Chandler rummaged in his basket, finally retrieving a journal that appeared to be written in French.

"But?" Wilde prompted, sure there was more to the story.

"There's an interesting rumor swirling around certain circles." Chandler flipped through the pages until he came to a short article. It barely took up a page. "A French explorer claims a new Forbidden City has risen out of the tomb of the First Emperor. An imperial city ruled by a Dragon Queen."

Wilde started at the name. A ticking sound, the mantle clock perhaps, jogged decades old memories of a certain Russian and his father telling the history of a bandit queen. "With her own cadre of female assassins?"

"Quite possibly." The professor rolled the hairpin in his fingers, making the pink diamond eye glitter. "There have been some unexplained murders. Hong Kong, Singapore, Bombay, San Francisco. All scientists or businessmen. All rumored to be supporters of the Communists and, thus, not necessarily our best friends. Quite possibly someone from our side is responsible."

Wilde raised one eyebrow in question. He had never seen the professor look so troubled.

"However," said Chandler, placing the white jade hairpin carefully on the table between them, "based on the inquiries I've received from certain people I cannot name, I suspect our covert friends are just as baffled as the police. But one common tale is told for all: each victim was seen with a Chinese woman of surpassing beauty shortly before they died."

"Would an Italian scientist with a fondness for volcanic explosions be a typical victim?"

"Not an unreasonable guess. Especially if he was seen as a threat. Could he be trading secrets to the Chinese Communists?"

"Almost certainly. And his death may well have saved hundreds of lives. I cannot say I will mourn the man," said Wilde slowly, revolving his drink in his hand, making the ice tinkle like a wind chime. "But I dislike murder in my city, no matter how noble the cause. If these ladies of death are here, I will find them."

"Do you need a bed for tonight? I can have Tidwell make up a room downstairs for you. We could talk more over breakfast."

Wilde shook his head. "I do not intend to sleep until this is solved. If I grow tired, a few minutes of meditation in a quiet corner will be sufficient. I find the public library very restorative."

Chandler chuckled. "Nice line. I may use it in my next thriller."

"I'm sure your own adventures are more than adequate fodder for the pulps. My life," Wilde said, "is not nearly sensational enough for your editor."

"Hmm," said the professor, "I do wonder if you ever tell me the entire truth of your investigations."

"More than any other man, Chandler, more than any other. I appreciate your help tonight." Wilde drained his glass and then replaced it on the silver tray on the bar to be taken away to be cleaned.

"And this deadly little memento?" Chandler held up the hairpin.

"Keep it safe," said Wilde, as he strode out the door.

Wilde waited until late afternoon, that hour when clerks tend to drowse and even the finest of secretaries ease their toes from their high-heeled shoes and dream about a second cup of coffee. Or, in the case of the sole lady working in the office of an importer of antiquities, a nicely brewed cup of tea.

Miss Hong, a secretary with steel-framed glasses and hair clipped too short for any type of ornament, looked longingly at her fragrantly steaming pot and waiting cup. Then she audibly stifled a sigh before turning back to Wilde.

"So you need to tour our entire warehouse? Could you not just give me a list of the items needed, sir?" she asked in a voice meant to be polite but sounding just a touch frustrated by the interruption in her afternoon.

"Oh, no, no!" Wilde waved his hands fluidly through the air, finishing with an emphatic flutter of the fingertips. "I am creating a palace, a true palace, of absolutely decadent Asian splendor... although, between you and me, nobody is going to notice my creative talents with the seventeen houris in peacock feathers rushing around, trying to distract the prince from saving his red-haired princess."

"I'm sorry," said Miss Hong, blinking her eyes rapidly at this speech. "I do not understand, Mister—?"

"Hawthorne, Septimus Hawthorne, set designer for Lew Large Productions." With his conjurer's fingers, he produced the white and gold business card he used for this persona. "We're creating a new spectacle in Technicolor based on *Aladdin*. When Lew's clever little scriptwriter discovered that Aladdin is from China, not Persia, Lew said to me: no scimitars and brass, no tacky flying carpets. Make it look like old China. The real thing. Emperor's palace."

Miss Hong sighed and reached into her desk to gather up the keys to the company's backrooms. She slid her feet slowly back into her shoes.

"Oh, dearie," fluted Wilde, "it can take me hours, simply hours, to find the right little knickknacks for Lew. Why don't you give Septimus those keys and enjoy your lovely cup of tea."

"I don't know if that would be allowed—" Miss Hong glanced with longing at her teacup.

"I'll be extra, extra careful, darling, I promise. And if I so much as crack a vase, Lew will pay for the lot." He tilted his head and flung his hands up in an exaggerated shrug he had copied from one of Cobalt City's most infamous art thieves, the Yellow Daffodil. "That's the delightful thing about working for a mogul: he never cares how much one spends on his little endeavors."

With a more refined shrug of her own, Miss Hong handed over the keys and eagerly turned back to her tea.

Past the inner doorway and out of sight, Wilde undid the buttons of his trench coat to allow free access to the deadly Webleys stored in the twin shoulder harnesses. He turned the pale purple ascot around his throat, an essential part of Septimus Hawthorne's character, inside out. Backed with black silk and lined with leather, the ascot became a collar to protect his throat from the garrote wire or the assassin's blade.

He pulled the porcelain mask from his pocket and settled it on his face. He was no longer Wilde the amiable night reporter or Hawthorne the flamboyant Hollywood designer or the half-dozen other characters he put on and off like Carnival masks. Now he was the Wrecker of Engines, the true man protected behind the gleaming black and white mask.

He made for the back of the building, stepping lightly through the cluttered bric-a-brac piled to the ceiling. Cloisonné vases large enough to hide a child, opium beds carved from rosewood, chests inlaid with mother-of-pearl decorations, fake antiques created for the export trade and meant to hide the true use of the building. For his sharp eyes spotted footprints in the dust of the far corner, a perfect outline of a lady's sole half visible at the edge of a seemingly solid wall.

The Wrecker of Engines ran his fingers along the wood boards of the warehouse wall, starting at the floor and working slowly upward. A few seconds of search, based on the position of the half visible footprint, and he found the catch that unlocked the secret door. Behind it was a staircase lit by bare lightbulbs leading upward.

He pulled the Webleys from their holsters, unwilling to climb weaponless to that obvious of an entrance to a villain's lair.

Someone had pounded the boards down tight on this stair, not a single tread creaking as he climbed. It seemed others using this particular route wanted to hide the sound of their passage. The straight staircase ended at a plain wood door, no keyhole, just a simple latch. He paused on the landing, pressing one ear against the panel of the door. Beyond it, he heard the musical rise and fall of Mandarin. He could understand enough to know the ladies were making travel plans, something about a boat in the harbor taking them north.

The Wrecker of Engines drew back a little and applied shoe leather to the door, kicking it wide open and leaping inside before the occupants had time to arm themselves.

Five women whipped around at his entrance. In the center was his scarlet-clad beauty. The four clustered around her were beauties as well, dressed in the colors of the four flowers in a mahjong set: the bamboo, the orchid, the chrysanthemum, and the plum blossom. Each, except the woman in palest pink, wore a jade hairpin in the form of a rearing five-toed dragon, an imperial dragon of death.

Behind the mask, his laugh rang like a mournful bell.

Strong men, murderers, had trembled when that laugh filled the room, exposing the rotted core of their souls. Scientists had clutched tubes of bubbling destruction and drank their own poison rather than face his knowing mockery.

But the Claws of the Dragon Queen were different. They drew a little apart. One unlaced a silk scarf from around her throat, another unfurled a paper fan, the third casually lifted a chopstick from the table, and the fourth reached up to her braids to pluck out her jade hairpin.

"The laughter of the Lonely Man cannot frighten us," said the scarlet beauty in the center, the killer of Dr. Caesar. "We too have walked the path of fire through the iron temple."

"Then you know that to corrupt the arts of the incorruptible way leads to madness," said the Wrecker of Engines, his voice deep as the ocean and more fearsome than a storm at sea. "And the punishment of the just."

Two of the women faltered as he used the Voice of Doom upon them. But the woman in golden silk threw her paper fan at him, whirling it through the air. He heard the slicing sound of its hidden blades and leaped to one side. The very tip of the fan caught the shoulder of his trench coat and ripped it open.

He raised the Webleys, always his last resort, and fired twice: Bang! Bang! Just as Sammy Mongo had before these deadly lovelies murdered him.

The first shot shattered the chopstick in the hands of the woman in pink. The second ripped the silk scarf out of the grasp of the pretty killer in pale purple. He wouldn't kill, but the next shot would wound. He hoped the next shot would not be needed.

With silent speed, a woman sprang at him, her black jade hairpin unsheathed to reveal the deadly steel tip. He leaped to the side, only to find the crimson claws of the fifth assassin slashing at the edge of his mask. With a twist of his head, he avoided her. Her nails scratched uselessly against the smooth porcelain protecting his cheek.

He rolled around her, reversing the gun in his hand to strike with the butt at the murderous beauty attempting to skewer him with her steel stiletto.

The woman gave a musical gasp and folded to the floor. Another of her sisters dashed forward to pull her from the fray.

The Wrecker of Engines flipped the gun again, lifting both Webleys now for a clear shot at his attackers. His back to the door, they could only come at him straight on.

"I can take you all with two shots." The reverberation of his proclamation conferred by the tricks of the porcelain mask made them hesitate.

The scarlet-clad leader held up one hand. The others froze in place.

"Our business is done in Cobalt City," she said. "The madman is dead, and our people are safe. I do not think many others will hurry to sell their services to the Chairman, not when they know the toll we demand."

"There are other ways than murder," he responded, the Webleys still and steady in his hands, one trained upon her heart.

"Blow up their laboratories by switching the labels on the chemicals they mixed in their beakers? Unscrew the wires so their own bombs consume them in flames? Pour sugar into the engines of airships so they crash into the fields rather than rain bombs upon the innocent?"

"There were always warnings," he said. "Shih Ho. If they turned aside, if they followed the just way, if they did not use their terrible engines of destruction, they would not have reaped that whirlwind."

"But did your tricks save Hiroshima? Did your methods shelter Nagasaki?"

He gasped. Beneath the hexagram, his tears ran swiftly, silently, down his cheeks. His greatest shame, his greatest failure, his soul slashed into ribbons of remorse by her gentle voice.

"I knew you when I first saw you," she whispered so low it

seemed only he and she were in the room. "The warrior with the heart of heavenly fire."

And then, to the startled cries of the others, she extended one hand. "Come with us. Help us. Together, we may save China from a terrible war."

He hesitated, nearly seduced by her simple request. The Webleys dipped the barest fraction in his hands. He stepped forward, trying to read the truth of her intentions in her face.

The blow came from one side, the forgotten dame in pink. She swung a clay camel with deadly accuracy, striking the base of his skull. He pitched forward, falling, falling into a cloud of crimson silk.

Two days later, Chandler watched him pour a scotch from the cut-glass decanter.

"Should you?" asked the professor. "After all, the concussion left you unconscious for hours."

"I hurt my pride more than my head," replied Wilde. "An imitation Tang Dynasty camel, of all things. And then to be discovered by Miss Hong in the warehouse."

"Decent of the Dragon Queen's ladies to remove your mask and hide your guns before leaving you on the warehouse floor."

"More decent to leave my mask for me in that hidden room. And the Webleys. I would have missed those. I've had them since my OSS days."

"So that's it," said Chandler. "Beaten by five ladies. I'm sure my editor would never accept that one."

Wilde shrugged. "We all have our defeats. As such things go, this one, I can live with." But still he could hear her whisper. "Did your tricks save Hiroshima? Did your methods shelter Nagasaki?"

He rambled around the professor's library, a restless striding to and fro. On the bookshelf, propped in front of the slim blue book, was the white jade hairpin.

Taking it from its place, Wilde rolled the hairpin between his fingers, making it appear and disappear. "Magic," he whispered.

The professor watched with the eyes of a man who had seen his own dreams of adventure shatter with his health long ago.

"So, at least, you have a small souvenir," Chandler observed.

"Pity to break up a set like that." Very abruptly, Wilde added, "She left me a note. Draped around the mask."

"You hadn't mentioned that before."

Wilde pulled the rectangle of silk out of his pocket and dropped it on the professor's lap.

The scholar unrolled the formerly white scarf, the center showing a neat bullet hole. Chinese characters, painted in crimson ink, swirled like dancers down the silk.

"Come to me," Chandler translated.

Wilde nodded.

"Will you go?" the professor asked.

Wilde shrugged, and the paper of the airplane ticket hidden in his breast pocket crackled like the first flame in a conflagration.

"The borders are closed. Nobody goes in, nobody gets out. A foreigner, a white devil foreigner, would be spotted in a minute."

"Unless he hid his face behind a mask," Chandler said.

Wilde laughed, and it was the carefree laugh of the man and not the hollow laughter of the mask. He tossed the white jade hairpin into the air. He watched it twist, end over end, claws over tail, the pink diamond eye glittering in the lamplight. Then he snapped one hand out. The dragon vanished into his pocket.

"I'll send you a postcard," the Wrecker of Engines promised his friend.

SIGNIFICANCE OF NUMBERS AND NAMES

TWO GHOSTS MET AT A BAR ONE AFTERNOON. ONE WAS AN eternal being. The other had been able to turn himself into a spirit since he was seventeen, an American Spirit. They talked, as old friends will, about how a city had changed. The bartender and the lone drunk at the end of the bar paid them no attention. That may have had something to do with the fact that it was mid-afternoon in a neighborhood where drinking was still a genteel after-hours activity. Or that it was a Tuesday. Or that superheroes regularly had a drink in the orange vinyl booth when they needed to exchange information, and everybody else pretended not to see them.

"There's more places decorated like this every year," said Simon Stolberg. He stared at the potted fern swinging in a macramé sling. The fern did not look well.

"One wonders why the knotted string," said the Black Hand, who had once been called Pharaoh's Ghost. He had stopped following decorative fashions after the Third Dynasty was dust.

"Trends," Simon said gloomily. "Like disco. Only worse."

"Disco? What is that?" The Black Hand's knowledge of music was only slightly more progressive than his knowledge of decorating.

"Oh, you know, disco. It's a dance craze." Simon waved his hand toward a miniscule dance floor and the mirrored ball that hung above it. "The Hustle? Bee Gees?"

The Black Hand raised one eyebrow and sighed.

"It could be worse," said Simon.

"I truly don't know how," replied the Black Hand.

Both surveyed the street outside with a distinct lack of hope. As the twentieth century entered its final decades, they were united in their belief that the city was deteriorating, evolving into a grimmer place with less hope. Urban blight did not just happen elsewhere. Evidence of it could be seen in neighborhoods like this, where Simon remembered crowds of men and women moving briskly between dozens of shops and small businesses. Now it was just a few seedy bars and pawn shops, along with an adult bookstore on the corner. The windows of the hopefully and unfortunately named Loft 45 were tinted, either deliberately or with dirt, so the world outside had taken on a brownish hue.

"It's like peering out of a beer bottle," said Simon.

"Have you tried that?" asked the mysterious mage across the table from him.

"Tried what?"

"Condensing yourself into a beer bottle."

"I'm not sure I could." Simon wasn't even sure if he wanted to. His abilities as the American Spirit allowed him to become intangible. But he couldn't squeeze himself into a space smaller than his actual body, as far as he knew.

"Disincorporation and then contraction into a limited space. Should be possible." The Black Hand was drawing arcane symbols on the window, possibly to protect the place or possibly just the magician's equivalent of doodling during a conversation.

"What about the beer?" Simon asked, because if he could fit

himself into a beer bottle, it would be a neat trick for listening in on villainous conversations.

"Drink it first," recommended his friend.

Simon almost smiled. "Well, if I ever need to hide in a beer bottle, I'll remember your advice."

The Black Hand steepled his fingers together. "I have been testing the limits of dematerialization. Removing one's physical self from the physical world."

"And going where?"

"Oh, remaining here. In the same locality but in a different location. As it were."

"Here but not here."

"In a manner of speaking." The mage swirled the beer in his glass and peered into it as if he was seeking a vision from a crystal ball.

"But where would you be?" Simon asked, after a few more minutes of contemplative silence.

"That's a very good question. More importantly, how would you find me?" Something in the Black Hand's tone suggested this was not a rhetorical question to idle away a slow afternoon.

"In the here but not here?" Simon wanted to make sure that was still what they were talking about. As a being of immense age and magical power, the Black Hand did drift off into his own thoughts quite often, and conversations had a way of leapfrogging into new territory with very little warning.

"As it were," the mage confirmed.

"Are you hiding, or do you want to be found?" Simon asked.

The Black Hand took a sip of his beer. "Assume that I wish to be found."

A phone rang on the bar behind them, and the bartender left off polishing glasses to answer it. "Wrong number," he said, dropping it back on the cradle with a crash that echoed through the empty establishment.

"Maybe I could call you?" Simon suggested.

"Interesting idea. How would you do that?" his friend answered.

"Use a number that has reached you in the past. You're rather predictable." Simon considered what he had observed during their recent battles with the vampire infestation of Cobalt City's darker corners. "Arithmancy and numerology always will draw your attention."

"As injustice draws yours."

"That, plus attacks upon innocents." Simon drained his beer. He kept thinking one more battle, one more bigot put down, and he could...what? Retire from being a superhero? He wasn't even fifty yet. Way too young for doing nothing. The city needed the American Spirit. Besides, he couldn't abandon his friends now. Not with Igor Chernystian threatening everyone with his vampire tricks. "Igor can turn himself into mist. Do you think he's been hiding in a beer bottle?"

"Unlikely." The ancient mage drained his beer glass and gave it a look. It immediately refilled with a nice head of foam across the top. "He would consider it too plebian. A champagne bottle, perhaps. He can definitely change his mass. As a bat, he escaped capture by slipping out of the attic where we had him trapped."

The phone rang three times before the bartender answered, growled "stop kidding around," and crashed the receiver down again.

"Not for me?" asked the drunk.

"Nah, just silence. Being doing that all afternoon," said the bartender. "Want another?"

The drunk banged his shot glass once on the bar. "Nobody ever calls me."

"So other than suggesting that I hide in a beer bottle, anything else you needed to tell me?" Simon asked.

In their corner, the Black Hand nodded. "Igor Chernystian is an ancient and powerful being. There are signs this war will not end well."

Simon shrugged. "I'm not afraid of Igor Chernystian. I've beaten worse creatures."

"No, you have not." The Black Hand took a deep breath. The light in the bar seemed to flicker. "I dislike predictions. But the calculations coming from the Adventurers Club should not be ignored."

Simon looked at his friend, more troubled by the solemn tone of the mage's voice than the words themselves. While the Black Hand often made the most mundane discussions mystical and dire, he never sounded as dire as he did today.

"That old place? What has that got to do with anything?" Simon asked. He recalled stories about the Adventurers Club, a hangout for explorers mostly, from when he was a boy. But there had been a few superheroes who frequented the place too. The Club was a relic of another time. Although it had lasted longer than this bar would, he thought, glancing again at the dying ferns and forlorn disco dance floor.

"The Adventurers Club is nearly gone." The Black Hand sighed deeply. "I spoke to Tidwell yesterday. The last member fell into a volcano on Kilimanjaro. Once her estate is settled, the place may be shut indefinitely."

"Can't they recruit new members?" Simon asked.

The mage shook his head. "According to Tidwell, there's nobody left who cares enough to bring in new members. A bank holds the accounts, and a law firm oversees the trust that finances the Club. Both entities have agreed to shut the place down until a new proprietor can be found. Of course, Tidwell will stay on as doorman and caretaker."

"Of course?" The name rang a vague bell in Simon's memories. When he had first started fighting crime as a teenager in the 1940s, he had gone to the Adventurers Club, he realized. A butler or doorman, a rather cadaverous individual named Tidwell, dispensed little cards with information on a group being hunted by the superheroes assembled there. But that had been almost thirty years ago, back when the Wrecker of Engines was still battling criminals in real life, before he became just a TV show superhero.

But Tidwell, the butler guy, he couldn't be the same individual the Black Hand was discussing, Simon thought. Then, looking at his ancient companion and considering others who dwelt in Cobalt City, he reconsidered.

"Tidwell stays with the building. As does another individual. One who is not here. But who is also here."

"Ah," said Simon, not quite understanding but fairly sure that this last piece of information was why the Black Hand wanted to meet this afternoon.

"I've put certain research off far too long. Where do the decades go? I swear it was only 1901 yesterday," said the mage with some sadness. "I need to go looking in the past for some answers. Which means I may not be completely present in Cobalt City."

"What if we need you?"

"I like your idea of using certain numbers to call me. You will find the right sequences placed throughout the city in the most likely areas for future battles."

"But I just mentioned the idea to you. How can those numbers already be placed throughout the city?"

"Magic. IBM isn't the only one who can multitask. I will split myself between past, present, and future. It's a clever solution. Thank you for inspiring me to think of it." The Black Hand almost smiled as he finished his second glass of beer.

Then he slid a card across the table to Simon. "This is for you. Do not be alone at night."

Simon snorted. "I'm not some newbie kid playing hero tag with criminals in the back alleys." At this point in his career, Simon counted himself as one of the veterans of Cobalt City's constant war between good and evil.

"No. But the calculations are dire. This is why we needed to meet."

Simon flipped the small white card over. The typed message read: "American Spirit is vulnerable to vampire attack."

"What? What is this?"

"The answer to a question I had Tidwell ask. I must leave. So I asked for as much information as possible to help you. It is my fault Igor escaped us and settled here. If we had only captured the bat!"

"Look, you did your best to save an entire town from an ancient vampire lord. The fact that he decided to settle in Cobalt City two years ago is not your fault."

The Black Hand shook his head. "You have done very well in thwarting him."

Simon suppressed a quick smile at the "thwarting." Only the Black Hand would use such an antique word in a casual conversation.

"But you must not overestimate your powers. Being incorporeal is your best defense. Otherwise, you are as vulnerable as any human. The American Spirit could be turned into a vampire as easily as any civilian."

"What a useful thing to learn," said the bartender.

Simon and the Black Hand stared at the man. The drunk at the end of the bar was now asleep, his cheek resting in a spilled puddle of whiskey.

The bartender grinned, flashing the extended canines of a newly turned vampire. "My master will be delighted to learn the American Spirit can become one of us."

The phone rang again, the bell now sounding like a harsh warning of danger. They had thought this place was safe, but Igor's minions were everywhere.

Simon leapt out of the booth, phasing into his intangible form to flow through the bar. He phased back to being solidly human as he punched the vampire bartender in the jaw.

The creature smacked into a rack of bottles, sending them crashing down in a shower of glass and liquor. Simon phased again, passing through the broken bottles without harm.

The vampire sprang up. Bloodless wounds on his face from the glass shards closed immediately.

Behind Simon, the Black Hand shouted some arcane command. The bottles flew back into the air, forming a glittering barrier between Simon and the vampire.

"Don't protect me!" yelled Simon. "I can take him down."

But the vampire turned and rushed through the door in the back of the bar.

Simon phased through the glass and followed. A dark stairway plunged down to a basement. Already the vampire had vanished into shadows.

"Stop," said the Black Hand, as Simon groped for a light switch. "He will be gone."

"You don't know that!" Simon switched on the light, illuminating a small and empty storage room.

"This place operated during prohibition," said the Black Hand, "with secret access to the sewers. If you follow the vampire into the dark, you will be lost."

Simon pounded a fist against the wall in frustration. "You met me here a month ago. I drank here last week! He was just a bartender. A regular guy. Not a vampire." And I didn't even know his name, Simon thought with regret. How many times had he come into this place for a quick beer or a chat with others like himself, trying to keep the streets safe? When had he stopped noticing, stopped caring, about the guy who poured the beer? When had he stopped asking for a name?

"Yes," said the Black Hand. "He was just an ordinary man caught up in this extraordinary war. As vulnerable as you are."

The phone was still ringing. With a grumble, the drunk roused himself and picked it up. "Look," he said into the phone, "either ask for someone or stop calling!"

The Black Hand reached for the phone. "The call is for me," he said authoritatively and a little ominously—in other words, using his normal tone of voice.

The astounded drunk passed the phone to the Black Hand. "Where did you come from?" he asked, but the Black Hand didn't bother to answer.

"My friend, be careful." The Black Hand held the receiver a little away from his face as he continued to speak to Simon. "There are so many lost souls in this city. I do not want you to join them."

"Igor will never get me." Simon peered down the stairs. He understood the risks. The best way to catch the vampire lord was to track his minions back to his lair.

The Black Hand repeated his final warning. "Be careful. Work with the others. I am sorry, but I must leave now." He whispered a few words into the phone. Then the mage dissolved into a shower of sparks that flowed into the mouthpiece. With a neat click, the handset hung itself up.

"Nobody ever calls for me," the drunk said sadly.

"It could be worse, buddy," said Simon. "What's your name?"

LOCATION, LOCATION, LOCATION

"IT'S PERFECT," BERRY YELLED INTO THIN AIR. "EXACTLY WHAT they wanted. The hardcore fans will get it, and Umberto can turn it into a huge Easter egg for his director's cut DVD." She scrambled within the oversized tote threatening to spill off her shoulder onto the wet stone steps, searching for her tiny digital camera, so tiny it was now buried under the marked-up script, her pens, the notepad, the measuring tape, the compass, and all the accumulated debris of a life spent constantly on the move from one end of Cobalt City to the other. With her other hand, she tried to keep her impractically small umbrella from blowing down the street.

Luckily the Bluetooth earpiece eliminated the need for hanging onto the cell, although it did make her feel like she'd been assimilated to the dark side. Berry often wondered what other people thought when they saw her working: a redhead yelling into thin air on street corners to her imaginary friends?

Because Marcus might as well be imaginary. Her business partner had once again managed to lose himself after exiting the freeway and was massively late to their meeting with the property manager. So here she was, wrestling her tote in a downpour to make it give up her camera, and somewhere out there circled Marcus in his SUV, touring past the high-end shops of Parkside and yelling at his off-track GPS.

"Look," screamed Berry to the ether, cutting off his diatribe about a GPS that couldn't find its electronic backside with both hands, "the guy from JMS isn't here yet either. Stop and ask someone for directions if you have to."

She switched off the phone before she heard his response to her suggestion.

Her questing fingers finally found the smooth metal case of the camera, and she pulled it out of her tote to snap a few pictures of the massive oak door in front of her. Huge wrought iron hinges, oversized brass knob, and a stylized carving of chains crisscrossing the door. The thing was gorgeous. Amazing somebody hadn't ripped the door off this vacant building long ago. Although, in Parkside, Cobalt City's premiere millionaires' neighborhood, the cops probably kept an eye on such places. Even more astounding was that none of Cobalt City's more flamboyant superheroes or mad geniuses had moved into this place after the Adventurers Club closed at the beginning of the 1980s.

If the interior proved to be in half as good condition as the exterior, Umberto Longhini would be ecstatic. Italy's biggest big-budget producer kept emphasizing "real, you know, like the commercial, the real thing," in every one of their Skype-connected conferences. And it didn't get more real than the actual home of the first author of Solomon Cree's adventures.

Now she just needed to get inside. Maybe she should call the building management company again. The JMS rep was supposed to have met her by now. Berry searched in her bag for the old envelope she'd written the number on. A deep thud sounded from somewhere on the opposite side of the door, startling her into backing up a step. The wind snatched the umbrella from her hand and sent it flying down the deserted street.

"Oh, crap," Berry swore. Thunder boomed overhead. Behind

her, the tortured screech of rusted metal rang out. Berry whipped around. The door was now open, and a shadowy figure beckoned with one pale hand.

"You should come out of the rain, miss," the man in the doorway said.

An absolute wall of water poured out of the skies. Berry dove through the open door, shaking drops onto the marble floor like a wet puppy. "Hi, hi, hi. Wow, what a storm. I'm so glad you're here. Sorry, they didn't give me your name—"

"Tidwell," said the cadaverous man in an old-fashioned black suit, white shirt, and skinny dark blue tie.

"Very nice to meet you, Mr. Tidwell. Thank you so much for coming out on this awful day to show me the Adventurers Club." Privately, Berry wondered where JMS had found him. She'd dealt with the property management company when arranging downtown office shoots and had the impression they only hired Ivy League grads who dressed in the latest fashions. Tidwell looked like his next job might be in a mortuary. Maybe that was why he was in charge of this mothballed building.

"I'm Berry Fields," she added, in case JMS hadn't given Tidwell her name, and he was wondering how to ask her. "My partner Marcus is a little lost, but he'll be here soon."

"Very good, Miss Fields. May I take your coat?"

Berry glanced down at the puddle growing around her feet as the rain dripped off her. "Yeah, maybe, I shouldn't go trailing this through the mansion." And, as she struggled out of the coat while keeping a tight hold on her bag, she added, "I hope the heat is on."

"The Club is kept at a pleasant temperature for all residents."

"Residents? I thought the place was empty."

For the first time, Tidwell appeared slightly nonplussed. At least, that's how Berry interpreted his suddenly raised eyebrows.

"Ah, certainly," Tidwell replied after a short pause, head cocked as if listening for footsteps or listening to somebody else. "There are no physical residents present at the moment. Other than myself, of course."

"You live here? I'm sorry, I thought you were with JMS, you know, the property managers."

"No, Miss Fields, I am the doorman."

"Well, I knew most of the Parkside buildings had a doorman... but it's a little odd for an empty place like this. Or is JMS planning to reopen the building? Turn it into high-end apartments or something?"

"I am unaware of these plans. This will change our recent calculations." Tidwell turned away to neatly hang her coat in an oak wardrobe standing to the left of the door.

Berry glimpsed a number of old coats hanging in it. One even appeared to be an ancient fur. "That's a pretty piece. An antique?"

"Shipped from England in the 1960s. It was thought to be too dangerous to stay there." Tidwell snapped the wardrobe door shut and started down the marble hallway. As he moved deeper into the Adventurers Club, lighted fixtures in the ceiling automatically sprang on, shedding warm golden rays from their etched glass shades.

"Dangerous? What's dangerous about a wardrobe?" Berry asked, as she trailed after him.

"Lost children, quite a few, as I understand. Until they arrested the mad professor responsible."

"I thought mad professors were a Cobalt City specialty. You know, like the guy who lived here." Berry snapped a few shots of the heavy entrance door from the inside and then swung around to snap a few more down the hall. Umberto would love the look of the place. But if the Club was crammed with antiques, they'd need to check into insurance coverage and maybe consider shifting a few things out of the way before the film crew set up. Or maybe Umberto would pay to use the original fixtures.

Tidwell sidestepped easily out of every camera shot. Berry thought about waving him back into the photo, just so Umberto could get a picture of the hall's size in relation to a man. But then, maybe the doorman didn't like having his picture taken. She'd run into that prejudice amazingly often in Cobalt City, and she didn't want to upset him. He was being very pleasant about her interruption into his day—maybe JMS had alerted him—but he didn't have to be her guide through the Club.

"Can we go upstairs? I need to see the top floor apartment. The place where Professor Chandler, the writer, lived."

"Professor Chandler's old rooms?" Tidwell hesitated at the copper and marble inlaid doors of the elevator. The floor indicator needle above the doors pointed to a lovely Art Moderne metal number "one."

The Adventurers Club's elevator looked exactly like the descriptions in Chandler's novels of the lift that rose to Cree's penthouse apartment. Berry tried, without complete success, to eliminate a small squeal of delight. The script called for Solomon Cree to have a fight in this elevator before setting out from Cobalt City to track the villains through the Himalayas. Of course, they'd mock up the elevator in the studio, but this would be perfect for set-up shots. She snapped a couple more pictures.

"Does it work?" she asked Tidwell.

"Of course." Tidwell pressed a button to open the heavy outer doors. He pulled back the interior safety cage door and gestured to Berry to step inside. He followed her, carefully sliding the interior door closed. The manual controls included a big brass lever.

Berry practically swooned. She was sure the script called for

Cree to pull the elevator handle out of the controls and reveal a hidden sword that allowed him to fend off the villainous Vikings attacking him.

"I do have the best job in the world." She beamed at Tidwell, who failed to beam back. If nothing, the man looked more solemn.

"You must visit Professor Chandler's rooms?" he asked, making no movement to engage the controls.

"Oh, yes. If they're as good as this, we'll totally be able to sell Umberto on filming here. Didn't JMS tell you about this?"

"I am the doorman. My purpose is to let people in and out and take them where they request in the Club."

"Well, they should have told you, because you'll be opening doors a lot if Umberto decides to film here. See, they're making this great big Euro-pudding of a blockbuster. Most of it's taken from the graphic novels, you know, after Cree became this demon-cursed character trying to regain his immortal soul. But the Italian producing and directing the whole thing, my client, well, he collects the old Ace paperback reprints of Chandler's stories. You know, the ones with the bulging muscle guy slinging some screaming chick on his back and smacking samurai warrior types with his shotgun. And Umberto wants the start of the movie here, in Cobalt City, and in Chandler's apartment, except, of course, it's going to be Cree's Parkside penthouse apartment. He wants it to have that retro look, which you totally have. At least downstairs. But if upstairs is half as good, I'm going to be Umberto's favorite location scout!"

"I am enlightened," Tidwell said, an amazingly bright smile lighting up his face. "You are a scout. You find things that need to be found. No wonder I heard you at the door."

"Location scout. Proud partner in Fields and Moore. Marcus is the Moore, and I'm the Fields—Strawberry Fields—Mom's a major Lennon fan. I was going to name it Strawberry Fields and Moore, but Marcus thought that was a bit much. If this Club works for Umberto, then we'll have scored some major Hollywood street cred. Up until now, it's mostly been docudramas. Those Discovery Channel recreations of the Protectorate's battles. Oh, and the Starcom commercials. They love filming that main shopping drag of Parkside, you know, with the well-heeled types hurrying out of the best shops and into their cabs with the latest Starcom phones clapped to their ears." Berry paused to draw a breath. She loved her job and knew she tended to overwhelm other people when she started to explain it.

"I am sure the Club will prove to be more than satisfactory. After all, your presence at the entry did summon me."

"Thanks, I really appreciate you picking up the slack since the damn JMS rep seems to be as lost as Marcus." Then, realizing JMS was Tidwell's employer, she added, "Ah, crap, I didn't mean to call him that . . . uh, sorry." Swearing in front of Tidwell made her blush. The guy looked like he was descended from Cobalt City's most pure Puritan families. "What if Marcus arrives when we're upstairs, how will he get in?"

"I will know if someone appropriate is at the door and let him in. This way, please."

"Great, perfect. Well, up, up, and away," said Berry, relieved Tidwell was continuing the tour. "I've always wanted to say that! Seems perfect for an elevator."

"Very good, Miss Fields."

It might have been a trick of the flickering light in the elevator cab, but Berry could swear the man looked happy and somehow younger than he had when he answered the door.

"It is pleasant to be of service again." Tidwell pulled the elevator's inner cage door shut and pushed the topmost button.

"Mmmm," said Berry, not paying much attention as she scribbled some notes for her presentation to Umberto. The elevator jerked a little but seemed perfectly functional as it rose through the building. With a soft and discreet ding, it stopped, and the outer doors slid open. Tidwell cranked back the safety door, gesturing at the entryway of the penthouse apartment.

Berry stepped out. A porcelain lamp shaped like an elephant carrying a howdah lit immediately, shedding little diamond squares of light across the wood-paneled walls.

"Wow!" Berry turned in a circle to take in the crossed spears affixed to one wall, the complete conquistador armor on a plaster mannequin in the corner, and the full set of framed book covers depicting Solomon Cree's adventures. She moved closer and realized the covers weren't the printed copies found in any fanboy's basement. These were the original 1940s and 1950s oils painted by Dunamis Macamber for the pulp magazines, showing the golden-skinned Cree battling Vikings, mad mullahs, and silk-draped dragon ladies. There was even a painting inspired by the final weird adventure written by Chandler: Cree being dragged across a temple floor by wiggling tentacles sprouting from an enormous Chinese bronze vase.

"I had no idea," she breathed. Some serious internet research into the lore of Cree when she was preparing to pitch their company to Umberto had turned her into an aficionado of the artwork depicting the fictional adventurer. Frankly, Macamber's paintings were far more to her taste than the bare-chested figure of the Ace paperbacks or the dark, distorted look of the later graphic novels.

"I'm surprised these paintings haven't been ripped off and sold at Comicon. Not that you should worry about Umberto's crew. He's adding so many layers of security to keep props and scripts from walking off the set, he can do something for these too. Or maybe he'll want to put them in a bank vault during filming."

"The Club has its own ways of keeping its contents safe." Tidwell remained inside the elevator as Berry slowly walked the perimeters of the room, jotting notes about the size, look, and possible use in the film.

"Miss Fields." Tidwell gave a small cough, much more discreet than the elevator's bell. "I must inform her about this film, and the telegraph key is in the basement."

"You have a telegraph, a working telegraph, in the basement?" Berry groped in her bag for her planner and jotted down a note. "Fantastic. Let me take the pictures of the apartment, but I'm sure we will be renting the Adventurers Club."

"Very good. When you need to return to the main floor, please press the button. Please remember, all you need to do is press the button to call the elevator and help will come."

"Oh, you've been so nice. If you can just send Marcus up...if he gets here before I'm done. I swear he stopped to shop! Tiffany's, if I'm lucky." She grinned at Tidwell. Then she waved her hand at his concerned look. "Just a joke. His apologies usually run to an extra doughnut with coffee, not diamonds. Oh, and that rep from JMS, he can come up, or he can meet me downstairs. Doesn't matter. I know Umberto is going to take this place as is. I just need to see the rest of the rooms in this apartment and take a few more photographs for him."

"Very good, Miss Fields. I will send help to this floor when it arrives."

The elevator doors slid softly shut. Berry shook her head at the doorman's odd turn of phrase. Fancy calling Marcus, or maybe the rep from JMS, the help.

A dark mahogany door with a beautiful octagonal glass knob

opened into a dimly lit library. The built-in bookcases were crammed with leatherbound volumes of all sizes, many tattered and torn across the top edges of the spines, as if they had been opened often.

Two leather club chairs flanked a small table. Berry caught sight of a crystal decanter set on one lower shelf, looking as if it still held a swallow or two of Scotch.

"That old joker. He really just wrote what he knew." The whole set-up perfectly matched Chandler's descriptions of Cree's inner sanctum, Solomon's personal library where he always found the first arcane clue that started him on his fantastic adventures.

"There's probably even a thirty-eight revolver and a chemical set in one of those cupboards flanking the fireplace," she said to herself, as she circled the room. As Berry moved closer to the tile-framed fireplace, the gas flames popped on, adding a cheerful warmth to the room.

Remembering the last Chandler book Umberto had mailed to them, Berry counted three bookcases to the left from the fireplace. There, as she half expected, she found a Celtic knot carved into the wood of the shelf. She snapped a quick picture and, with one trembling finger, pressed the center of the knot. With a distinct click, the bookcase slid silently away from her, revealing a tiny inner chamber crammed with dusty boxes and odd shapes covered with canvas and rope.

"Umberto will buy this place and ship it back brick by brick to Italy," she said to the long-forgotten contents of the little room. "Or maybe I can rent it from JMS and lead tours through here after the movie comes out."

She considered the reaction of the Solomon Cree Fan Club. They had flooded the comments on her blog already when she posted about scouting possible Cobalt City locations. One of their members, George, had tipped her to the Adventurers Club in Parkside and the fact that Chandler had lived there. Berry decided she had to invite George to the filming so he could see this. Of course, she'd need 911 on speed dial. He would have a heart attack if he knew Cree's secret treasure room really existed.

Her camera light was flashing, warning her the memory card was nearly full. Her backup was down in the car, but she really didn't need any more pictures. Except ... well, why not take the last one? What should it be? Berry stared at the tall chunky shape hidden just inside the treasure room door. Oh, it couldn't be? Could it?

With eager hands, she pulled the canvas covering away to reveal a giant bronze funeral urn. She knew it was from the Qin Dynasty, because that was exactly how Chandler had described it in his last Cree adventure. Three triangular feet, weird pictographs encircling the greenish bronze sides, and a lid topped with a jade finial.

This vase looked so much spookier than the mock-up Umberto had emailed her last week. It appeared as though it could contain the soul-sucking tentacles of Wen Chang's demon from outer space.

She grabbed the jade finial, intent on lifting the lid and getting a shot of the interior, something Chandler had failed to mention in his novel. Of course, it probably held the opium or whatever the old professor had been smoking when he came up with his extraterrestrial demon.

Berry struggled with the lid, which seemed to be jammed tightly into the neck of the vase, but she finally managed to drag it off. Unfortunately, her final mighty tug set the vase rocking wildly on its tiny feet.

Berry leaped back as the vase tipped with a crash onto the floor.

"Oh, shit!" She prayed she hadn't just broken a valuable antique. What would Tidwell say?

As the first long, greasy, black tentacle came snaking out of the vase, stabbing across the room, Berry swore again and lunged for the door. She remembered the drills in school with a chilling clarity that would have made her first-grade teacher proud. "When you see a monster, or even the tip of a monster, children, remember this is Cobalt City, city of superheroes. Don't hesitate," Miss Anselm would say, shaking one bony finger at her small charges, "leap, run, drop, roll, and scream! Remember, some hero will hear you if you yell loud enough, children!"

Berry found the screams came naturally as she dodged a second tentacle slashing out of the bronze vase, as did the running jump, weave, and hop over one snake-like writhing black tip. She sprang into the entry hall. Berry tried to slam the door shut behind her, but the tentacles grasped the edge of the door and whacked it back into the wall.

Grabbing the plaster mannequin dressed as a conquistador in both arms, Berry hurled it at the three tentacles now blossoming out of the vase.

The trio of black tentacles wrapped themselves around the mannequin, dragging it backward with crushing force that dented the armor. Berry winced at the destruction but did not pause in her rush to the elevator button. She pushed it hard and repeatedly, hoping Tidwell was right. That help would arrive.

Another crash came from the library, and the mannequin was hurled back into the entry.

Berry jumped to one side and ripped down one of the African spears on the wall. She swung it so the sharpened end pointed toward the door. With luck, the thing had been dipped in some arcane poison venomous to tentacles. Given the rest of her experiences in Chandler's rooms, that would be appropriate.

The tentacles, now four in number, slid through the door, sending questing tips across the floor. Berry slashed down at the one nearest to her, skewering it like sushi on a toothpick. With a force that dragged the spear out of her hands, the tentacle recoiled, snapping into its fellows.

Behind her, the elevator made its soft little ding and the doors slid open.

"This way, sir," said Tidwell, gesturing to a shadowy figure dressed in a fedora and trench coat.

For a brief second, Berry believed the original Solomon Cree had appeared to save her. But the face that glanced briefly toward her was masked in white bandages, not the famed glowing golden features of Cree. She recognized Mister Grey, the spectral man who fought as part of the Mysterious Five and Protectorate.

"Come here, Miss Fields," called Tidwell.

Mister Grey spun into a whirlwind of stinging ash, blasting past her as he herded the thrashing tentacles back through the library door.

"Miss Fields," said Tidwell, sounding almost urgent, "the rest of your party is waiting for you downstairs."

With a gulp and nod, Berry hurried into the elevator. "Shouldn't we wait for him? Help him?"

"If Mister Grey needs any help, I am sure he will ring the bell." Tidwell swung the brass handle to take the elevator to the ground floor.

Berry wrapped both arms around her bag and hugged it tightly to her chest. In some part of her brain that wasn't still screaming, she felt incredibly proud that she had managed to hang onto her things throughout her brief fight and flight. And follow Miss

Anselm's instructions. Apparently screaming loudly did attract heroes, or at least one famous hero of Cobalt City.

As the elevator slid to a halt, she couldn't resist asking, "Tidwell, does that handle pull out and become a sword?"

"Of course, although I never recommend using it." He twisted the handle and revealed a quarter inch of shining steel before pushing it back into place.

The outer doors opened. Tidwell neatly swung back the brass cage door.

Thinking about the movie, because that was less terrifying than the tentacles battling Mister Grey a few floors above their heads, Berry asked, "Why wouldn't you use the sword?"

"Once you pull it out completely, the elevator is disabled. And the sword rarely goes back in easily. It tends to stick. Poor engineering, if I do say so myself."

"Good to know." Berry stepped out of the elevator.

Across the hallway, she spotted Marcus talking to a slender guy in a suit that obviously came from one of Parkside's most exclusive tailors, a rep from JMS if she ever saw one.

"Marcus!" Berry screamed, as she hurried across the floor, hugging her surprised business partner as her bag tumbled to the floor and sent a jumble of stuff rolling in all directions.

"Berry," Marcus said, doing the awkward guy pat between her shoulder blades. "What's up? How's the apartment upstairs?"

Beside her, Tidwell gave one of his soft little coughs. "I believe Miss Fields found that Professor Chandler's rooms would be most pleasing. Once a small pest problem is cleared away." He looked almost imploringly at Berry. "It will be nice to have people using the Club again."

"Oh, Berry, not a rat?" Marcus shuddered and turned to the JMS rep. "You know, no matter how many times they clean out the sewers, there's always mutant rats trying to move into abandoned buildings. Was it a big one, Berry?"

"I just saw the tip of a tail, or something," said Berry with a glance at Tidwell, who bent to swiftly retrieve her things. He handed her bag back to her with a small bow. "Tidwell, are you sure it'll be gone before the filming starts?"

"I have no doubts about the gentleman upstairs. His expertise in removing such pests is exceptional."

Berry nodded at him and took a big breath to calm herself. She turned to Marcus. "Other than that, it's perfect. Exactly how Chandler described Solomon Cree's apartment."

Marcus beamed at her and shook the JMS rep's hand again. As they went out the door together, Tidwell glided over to the wardrobe to retrieve her coat. He held it for her to put on.

"Will it be alright, really? Filming here? I mean, are you sure you want strangers here, going in and out? It won't stir up more trouble for you?"

"Oh, no, Miss Fields. I think your movie is exactly what the Club needs. A little advertisement, as it were, to attract the right tenant. And anything that is found, like that vase you noticed today, needs to be found. I simply cannot remember the last time an accident occurred in the Club."

Berry smiled at him.

On the sidewalk outside, Berry thanked the JMS rep for coming out as Marcus gallantly held his umbrella over both of them. The rain slackened into a light drizzle, and the thunderclouds began breaking up to the east.

"I'm sorry I was late. To tell the truth, I hate this place. That Tidwell gives me the creeps," said the man from JMS. "Half the time when I knock, he won't open the door. I was a little surprised he let you in."

"Well, Berry's a charmer. She can talk her way into anything," said Marcus.

"Did you see the guy in a trench coat and a fedora?" Berry stared up at the top of the building. She wondered if any of the darkened windows there were connected to Chandler's rooms. "Did he come in with you?"

"A man wearing a fedora? Sounds like Solomon Cree in his city clothes." Marcus laughed. "Nah, didn't see anyone else. Maybe you spotted a ghost."

"Maybe I did. I bet there are a lot of ghosts and stories behind those doors."

"Hey, it's Cobalt City, of course there are. Can I buy you a doughnut and a cup of coffee? Since I was late and left you to do all the work."

"Sure," Berry said. "That sounds great."

FORTUNES FOR
THE BRAVE HEART

THE AIR FILLED WITH THE SPICY SCENT OF SIZZLING HOT DOGS, the delicious whiff of frying doughnuts, and the buttery burnt smoke of fresh popcorn, all underlaid with the subtle sweetness of sticky children clutching caramel apples or cotton candy.

Excited couples on dates passed by, arguing whether they should try the sideshow tents first or seek passage on the boats swinging through the Haunted Tunnel of Love. A red-haired woman laughed up at her stocky date as he draped a lazy arm across her shoulders and teased her with a sugary doughnut plucked from a white paper bag.

Teenagers pushed and shoved in their own group mating dance. At the other end of the spectrum, an elderly pair fell into amiable wrangling over who was the best shot at the rifle booth and who always won the most prizes.

Katherine Wilde felt her inner feline sit up and sniff hungrily at the tasty toddlers being pushed or pulled by frazzled parents searching out the sparkly rides at the Golden Apple Carnival. "Down, kitty," she muttered. Now was not the time for a snack—nor were fat babies ever appropriate food for her inner tiger.

She hated carnivals. Even with all her feline senses stuffed under her seemingly normal human exterior, the noise, the smells, the flashing lights, it all made her twitchy. If she had a tail, it would be lashing from side to side. As it was, she struggled to keep her canines from descending into sharp points and curled her fingers into her palms to prevent instinctively swiping with razor-sharp claws at the next person who jostled her.

She wished she wasn't there, but she'd heard stories all week from the others about strange happenings at the Golden Apple Carnival. Trouble had come to Cobalt City, disguised as a fun fair, and she needed to keep her wits and not be distracted by the memories dredged up by the smells and sounds of this carnival.

A dreadful night in Switzerland…a girl running down a dark mountain road to the brilliant lights and calliope music…

A dare sent young Katherine to the carnival. The expensive Swiss finishing school her parents decreed necessary after the hat incident at Ascot had a nighttime curfew, of course. But even then, she'd been a bit of a daredevil, a bit of an acrobat. She hadn't needed enhanced feline powers to unlatch an upper story window and climb down a drainpipe.

It began as a bet with her roommate, Claudine, that she could get out and visit Le Carnaval Pomme d'Or and see all the wonders promised on the posters plastered throughout the village. The most intriguing one showed a two-faced man with slips of paper spilling from his fingers. Across the bottom was written: "audentes fortuna iuvat." Being overly educated young ladies, she and her classmates were certain they were the brave, the audacious, who fortune would favor. As the daughters of aristocrats, wealthy industrialists, or famous artists, they had every right to expect the world's riches to fall into their eagerly outstretched and perfectly manicured hands.

The beautiful Claudine, the daughter of an equally beautiful and chic former model, spent her nights whispering about the fortuneteller. "I want to know how wonderful my life will be," she told Katherine once.

"What will you do if you don't like your fortune?" Kat could never resist teasing Claudine, trying to ruffle the other girl's self-possession.

But the swift reaction startled her.

"Oh, if I was not going to be famous, I would die!" Claudine said.

The school wasn't a prison—they regularly took trips to theaters, museums, and other amusements. But Katherine still remembered the ripple of shock that ran through the assembly when, just hours before the carnival was to open, the headmistress flatly announced that no girl in her care was to visit it, that even attempting to see it would be grounds for expulsion.

And, of course, Katherine ranted about this ridiculous curtailment of their freedom to Claudine. She never meekly accepted the dictates of others—that quirk of her personality led to the disaster with the Queen Mother's hat, among other things.

"If you're so bold," Claudine said finally, "why don't you go?"

"I'll go, and I'll ride every ride," Katherine recklessly promised. "And I'll bring you back a prize from one of the booths."

"Bring me back my fortune," Claudine insisted. "One of those slips of paper."

"I will." Katherine never stopped to consider that she was taking all the risks. If caught, she, and not Claudine, would be expelled.

So, later that night, she slipped between the black curtains of the fortuneteller's tent and met a small, remarkably plain little man, seated on a folding stool behind a simple wooden table. On the table—and this memory burned strangely clear in her mind—was a clay bowl filled to the brim with slips of folded paper.

"Take one," said the man, and she'd been startled that he spoke English to her, not the more common French or German. "Take it and give it to me."

She'd plucked a strip of paper from the bowl and handed it across the table.

He had unfolded it and spent a long time staring, until she began to squirm under the pressing weight of his silence.

"Cave felem." His face was blank, and the sound of his voice came from everywhere and nowhere. For a moment, she was scared, but then she told herself it was only a ventriloquist's trick.

"Beware the cat?" Katherine translated from the Latin, showing off her expensive education.

He nodded. "If you do not take control of it, it will devour all. Even you."

"What nonsense! I thought you told fortunes, predicted the future."

"I have. Next time I can only tell you your past."

"That's foolish," seventeen-year-old Katherine retorted. "Completely bonkers. Who wants to know their past?"

"You will. Some day. But now you must leave."

He stood up then and crossed the tent to hold the curtain open for her. The glare of the midway lights outside created a crooked shadow man against the far wall of the tent. The shadow had two faces: one looking forward and one looking back.

Katherine pretended to fumble with her purse, dropping an extra fifty-franc note upon the table and, at the same time, filching one of the paper fortunes from the bowl for Claudine.

"You needn't steal one," said the little man. "Or pay for your theft with so much money."

Startled, she swung to face him.

"Tell Claudine to heed her fortune if she wants to keep her future."

Outside, the music blared through loudspeakers strung up in the trees and atop tent poles. The crowd shrieked in a babble of languages that made her want to clap her hands to her ears. Strangers swirled around her, shouting and pointing at the garish entertainments, and suddenly she wanted to leave. The carnival wasn't fun at all—it was hectic, and bewildering, and everyone seemed desperately hungry for something they could never have.

For the first time in her life, and for the last, Katherine fled before her vague fears. She ran up the dark mountain road, escaping the maniacal confusion. She clawed her way up the drainpipe and fell, panting, into the moonlit bedroom.

"What took you so long?" asked Claudine from her bed, switching on a small bedside lamp and sitting up. "Did you get it? Did you?

"Here," said Katherine, dropping the paper fortune on her lap. "I stole this for you." She didn't quite dare to admit the strange fortuneteller had caught her in the act or tell Claudine his words of warning.

The French girl reached out her hands and unfolded the paper. "Fortuna vitrea est; tum cum splendet, frangitur," she read. Her face was puzzled. Latin had never been Claudine's favorite subject.

But Katherine recognized the motto. They had spent a long and weary hour dissecting it in class. "Fortune is like glass, when it glitters, it breaks."

Claudine stared at her blankly when she translated it, and then, with a cry, crumpled the paper and tossed it away. "That's horrid."

"Well, it's your future," said Katherine, dropping exhausted onto her own bed.

"I don't want it," wept Claudine, her sudden sobs shaking her slim body.

Footsteps pounded down the hallway, attracted by the girl's mounting hysteria.

The door of their bedroom was thrust open, followed by shouts, alarms, and accusations of rules broken and curfews confounded. In the end, Katherine returned to England in disgrace. Claudine left the school a few months later.

A year after appearing on the cover of the French *Vogue*, Claudine was found dead in her Paris apartment, the victim of an overdose. Recently embarked on the genetic modifications that would turn her into Wild Kat, Katherine only learned of Claudine's death while reading an ancient gossip magazine one night to distract herself from the pain and insomnia created by the beginning transformation of her body. In the obituary, some young writer decided to get fancy and quote an obscure Latin phrase, talking about a glittering career shattered by the emotional fragility of the unfortunate Claudine.

In the darkened waiting room, Katherine could not suppress a shudder. Was the paper slip she gave Claudine merely a chance prediction, or had it been a curse that set the girl's feet on the path to ruin?

Unlike Claudine, Kat mastered the fate thrust upon her by the fortuneteller. The cat did not consume her. But, sometimes, she dreamed she heard a calliope whistle and a strange voice whisper, "You still have a fortune waiting. Do you dare to hear it?"

Years later, the Cobalt City carnival shattered the night with its noise. In the middle of it, Katherine stood frozen, staring at a poster advertising Unfortunate John the Two-Faced Oracle, a small man with slips of paper dropping like petals from his out-stretched fingertips. A feline snarl escaped Katherine's curled lips. It couldn't be true. Yet it looked like the same man who had ruined poor Claudine with his paper slip of a curse.

Intent on finding the fortuneteller, Katherine stalked down the narrow alley where the carnival's sideshows were located, searching past Questo the Mentalist, Ice Hair Tom, the China Doll Family, and Sateen the Razor Dancer for the fortuneteller's tent. Pushing past her, several couples headed for the Haunted Tunnel of Love, where they were promised the ride of a lifetime.

"Excuse me," a red-haired young woman clutched at Katherine's arm. "But can you help me?"

"I'm sorry. Do I know you?" To her own ears, her clipped vowels sounded terribly unfriendly. She softened her words with a quick and slightly apologetic smile.

"No, no, it's just—" The redhead swayed where she stood, her pale complexion turning almost ghostly under the garish neon of the carnival lights.

Katherine glanced around and spotted a bench near Questo's tent. She guided the young woman to it and sat down beside her. "Are you ill? Should I call someone?"

"No, I'm okay, at least, I think I am. It's just…well…this is going to sound so weird…but I think I lost someone. I think I lost someone important." Tears started to well in her large green eyes.

Katherine dug into the pocket of her leather jacket and pulled out a large clean handkerchief, one of the most important tools that any superhero (or heroine) could carry. She thrust it into the hands of the redhead. "Tell me what's wrong. But, first, blow."

With a hiccup, the young woman blew her nose and mopped her eyes. "You're so nice, and I'm sorry, I never meant to stop you. You must think I'm out of my mind." She straightened up a little and thrust out her hand to Katherine. "I'm Berry, Berry Fields…it's Strawberry, really, my mom was a bit of a Beatles freak…but everyone calls me Berry…even—" She trailed off and sat staring at Katherine. The tears continued to pour unheeded down her face.

"Even who?" prompted Katherine.

"That's it. I don't know. Except I do know. I know it's somebody important. Somebody who calls me Berry and buys doughnuts." Berry reached into the large satchel purse slung at her side and pulled out a crumpled bag of carnival doughnuts. "See, it's still warm. And I didn't buy it. I know I didn't. Somebody gave them to me. But I can't remember who. Except I'm sure it was a guy."

Katherine looked at the bag. It appeared completely normal and was, as Berry said, slightly warm to the touch. Why such a thing would send this young woman into such despair, she couldn't imagine.

"Let me take you home." Katherine suddenly felt a wave of guilty relief. She didn't need to face the fortuneteller. This young woman clearly needed her help. She could leave the carnival.

Berry shook her head vehemently. "No, no, we have to find someone."

"Who?" asked Katherine.

"I don't know," Berry admitted. "But I know it's important to find him. You see, I have this talent. I think it comes from growing up here. It's not like I'm a hero or anything, but I can find things, when I need to. That's my business. I'm a location scout for TV and movies. I find places around Cobalt City for people to film. I recently finished my first big budget commission, this huge action film. They're going to use this old mansion in Parkside for the opening sequences."

"Really? I live in the Parkside neighborhood." Katherine hadn't heard of any filming, but she hadn't been paying much attention to local news recently.

"It's the old Adventurers Club. They're filming the first part of the new Solomon Cree movie there."

Katherine nodded. She'd driven by the building numerous times and always thought it a pity that something so lovely was closed up. "And why are you at the carnival?" she asked Berry.

"That's it. I'm not sure. We...I...the check just came through from Umberto. It's the most I've ever been paid. So I...we...came here to celebrate." Berry stopped and rubbed her forehead.

"You came here with someone?" Katherine was troubled now. She vaguely remembered seeing this woman when she first arrived at the carnival. Had someone been with Berry? It seemed her own memory was playing tricks on her, because she could not recall exactly what she had seen.

"I think I did, but how can I not know for sure?"

Katherine delicately shifted her sense of smell, letting the tiger inside inhale the fragrance of the young woman sitting on the bench. There was something else, a trace, very subtle, of someone else, someone masculine, lingering about her jacket. Someone else had handled Berry's coat, and fairly recently. She could probably tell more if she leaned into the leather and gave it a good snort, but she couldn't explain that to the unfortunate Berry.

"Turn out your bag," Katherine suggested. "Let's see if there's anything else in it."

Berry dumped the bag upside down on the bench, the usual litter of a busy woman's life, except for one thing. A man's leather wallet, very worn.

Katherine noticed the same scent on it that she detected around the shoulders of Berry's jacket.

Berry opened it up. "There's nothing in it, just some of my

business cards and some cash." She ran her fingers along the leather. "He dropped it…After he paid for the tickets. I picked it up and stuck it in my purse to keep it safe."

"Paid for what tickets?"

"The Haunted Tunnel of Love." Berry sounded definite now, more sure of herself. "I was there. Then I knew something was wrong, and I had to find someone to help me. That's when I saw you."

Katherine nodded. She knew a cry for help when she heard it, and she couldn't turn away. This woman needed Wild Kat.

"Stay here," she instructed Berry. "I think somebody has been playing tricks on you. It's probably nothing, but I'm going to get help. Just stay here."

"Okay." Berry clutched her bag to her chest.

In the shadows behind the carnival booths, Katherine Wilde found an appropriately private space for a quick change. The tiger deep inside her soul stretched and let out a satisfied snarl. The hunt was on.

As always, the change from human to feline-enhanced senses took a moment of orientation. Then, costumed now as Wild Kat and with her Katherine clothes neatly rolled up and stuffed out of sight, she stepped back into the flow of the crowd.

She didn't need her heightened hearing to note the whispers and hissed comments. But this was Cobalt City, and people hung back, gave her space. A few of the more timid pretended to check their watches and then pulled their families away toward the exits. The bolder ones whipped out their digital cameras, ready to click pictures if a superhero versus supervillain battle suddenly engulfed the place.

The carnival still swirled around her, but now her sense of smell formed shapes, trails of color, like ribbons attached to each of the individuals crowding up the midway. Wild Kat stopped looking with her eyes and let her other senses take command.

Couples, like pairs of ribbons entangled in their overheated pheromones, entered the Haunted Tunnel of Love. But around the red-lit exit, the ribbons of scent broke apart, each heading in a separate direction, no longer entwined.

Wild Kat cocked her head, standing as still as a cat contemplating a mousehole. The dark entrance to the tunnel was empty. Too many couples had passed in and out of it to clearly distinguish Berry's scent, or that of her lost companion, but the feeling of something evil prickled her hair. With a low growl, Wild Kat glided forward.

Inside, the tunnel seemed larger than it appeared outside. A boat rocked upon a pool of black stagnant water. A dark figure stepped forward, an old man cloaked and hooded. "Silver for the ferryman. Coins, please, no paper money."

Wild Kat snarled at him, and the old man shrank back.

"Couples only," he said. "No singles. She only wants couples."

"Who?" Wild Kat asked.

"Madame Proserpina."

Wild Kat looked into the tunnel. The boat seemed the only way to go forward, unless she wanted to wade through the dank water. Like any good cat, she hated getting her feet wet, so she leapt lightly into the bobbing little boat.

The old man hesitated for a moment longer, then he pulled on a lever shaped like a long oar. "You can pay me next time. Enjoy the ride."

The boat rocked and then jerked forward, gliding deeper into the tunnel. Scenes slipped past her, painted upon the fake rock walls. A young girl collecting flowers, a dark man erupting from the center of a meadow, flames shooting into the sky, an abduction into the dark earth.

The woman who lived at the center of the cat recognized classical themes and the crudely painted rendition of the story of Persephone and Hades. She also wondered when the "love" would replace the "haunted" in this tunnel.

The ride grew even darker. The tang of wet stone and mud, an underground smell, gave way to a strange, seductive odor, a mixture of wild thyme and catnip, of summer sunshine and winter snow, of coffee mingled with a man's spicy aftershave—and then the air was clear and free of everything except a cold dusty scent, like an open empty tomb.

Wild Kat tensed. The boat rocked around a corner, gliding to a halt in a large dark pool, facing what seemed to be a cave. Behind the gauzy curtain stretched across the cave's mouth, something rustled. The tiger inside her head yowled a warning.

"Are you alone, my dear?" a woman whispered behind the curtain. "Madame Proserpina has nothing for you. Why don't you come back with your young man later? I'll tell you if his heart is true. Just a whiff of my cauldron will let you know."

The boat jerked, starting forward. Heedless of years of warnings about the dangers of standing in small boats, Wild Kat rose and tensed her muscles. She glanced up. Pipes spewing mist ran across the ceiling.

She flung herself up, caught hold of one pipe, and swung herself to the ledge running in front of the cave.

With one swipe of her claws, Wild Kat tore down the curtain to reveal a slender woman standing next to a steaming cauldron, a wand raised in one pale white hand.

"Go away!" commanded Madame Proserpina. Steam boiled out of the cauldron, a cloud of icy fragrance that drove Wild Kat back.

"Sorcery!" screamed the human part of her brain. "Prey!" prompted the tiger inside her. The strangely scented steam began to envelop her, and suddenly, all her senses seemed dull. She shook her head, trying to focus on the woman behind the cauldron. Her face wavered, out of focus, and Wild Kat felt her anger starting to drain away.

"You haven't any heart left to break. You're useless to me." Madame Proserpina raised her wand again and gestured toward the door. "Go on, be a good kitty, shoo!"

"I am never a good kitty!" Wild Kat spat back, the tiger's rage overcoming the dull lassitude of Madame Proserpina's bubbling potion. She leaped over the cauldron, kicking at the wand in Madame Proserpina's hand.

The wand cracked in two. Madame Proserpina screamed as she staggered back, upsetting her cauldron so the contents spilled across the floor and drained away into the dark river flowing past her cave.

Far off, Wild Kat heard the howling of dogs, a deep baying like a hound. She could smell something else. Something old, ancient, vast. Something like Doctor Shadow, only worse. Around them, the cave stretched, seemingly without end or hope of exit.

Years of battling the supernatural let Wild Kat close her senses to the expanding darkness around her. Instead, she grabbed Madame Proserpina's long white braid, hauling her to her feet. She shook her hard, just pricking through the long black cloak with her nails. "Don't play tricks."

The sorceress snarled at her. "I married Death, why should I fear you?"

"I'm the one with claws and teeth. What did you do with the couples who came in here?"

"I'm saving them," Proserpina said with utmost conviction.

"What?" Wild Kat looked at the other woman. This was no

maniacal cackling witch. The sorceress looked almost sad but also determined.

"All those foolish couples, thinking love will last forever, that they can be happy if they are only with each other. You and I, we're cleverer than that, aren't we?"

Wild Kat shook the woman again. "What are you talking about?"

"Better to forget than to be in love. You should know that. I can see these things. You lost your heart long ago."

"I think you're quite mistaken," Wild Kat replied quickly. Her love life wasn't the thing on trial here. "What did you do to Berry? And the others who came in here?"

"I stole their memories. I stole their memories of each other. I made them forget the one they were with."

"Can you restore them?" Wild Kat thought of the shattered young woman sitting on the bench outside, convinced she had lost someone very important. How many more scenes of heartbreak were playing out across the city?

With a grimace, the sorceress pointed at her shattered wand and upset cauldron. "The spell is already broken. They will go back to being the same foolish, lovestruck idiots that they were." She pulled away from Wild Kat and wrapped her cloak more firmly around herself. The sorceress began to sink into the ground, melting away like a certain Wicked Witch.

As she disappeared, she made one last mocking comment. "Go ask the fortuneteller for one of his slips of paper. He knows what happened to your heart."

Then the cave was only an empty alcove, built out of canvas and metal piping. Wild Kat looked over her shoulder. A boat glided into the pool carrying a young couple. The woman screamed when she saw Wild Kat crouched at the edge of the now tiny pond. Her date pulled her tight into his embrace. "It's only a wax dummy," he said to the girl and kissed her soundly. The girl giggled. The boat jerked and passed through a curtain.

An empty boat slid past. Wild Kat jumped onboard. It carried her out of the Haunted Tunnel of Love and back into the garishly lit midway of the carnival.

She made her way back to the bench where she had left the distraught redhead, but Berry didn't need her anymore. A stocky young man was sitting next to her, clutching both her hands tightly in his.

"It was so weird. I was halfway home when I realized I'd left you at the carnival. So I turned around and came right back. We need a vacation, babe, we've both been working way too hard. How could I forget and leave you here?"

"It's okay now, Marcus. You found me." Berry snuggled closer to him, resting her head on his shoulder.

Wild Kat smiled and turned away. All around her, couples were reuniting, with glad cries and quick kisses, hugs and exclamations.

Then she spotted it, the sideshow tent with the poster advertising Unfortunate John the Two-Faced Oracle.

Forgetting she was still Wild Kat and not Katherine, she stepped through the entrance. Once again, she faced a nondescript little man seated behind a plain table. But there was a scent lingering in the air, a scent of something ancient and powerful. Something like what she'd smelled in Madame Proserpina's cave but different also.

The man looked up at her and then pushed the clay bowl full of strips of paper toward her. "Pick one, and I will tell you your past."

"I don't care about my past," snarled Wild Kat, leaning on the table with her claws out. She scratched long furrows into the wood.

"You should. Knowing your past can change your future."

"Your fortune killed Claudine!"

"Did it? Or did it show her a fate she lacked the will to change? Did your fortune kill you?"

"Omnia causa fiunt," said a second voice from the back of the tent.

Once again, Wild Kat saw shadows crawling up the walls, the shadow of a man with two faces.

"Indeed," said Unfortunate John, "all things happen for a reason. Like old gods trapped in a carnival or a young girl seeing her future written on a slip of paper."

"How can you stand it?" she asked. "To ruin people's lives like that?"

"I don't do anything. I give them a glimpse of their future and their past. If they are wise, they learn from what I tell them. If not, then what can I do? I'm just a sideshow freak trapped in a carnival. That's why they call me Unfortunate John, even though I would prefer them to call me Janus. Now, do you want to draw again and learn about your past? Or are you done?"

"Madame Proserpina dared me to do it." Wild Kat stared down at the simple clay bowl filled with slips of paper. It both drew and repelled her. She withdrew her claws and leaned away from it.

"Another relic of another era. And far angrier about her fate than me. Go on, draw one. You're strong enough to face backward." He turned so his profile faced her. Two profiles, one facing forward, one facing backward.

She stretched out her hand and snagged one slip of paper on the tip of a claw. As she opened it, Unfortunate John's second voice stated, "Abstulit qui dedit."

It had been too many years since she studied Latin. She looked to the little man for translation.

"He who gave it, took it," he said.

"What?"

"Once you held a man's heart, his love, and when he left, he took your heart with him."

Wild Kat shook her head. "No. There's never been anyone like that. Not in my past."

"Now you have the fortune you paid for. Fifty francs worth of knowledge you did not want." Unfortunate John smiled at her. It was not a warm smile. "Only you can truly interpret the phrase. But I can tell you this. Until you understand it, your heart will remain frozen. That much I can see clearly."

Suddenly all Wild Kat wanted was to retrieve her clothes. Like her teenage self, she longed to flee the carnival. However, she didn't throw away the paper fortune crumpled in her hand. Instead, she carefully tucked it inside her costume, next to her heart, to contemplate another day.

"I am finished with your games," she told Unfortunate John.

He nodded and then cocked his head to one side, as if someone or something had just whispered in his ear. "Unusual. But fair enough. You can draw once more."

"What?"

"Draw again, one more slip. For the city's fortune this time. Apparently, you are the keeper of its doorways as much as I was when I once held Rome in my protection."

"You are a very strange man."

"No. I am one old and very tired god. Draw and let me finish this night."

Some compulsion pushed her hand forward, and she drew out a final strip of paper. This one was black with white writing running across it.

"Ah," said Unfortunate John, "one of those."

"Novus ordo seclorum," his second voice said.

"A new order for the ages," he translated.

"And what does it mean?" But even as she asked, she felt the answer blossoming inside her. "Are changes coming to Cobalt City?"

"Old heroes will fall."

A shudder ran through Wild Kat. Because the heroes of the city were her friends. Because she was a hero of the city.

"But we can shape our futures. You said so," she argued with the man, the god, who told the future and the past.

Unfortunate John nodded at her.

"Then, no matter how many heroes fall," said Wild Kat, clutching the fortune tightly in her hand and feeling a sudden unreasonable but undeniable lightness in her heart, "new ones will rise. Because this is Cobalt City!"

She left Unfortunate John to his dark little tent and his bowl of obscure phrases. The world was changing, Wild Kat could feel it as surely as the tiger roaring in her soul. But she could face her past, and she could confront her future. All the choices in the world were hers to make.

Soon, the carnival would pull up stakes and leave. But the city, her beloved Cobalt City, would endure. She carried that certain knowledge with her into the night.

COBALT CITY 2012

..--- ----- .---- ..---

WRECKER OF ENGINES

.----

CHAPTER 1: THE ADVENTURERS CLUB

MORGAN LEE MISSED HIS VESPA. ON THE BACK OF HIS 1967 black and white sweet machine, he had zipped past cars stalled in traffic, grabbed lunch from the outstretched hands of Hong Kong's hawkers, and seriously impressed the girls.

But, most of all, he could see his city: from the jostle of folks spilling off the sidewalks to the tall buildings with the walls of windows reflecting the neon lights. Riding the Vespa felt like he was whizzing through the data and bytes that made up the metropolis.

But he left the Vespa behind, part of the life he was forced to flee. Everyone in Hong Kong knew about his antique scooter. Some lackey of the tong might have the bright idea of tracing the Vespa if he shipped it to Cobalt City.

So here he was. New city, new sights, and he was traveling through it trapped in a town car with tinted windows. Even tilting his head at an angle, the tops of the buildings disappeared above him.

Morgan regretted the limo rental. It smelled stuffy. He was traveling locked inside a leather-trimmed tin can. It wasn't him. But then again, the fancy wheels were probably necessary for the stiff-backed business dude sitting next to him.

When he'd shown up at the JMS office on the fiftieth floor of a downtown skyscraper, the real-estate guy kept looking at him funny. Even after he'd double-checked Morgan's bank accounts, the man stared at him a little oddly. When Morgan asked to rent the Adventurers Club, his expression became even stranger.

"Mr. Lee, how did you know about the Adventurers Club?" asked the JMS agent, Mr. Brown-Harwich.

Morgan resisted the urge to check over his shoulder for Mr. Lee. Being seventeen, and with the purple not completely washed out of his spiked black hair, people rarely called him "Mister." Of course, showing up with bank statements documenting that he was currently worth several million American dollars did help with the "Mister" thing.

"I saw the movie," said Morgan. "You know, the Solomon Cree flick."

At the word "flick," the agent's eyebrows rose slightly. Morgan pretended not to notice. His English was a little off. He knew that. Sometimes he sounded way too early twentieth century. It came from learning the language by watching Mr. Wong's collection of classic movies. But he hoped his modified Cary Grant mid-Atlantic drawl gave him a prep school vibe. Possibly a foreign prince. Whatever would make Brown-Harwich believe that the seventeen-year-old Eurasian with a shaggy haircut, hoodie, and jeans could rent a Cobalt City landmark. Maybe internet genius? Wasn't this America, the land of teenage super-minds and young heroes, at least here in Cobalt City?

More than anything, Morgan hoped all those stories on the internet about Cobalt City were true. That here he would find what he could never meet in Hong Kong: somebody like him.

"They never used the Adventurers Club name in the movie," Brown-Harwich said. "The current caretaker insisted on that. Also, we never advertised that we handle the lease for that building."

"A blogger wrote about scouting Cobalt City locations for films and mentioned you rented it to the producer," said Morgan. "I looked it up after I saw the film." And the building's real name is in your database, which I hacked this morning to figure out how much rent to offer, Morgan thought, but didn't say out loud.

"Well, you certainly have the funds to cover a long-term lease. However, the legality of renting to a foreign minor—" Brown-Harwich's voice trailed away.

"You will be renting it to a corporation," said Morgan. "One with a controlling board stuffed with many adults over the age of twenty-one." *Who I will have to create this afternoon*, he thought. "My lawyers will call you with all the details."

I'll create a law firm too, he added to his mental list of things to do in Cobalt City. Sometime around age ten, Morgan discovered he could recreate the world to suit his needs just by manipulating bits and bytes—except he could never create anything real, anything that truly mattered to him.

His teacher, Mr. Wong, had often shaken his head and muttered, "Magic is easier." But Morgan wasn't his mother, Mr. Wong's adept pupil of spells and fighting techniques. The physical came easily to him, but the psychic never made much sense. He liked computers better.

"Real depends on what you want," Mr. Wong once told him after they watched an ancient black and white film about a man who spent all his time talking about a giant rabbit. "This man, he created a true friend, a spirit who answered his call. You can do the same thing."

"I can create avatars online when I want," said ten-year-old Morgan. "But it's not the same."

"The same as what?" asked Mr. Wong.

But Morgan couldn't explain, other than to say, "It's not real."

Now his last real friend, his personal guide for so many years, was gone. Mr. Wong was journeying west to a kingdom the Chinese government said didn't exist. And Morgan ended up taking his own voyage, which now had him trying to convince a man to rent him a near mythical building in the heart of a legendary city.

All through their meeting, Brown-Harwich kept glancing at his computer screen, which Morgan knew was showing him bank balances of exceptional size. The Adventurers Club represented a huge rent for his firm. Morgan could see the agent mentally calculating what his own percentage of the deal would be.

The place had stood empty for years, until it became the backdrop for the beginning of the Solomon Cree film. After the filming was done, the Adventurers Club went back to empty. Not even tours for Cree fans, which both surprised and relieved Morgan. He wanted the apartment on the top floor; he'd wanted it since the first time he'd seen it on the giant screen in Hong Kong's biggest multiplex. He wanted it more every time he went back to watch the movie. But he didn't need busloads of ubergeeks traipsing through his space.

Deciding it was time to push the foreign prince persona, which he wasn't, or act like a snotty foreign internet genius, which he certainly was, Morgan said, "My car and driver are waiting. Shall we go see the space? Maybe it won't do after all."

Brown-Harwich, appearing slightly sick at the thought of losing all that rent for his firm, had agreed.

As Morgan rolled through Cobalt City in a fancy car, wishing he was riding his Vespa, he wondered if the Adventurers Club would turn out to be fake, some green screen thing. Except it looked so much like the faded photo he'd manage to salvage from his firebombed apartment before fleeing to the airport.

"Here we are," Brown-Harwich announced unnecessarily when the town car stopped in front of a tall brownstone building with wide stone steps leading up from the sidewalk. The silent driver got out and opened the door for Morgan.

Morgan uncurled from the backseat. The massive oak door

was real, at least, and looked just like it had in the movie. Huge wrought iron hinges, oversized brass knob, and a stylized carving of chains crisscrossing the door.

Brown-Harwich hesitated by the car. "I should tell you about the caretaker. He can be a bit difficult. And he can't be fired or replaced. It's in the lease."

With an indifferent shrug, Morgan brushed past him on the way up the steps. Now that he was here, really here, he couldn't wait to go inside. He spotted the ornate doorbell with the letters "AC" branded into the brass frame. When he leaned his thumb against it, he could hear a big electronic bell pealing on the other side of the door. "Wicked," Morgan murmured and then snagged his hood up to hide his face. Didn't want Brown-Harwich to think he was impressed or anything. He slouched a bit, playing like he was bored with the whole thing already, even as his heart thumped faster. He could hear steps on the other side of the door and the scraping of a bolt.

"Actually, I should warn you about Mr. Tidwell," said the nervous agent behind him. "Sometimes he completely refuses entry."

"Good afternoon, Mr. Lee," said the pale gentleman who opened the door. "Mr. Brown-Harwich, how are you?"

Tidwell might look like he was out of central casting for one of Mr. Wong's favorite English vampire movies, but Morgan couldn't understand why Brown-Harwich kept edging away from the man. The Club's caretaker seemed friendly, leading the way into various rooms and pulling the sheets off the old furniture.

"The producer paid for the cleaning and restoration of several rooms," Tidwell mentioned. "A most pleasant Italian gentleman, although quite excitable at times."

"I saw the movie ten times in the first week," said Morgan, a bit to his surprise. He didn't usually admit things like that.

But Tidwell smiled and nodded. "I understand it was a very entertaining experience."

"You haven't seen it?"

"Miss Fields very kindly sent me tickets to the premiere. However, I find attending such events unusually difficult these days." Tidwell opened another door and waved a hand at a book-lined room. "The smaller reading room. The greater one is upstairs, of course."

"Is that Berry Fields, the one who writes about being a location scout in Cobalt City?" Morgan asked.

"Certainly. She arranged for the filming here. A most charming young woman, although I have seen less of her since her marriage." Tidwell started to open another door, frowned, and shut it rather quickly. "The supply closet. Nothing terribly interesting in there today."

"So about the apartment? The one at the top of the building?" The place was amazing and all that, but Morgan couldn't see sleeping in the smaller reading room. Although he could always camp out in what Tidwell called a smoking room, the one with the weird pool table. As their trip through the Club progressed, Morgan noticed a serious lack of outlets along the baseboards. He wondered if he would need to run some cable for high-speed access, and if Tidwell would have a heart attack about him cutting holes in the walls and messing around with the wiring. There were definite possibilities in rewiring the smaller reading room.

But first, Morgan wanted to see the apartment. See if it looked like the one in the movie and in the photograph at the bottom of his backpack.

"This way." Tidwell gestured to the copper and marble inlaid elevator doors at the end of the entrance hall.

At the press of another ornate button, the doors slid open with a silken whoosh. Inside the brassbound elevator cage, Morgan couldn't resist pulling at the antique lever with a twist and a turn. It slid out a few inches, revealing a steel blade.

"Please, sir," Tidwell said, "push it down. If it becomes fully disengaged, it will take a fair amount of fiddling to put it back."

"Yeah, okay." Morgan shoved the sword into its hiding place.

Brown-Harwich, stuffed into the back of the tiny elevator, looked confused.

Morgan took pity on him and explained. "There's this fight in the elevator, and Solomon Cree pulls out a hidden sword. It's one of the things from the stories, not the graphic novels, and it was in all the trailers."

"Stories? Graphic novels?" Brown-Harwich asked.

"There was this guy—" Morgan began.

"Professor Chandler," Tidwell said, pulling the safety door of the elevator closed.

Morgan nodded. "Professor Chandler. He lived here. On the top floor. He wrote about this other guy—"

"He called him Solomon Cree in the stories," Tidwell added.

"—who went on these weird adventures," finished Morgan. "And then, lots later, there were the graphic novels, and then the movie." Once, Morgan had owned an entire run of the graphic novels, filling up the boxes under his bed. Those were gone, too. He could order more, but they wouldn't be the same. They wouldn't be the companions the old books had been, helping distract him from the dreams and worries, keeping him company in the lonely hours before the day began.

"I remember something about a movie made in Cobalt City," said Brown-Harwich. "But it was several years ago."

"Six," said Morgan, who could have added the number of days

and months since the film opened in Hong Kong too. Because that was the day his mother dropped him off at the movie—the one based on his favorite graphic novels that he'd been begging to see—and told him if she wasn't there when it ended, to go to Mr. Wong's apartment. To go straight to Mr. Wong and, whatever else he did, not to look for her.

But he had waited in the lobby for hours before he followed her orders: "Stay in the shadows, look behind you often, and do not stop for anyone." Just as she had trained him. He took the alleys and the hidden ways to Mr. Wong's place. When he told her teacher what had happened, Mr. Wong followed her orders too. He shut up his apartment and moved both of them across town to a new place with new names.

After that, Morgan changed schools, and then changed schools again. Eventually, when someone started to make inquiries and he'd run out of schools, he just disappeared into the crowds of "privately educated" children living in Hong Kong who didn't need to answer roll calls or awkward questions about parents.

But despite all that, he disobeyed his mother. They both did, him and Mr. Wong, because they had looked for her. They looked all the time. They looked until Morgan's poking, prying, and general interference in the lives of the tong leaders forced him to flee east and Mr. Wong to disappear west in search of the hidden realm of the Dragon Queen.

Now, he hoped Cobalt City would yield more than a place to live. That, with the smallest of clues, he could find out more about his mysterious family. That he could live a life outside the data streaming through his computers.

But first, he was going to see Solomon Cree's apartment. Or at least the apartment that inspired the one shown in the movie he watched day after day, hoping his mother would show up in the seat next to him and laugh and shake her head at all the stuff exploding all over the screen.

The elevator rose slowly, with an audible creaking of cables and nervous swallowing from Brown-Harwich. Tidwell frowned slightly, and the noise from the elevator decreased. Brown-Harwich gave a nervous little cough.

"Makes some noise," said Morgan.

"Old buildings have their quirks." The elevator shuddered to a stop, settling into place. Tidwell slid back the safety door and then the outer door. "Your apartment, Mr. Lee."

"Well, umm, not yet, not technically," said Brown-Harwich.

But Morgan already was halfway across the foyer, circling the walls to look at the oil paintings depicting the golden-skinned Solomon Cree battling various creatures and rescuing a series of women with only half a bodice still attached to their dresses, ceremonial robes, or, in one picture, a furry tunic.

"These aren't from the graphic novels," Morgan said. "Not the covers we got in Hong Kong."

"No, sir," Tidwell responded. "These are the paintings for the magazines that first printed Professor Chandler's stories. The pulps, as they were called then."

"Wow," said Morgan. "Must be ancient."

"The last was completed seventy-five years ago," Tidwell said.

"Ancient." Morgan drawled out the syllables as he wandered into the next room. He stopped. This was it. The room where Solomon Cree always began his adventures—just like the movie, just like his photo. Two leather chairs on either side of a battered old Chinese table, a fireplace to one side, and shelves of books circling the room.

Morgan resisted the urge to pull the snapshot out of his backpack, to check it one more time. He didn't need to look. He could see it so clearly in his head. The black and white photo of the man in the suit and loosened tie, sitting in the very chair he was facing, the man raising an old-fashioned glass in a mocking salute to whoever was taking his picture.

"I'm moving in," announced Morgan to the world.

"Certainly, sir," said Tidwell. "Welcome to your home."

Brown-Harwich made various protesting noises as Tidwell neatly herded him back into the elevator.

"Shall I retrieve your luggage from your driver and bring it up?" Tidwell inquired.

"Got everything right here." Morgan swung his backpack off his shoulder. He pulled his phone out of his pocket and began tapping the screen. "But I'm having some stuff delivered. Computers and things."

"Very good," said Tidwell. "I will bring the packages up when they arrive."

Morgan nodded, already engrossed in sending through orders for the equipment he wanted, with rush delivery selected for every purchase. When he looked up, the two men were gone.

He thought about exploring the rest of the apartment, but something even stronger than his curiosity compelled him to open his backpack and pull out the faded photograph. He flipped it over so he could see clearly the two lines of handwriting on the back. The first, in an unknown block printing, said simply in English: "Wrecker of Engines, Cobalt City." Below that, in his mother's elegant calligraphy, were the Chinese characters for grandfather.

Across town, the librarian dropped her greasy rag into a bucket and stepped back to survey the basement room. The machines all shone with the brass polished, the copper gleaming, all the dials and tubes glistening. More importantly, next to every one was a neatly printed card, important points laid out in bulleted lists, and below those cards, a dozen or so books from the collection were lined up on the newly hung shelves, jacket side out, to hopefully entice requests from the public. Maybe someone would even check one out and read it.

Ms. Garnet sighed. Probably reading was too much to expect. Still, it might attract school groups, which would boost their attendance numbers. Kids, she told herself, loved this type of stuff. More importantly, in the final weeks of the school year, teachers loved an excuse to take their charges out of the classroom. Then it would be summer, and Cobalt City's tourists would arrive. Rather than just snap a few pictures of the outside, this should lure them through the doors. It was shiny, it was different, it was sure to attract attention. Ms. Garnet suppressed her inner doubts firmly.

Because she believed, in a city filled with fantastic museums and monuments to superheroes, this truly fine collection of artifacts from one of the city's greatest and now-forgotten villains would do what all their other efforts had failed to do. It would bring people back to the library.

All she had to do was plug it in.

She reached down and picked up the new, rewired plug and stuck it into the wall. All around her, the machines began to hum, to light up, to look important. With a smile, Ms. Garnet flipped off the switch that controlled the outlet, because she wasn't such a fool as to leave any century-old machinery running unattended with all her lovely books upstairs.

The machines shut down with an aggravated whine, the purple mist swirling in one glass bulb slowly filtering back into the tubes beneath.

With one last loving glance at her latest exhibition, Ms. Garnet switched off the lights and headed home. Unseen in the dark, the purple mist trapped in the test-tube like bulb began to glow, casting an eerie light across the silent and waiting apparatus.

Sometimes, Lizzie saw the place she could not leave as a room. A room as bare and plain as any tenement boarding house. A single straight chair, a window whose panes were so dusty that the outside appeared only as a cloudy image, a desk with drawers empty of paper or pen, and, on the wall, one of the new-fangled gaslights flickering. The flame in the frosted glass bowl flared up and turned a brilliant, ominous purple. Then it faded down again.

She remembered a flame like that, one that burned away everything, everyone, that she knew. She reached out in the manner she'd taught herself during her long captivity, feeling the zip and zing of the currents as they raced through the city. She was never any good at magic, as she always preferred experiments and gadgets.

Still, when she peeked through the dusty windows, she saw the edge between the real and the imaginary, between the physical and the psychic. The lines of force running between her "here" and the City's "there" matched the memories in her head of the streets and sidewalks she once traveled. Maybe it was more Pharaoh's Ghost than Faraday's principles, but there was a science to her method of observation, one that might eventually yield a way out of her trap.

Lizzie reached out her hand, and after a moment of intense concentration, the telegraph key appeared under her fingertips. She began to tap urgently, sending her words out into the world she lost so long ago. A warning to her last friend in the City that an old enemy was stirring. Her miniature thunder heralding the deadly possibility of a lightning strike.

A series of clicks came back, a reassuring message she desperately wanted to believe. A new hero had arrived in Cobalt City.

FOR THE FOURTH TIME, MORGAN CHECKED THE STATUS ON HIS online orders. Nothing was arriving today. Which meant he was stuck with only his smartphone for another day.

"Perhaps you would like to try the gymnasium on the second floor?" Tidwell suggested when he found Morgan in the largest reading room practicing parkour, leaping between the oak table, the shelves, and the rolling ladder. Morgan had started parkour after discovering the videos on YouTube—he thought it looked amazing—and it was certainly less boring than the Tai Chi Mr. Wong insisted on practicing every morning when he was a little kid.

"The point," Morgan panted, as he swung over Tidwell's head and scaled a wall of bookshelves, "is to turn your environment into the challenge. And defeat it."

"Ah." Tidwell neatly sidestepped three old volumes that thumped to the floor in the wake of Morgan's passing. "An admirable philosophy."

"My idea. Indoor parkour. Morgan-kour." He performed a handstand on the back of a leather wingchair and, when the chair began to tilt, somersaulted to the couch and then vaulted off the tips of his fingers, feet above his head, to the library ladder.

Tidwell caught the falling wingchair with one hand and pushed it upright.

"But perhaps you should explore the city?" he suggested to Morgan. "Learn that environment too. So you can…ah…master it."

Morgan flipped off the ladder. "Not a bad idea. Where would you go?"

Tidwell looked a little puzzled. "I never leave the Club."

"Where do tourists go?"

"Ah. Wait here."

A few minutes later, Tidwell arrived with a map on a silver tray. "This was sent out by the Cobalt City Chamber of Commerce. I received it in the mail yesterday. Most opportune."

"Things To Do This Summer" was written in bold, bright green letters across the front of the map. "Support Your City" was in slightly smaller type below that. And "Be A Hero, Be Part of the Action" was printed along the bottom.

On the back, a brief paragraph extolled the many wonders of Cobalt City. Inside, the map showed a walking tour that would take the informed tourist to historical scenes of battles between superheroes and terrible villains—all perfectly safe today, the map promised—or to more ordinary delights like the zoo or the aquarium.

Morgan ended up at the aquarium. He paid for a ticket and wandered past the tanks of slowly circling fish. The place was dimly lit, smelled damp, and filled with the echoing cries of a local school group long before they rounded a corner and overran the section where he was.

A bunch of boys, all about his age, shoved and pushed against each other, while the girls hung back in their own group, snapping pictures with their phones and then giggling while they passed the results back and forth.

As with any herd or pack, there was one weak one in the group, a kid with big glasses and an overstuffed backpack. He had a clipboard with him—as they all did—but he seemed to be the only one actually checking the labels on the tanks and marking something on a sheet.

Watching the group, Morgan guessed things weren't going to

go well for the young scholar. After a couple of minutes of random pushing, the larger boys drifted toward the smaller one.

"Hey, dummy," yelled one, cannoning into the kid, "get out of my way." The little guy went sprawling to the snorting laughter of the others.

Morgan shifted position so he moved directly behind the bully. A simple sideways strike of the elbow, a quick insert of his foot behind the other's ankle, and a swift "accidental" bump, and the larger boy went down.

"I am sorry," Morgan said, stepping over the bully and helping the smaller boy up. "Did you trip?"

"I'm fine," said the smaller boy, climbing to his feet and retrieving his clipboard. "What happened?"

"I knocked into your friend, and he knocked into you," Morgan said, as he stepped backward and casually interfered with the bully's attempt to get up. The bigger boy went down again, to the giggles of the girls watching.

A frowning adult rounded the corner. "What are you kids doing?" the man, obviously their teacher, asked. "Finish up your assignments and move to the entrance. The bus will be here in ten minutes."

The group cleared out of the room except for the smaller boy, who looked back at Morgan and whispered, "Thanks, dude. I'm Adam."

"Morgan." Morgan tapped on his chest.

The teacher stared at Morgan as he rounded up his charges. "You're not in my class."

Morgan waved his map of the city and smiled. In Cantonese, he said, "I'm observing the habits of the American teenager." And, in English, with a bigger grin and a shrug: "Tourist. First time here."

"Oh." The teacher blinked a bit at the bilingual explanation. "Well, enjoy your visit. There's plenty to see."

Morgan nodded, waved, and moved out of the tropical fish area onto an open pier. The wind off the water hit him like a slap. It was almost June, but the weather felt like winter to him. The sky was full of clouds, and whitecaps topped the waves in the harbor. But as he looked across the water, he could see towering orange cargo cranes, so much like the ones back in Hong Kong.

It wasn't home, but it wasn't completely unfamiliar either. The towering glass and steel office buildings, the busy harbor full of container ships, and even the steady roar of traffic rumbling off the elevated highways and bridges, all held echoes of the city where he had grown up.

Behind him, Morgan could hear the loud chatter of the school group. With a shift of position, he watched them piling onto an orange and black bus marked with the name of their school. The small kid, the one he had helped, hung back, scanning the parking lot. Morgan almost raised a hand to wave at him, but his training drove him back into the shadows. The other boy shrugged and then swung himself onto the bus.

He couldn't imagine being trapped in a class like that all day long, but he also wondered what it would be like to be part of a group. To have people know your name, to have a place in the herd, to date one of those girls who nudged each other and laughed as they ran lightly up the steps onto the bus.

Morgan had spent his whole life watching groups like that. It had never been safe for him to be enrolled for more than a few weeks in any school. To stay longer would have made his location far too easy to find. Those were his mother's rules. And he'd never questioned her rules or Mr. Wong's advice.

But now he was completely on his own. And keenly aware of it.

Lizzie never understood those who complained about the noise of living in Cobalt City. She once loved every sound, from the early morning cries of the dairy and icemen making their rounds to the slow clip-clop of a tired cab horse taking his last fare home after midnight.

The whistles of the trains and steamships carrying across the harbor had reminded her of a world of possibilities beyond her doorstep.

But, most of all, she had loved the clatter of her own shoes as she hurried down the bare wooden hallways in the newspaper offices, practically racing to the frosted glass office door with the words "Editor" painted in gold across the top pane.

Now, she was lost in this place of silence, where no sounds could be heard past the walls made of shadows.

But she could remember. In her memory, she heard the clicking of the telegraph key as new stories came tumbling into the newspaper's office.

At the Adventurers Club, the lights were coming on, the elevator was humming up and down, and life was returning to the building. She knew this, in the same vague sense that she felt the power running through Cobalt City, the millions of messages bypassing her as they whizzed to some other destination.

Power, electrical power, that was always the key for her. Once she'd used the amazing discoveries of Thomas Edison and his brethren to fight crime. Now she needed just a little more, so she could push beyond the prison surrounding her, so somebody could hear her cries for help.

Unable to sleep that night, Morgan spotted the probability of a secret staircase during his nocturnal prowling about the apartment. Just a glance confirmed the doors of the bathroom and bedroom in the apartment were too far apart.

Some checking with the measuring tape app in his phone led to the missing space between the two rooms.

Unlike the den, covered in bookcases on every wall and the elevator lobby covered in Professor Chandler's memorabilia, the bedroom walls were remarkably plain. But the wall facing his bed, the one that should have backed the bathroom, had two odd cracks in the plaster, cracks too straight to be made by the settling of an old building.

Morgan ran his fingers along them. No latches, no bumps, nothing obvious. He pulled a chair from the desk by the bed and climbed on top of it. Nothing near the ceiling. Hopping off the chair, he began investigating along the baseboard. He found the latch concealed by what appeared to be an old-fashioned phone outlet. Using the screwdriver on his Swiss Army knife, he pried off the plate and tripped the concealed switch.

The door in the wall slid back with a satisfying hiss of hydraulics.

"Nice." Morgan switched his phone over to flashlight mode. The glowing white square of light revealed a pair of dusty stairs trailing upward into the darkness.

He took a moment to drag the chair to the doorway and prop it so the door couldn't snap closed behind him. He'd made that mistake once in Hong Kong, and Mr. Wong never tired of reminding him.

Morgan followed the narrow staircase upward.

It ended at a trapdoor that took only a minute to unlock with the pick Morgan always carried in his sock. Then he stepped onto the flat roof.

Morgan whistled.

By some trick of geography, or good planning by its architect, the rooftop of the Adventurers Club gave him an unparalleled view of the glimmering towers of downtown Cobalt City. Above hung a full and glowing moon.

The night wind cut through his t-shirt, but Morgan scrambled up to the parapet. Propping himself against a friendly gargoyle, he surveyed his new city. It seemed so close and yet so impossibly distant. His world spun away from him in Hong Kong, a blur of fires, explosions, and gunshots. Now he was here, alone, and nobody knew where he was. Nobody cared that he'd lost himself in this city so far from all that he'd known.

For the first time in days, Morgan sat completely still. He'd made the journey. He'd found his destination. Now what?

Thunder rumbled in the distance, a dry summer storm building up. Automatically, Morgan began counting under his breath to judge how far away the lightning would be. The air smelled electric. Static built up around him. When he brushed a hand against his jeans, the blue sparks followed the arc of the movement.

Lightning cracked. Morgan looked across the city. Jagged streaks of electricity lit the sky. Bolt after bolt zigzagged overhead. He'd never seen a lightning storm like this in Hong Kong. One enormous bolt seemed to rocket out of the earth into clouds.

A single bolt of lightning arced overhead, grounding itself in an old-fashioned lightning rod set in the northeast corner of the roof. Morgan automatically squeezed his eyes closed as the flash turned his vision to brilliant, bloody red. He heard the pop as the decorative glass ball at the tip of the rod shattered.

Then, as suddenly as it began, the storm disappeared. The sky cleared.

Rubbing his eyes and blinking, Morgan ran across the roof to see how bad the damage was. As he ran, he automatically fished his phone from his pocket.

The rod on the corner looked fried, the metal corroded and pitted by the strike, but the roof appeared unharmed, and Morgan could see no sign of fire.

He prowled around the roof, looking for any sign of damage, but found nothing. Hanging over the parapet, he could see where the grounding wire ran down the side of the building. Apparently, the old lightning rod worked.

His phone buzzed in his hand.

A text message glowed on the screen. "Lost," it said. The sender was blanked out.

His phone was an untraceable one. He'd given the number to Mr. Wong, but nobody else.

"Where are you?" Morgan typed back, cautious but hopeful his old teacher sent this message to him, perhaps a mission, a purpose to occupy his mind.

"Lost." The word appeared again on the screen of his smartphone and then erased itself.

Mr. Wong favored cryptic, but even for him, that was unusually short. Suspicious, Morgan typed, "Who are you?"

The screen stayed blank. Morgan cursed his lack of equipment downstairs. No way he could track this mystery message to its source.

Then he wondered if it was a trap, a trick of the tong to find him. The phone should be clean, but he couldn't take chances. He popped the back and removed the chip. He crushed it under his foot.

Then he leaned over the parapet. A dumpster sat against the side of the building, the lid propped open by a careless hand. Morgan dropped the phone into it. He was rewarded by a startled squeak as a rat scuttled over the dumpster's side and fled down the alley.

A door opened. In the golden square of light thrown down the kitchen steps, Morgan saw Tidwell step out into the alley and carefully close the lid of the dumpster. The man looked up as Morgan withdrew into the shadows of the roof. Then he turned and went back inside the building.

Morgan watched the moon, thinking about messages and long flights from home. About storms and electricity. When a new collection of clouds began to obscure the moon's face, he uncurled from his perch and made his way downstairs.

On the table beside his bed was a pot of tea. He put his hand on it. It was comfortingly warm. He poured a cup. The smell of flowers and spices tickling his nose reminded him of other kitchens far away. Morgan kicked off his shoes and his jeans. Curled up under the blankets, he cradled the cup in his hands and began to design in his head how he would fill this room and the next with the array of screens and servers he had ordered earlier.

Once he had his computers again, once he was the Wrecker of Engines again, then this place could become home, he decided.

He placed the cup back on the nightstand. Automatically, he reached for his phone, for one last check to see if there were any messages from Mr. Wong.

But, of course, he'd killed the phone. He could survive what was left of the night without a computer, Morgan told himself. He didn't need to have access all the time.

But as he slid under the sheets, he was acutely aware of the silence of the room. He rolled out of bed and padded on bare feet to the window. He pulled back the curtains. Outside his window, he could see the distant lights of the office towers and apartment buildings.

Returning to bed, Morgan lay on his side, staring at the window, watching the lights wink on and off in windows of other rooms, with other restless sleepers, like points of data appearing and disappearing in the giant network of Cobalt City.

Eventually, the sky lightened, and the cool, gray light of the false dawn filled his room.

The telegraph key faded into a shower of electric sparks. Lizzie smiled for the first time since she had raced up the steps into her prison. Something had changed, finally, just as she had been promised. The current running through the city felt different now, charged with something new. If she had ever been a superstitious girl, she might have called it magic or even mythic power.

With a moment of desperate concentration, she'd even been able to send a message to one of those newfangled communication devices.

Around her, the room disappeared into shadows and faint flickers of light, signals from a city that had forgotten her. But she had not forgotten it.

"Another package, sir," intoned Tidwell on the house phone.

On his third day at the Adventurers Club, Morgan had bought Tidwell a smartphone from the mall, preloaded with six of Morgan's numbers, his IM, and a couple of his email addresses. He showed Tidwell how to text. Tidwell thanked him and continued to call on the black house phone connected by a cord to the wall.

Morgan recognized an immovable object when he met one. So he trained himself to pick up the heavy black receiver when he heard bells ringing, rather than patting his pockets for his current smartphone.

"Thanks," Morgan said into the phone. "I'll get it later."

He rolled his chair back to his desk with a kick of one boot off the wall.

After two weeks in the apartment at the top of the Adventurers Club, his world was starting to spin in the direction he wanted. A half dozen screens streamed an amalgam of code and live video, news broadcasts overlaid with social media chatter, and hook-ups to satellite cameras showing him the corners of the city not normally visible to human eyes.

Things looked peaceful, unfortunately. Morgan wished a supervillain would surface in the harbor or carve jet trails through the skies. He wanted to see some of the famed Cobalt City cape and cowl set in action. Maybe even lend a hand, make some new connections with the crimefighters here. Although he had promised Mr. Wong to keep quiet for a few months and see which way the tongs jumped after the last dust-up.

"The cat outside the mouse hole does not growl and lash his tail," Mr. Wong counseled him at that last parting. "He stays still until the mouse feels safe and ventures out."

"At least you see me as a cat and not a mouse," Morgan had said, as he shrugged his backpack over his shoulder and prepared to leave the city of his birth.

"Your family will always be the tigers," said Mr. Wong with a smile. "It is in your blood."

And then the old man had disappeared, blending into the Hong Kong crowds.

Morgan checked their private online drop box. Still no message. Probably good news, as it was unlikely Mr. Wong would break silence without some powerful reason. Also, his teacher said he intended to walk home, which meant several hundred miles across the interior of China and out of range of most modern connections.

Morgan slid his hands across a touchscreen and brought up the latest headlines. It seemed like most of the city's commentators felt the lack of superhero activity as keenly as he did. Some blamed the current mayor for the latest ramping up of the city police force, for spending money on the type of protection they once received for free from the superheroes. Others, to be contrary, stated that superheroes led to super destruction and increased expenditures. Look at the past, at the wreckage caused when even something as innocent as a carnival came to town, they said.

Still others wondered why the exotic Wild Kat and the billionaire genius Stardust were appearing at functions outside Cobalt City, opening museums and hospitals in places ranging from London to Timbuktu. Didn't they owe their first allegiance to the charities and institutions of this city, the pundits argued around tables in TV studios.

Liberal or conservative, nobody liked what they were seeing—a general feeling that Cobalt City was somehow losing its unique status in the world.

Finally, old Art Guildestein summed it up in his usual broadcast about how things were always better in his youth. Looking at his wrinkles and the tufts of white hair that seemed to sprout directly from his ears, Morgan wondered what century that was: twentieth, nineteenth, or earlier. If somebody said Guildestein was running around Cobalt City in the Revolution with Paul Revere, Morgan would have believed it.

Guildestein was going on and on about the big fights of the past, how the skies had been filled with the snapping of capes and the whoosh of jet-powered flying boots, while the streets buzzed with masked motorcyclists chasing down madmen with plans of world domination. Then he waxed nostalgic about how a man could barely walk across the street without encountering some glamorous heroine like the Worm Queen.

Today, the world was a drabber, more boring place, he argued.

"What we have to ask ourselves," said Guildestein in his usual wrap-up, "is the time of heroes ended for Cobalt City?"

"It seems most unlikely," Tidwell said from the doorway.

Morgan spun around. "I was coming down for that box."

Tidwell advanced into the center of the room to set down the latest oversized hard drive Morgan had ordered. "It posed no problem to bring it up."

The caretaker looked over Morgan's array of cables, screens, and plastic gray boxes with single green blinking lights. "Efficient, I am sure, but it lacks something of the elegance of our communications room."

"There's a communications room?"

"Certainly. Directly under the smaller reading room."

Morgan bounced out of his chair. "I'd like to see it."

"Very good, sir."

The elevator purred down to the basement, the button marked "A" on its panel. Tidwell led the way down the hallway lined with faded velvet wallpaper.

"Here," he said, opening the door.

Morgan sauntered through, prepared to be unimpressed, only to exclaim as the overhead lights snapped on. "Whoa."

Brass levers and scrollwork decorated gleaming wooden boxes topped with old-fashioned tubes and flickering Edison bulbs. Cloth-covered cords crisscrossed the walls, while glass pneumatic tubes disappeared into the ceiling.

The place was a museum of nineteenth- and very early twentieth-century technology, the forerunners to the computers humming upstairs in his room. He'd seen stuff like this in museums and pictures online. But he'd never been in a room like this, where all the gleaming equipment looked like it could, with a flip of the right switch, start clicking with life.

"That's a Marconi wireless!" he said, as his fingers almost reverentially tapped the telegraph key sitting in the center of a heavy oak table.

"One of the very first," Tidwell said. "And installed personally by him. As was the antenna on the roof."

"Lucky it didn't get hit by the lightning last week."

"Quite unlikely. As you saw, the rod was more than sufficient to protect the other equipment. It was installed by an Edison."

"Thomas Edison? Not possible."

"A rather distant relative. He maintained that such rods would eventually draw power from the sky to light the world. For many years, the Club prided itself on not only encouraging those who adventured in unknown regions but also in the new sciences. We were the first building in this part of the city to have gas lighting installed and, later, to be fully electrified," Tidwell said, almost a little sadly.

"Wouldn't have guessed, because it looks frozen in time upstairs."

Tidwell sighed. "After his accident, Professor Chandler desired a quieter place, more like the homes he knew in his youth. His was a powerful imagination, and he was a powerful influence on those around him. The Club became less of a place of innovation and more a place of nostalgia. And, following his death, many felt the Club no longer served a purpose. A few members stayed on, but it became a place of nostalgia for them as well."

While Tidwell was talking, Morgan crawled under one of the tables to check out the hook-up for the telegraph. Still intact. Just needed an operator on the other side, listening. He scooted out from under the table and reached for the key. In American Morse code, just one of the many ciphers and languages he had taught himself as a little kid, he tapped out: "Hello. I want to be your friend."

Then, embarrassed that he remembered that particular message so clearly, he turned away from the table. Lights winked and flickered all around him. Morgan randomly hit a few buttons and levers and was rewarded by a deep ticking, like the slow beating of a reviving heart.

"Ah. Not so much a wrecker as a restorer."

"Uh?" Morgan was lost in contemplation of something that looked a bit like a clock and a bit like a pressure gauge. He wondered if twisting the needle so it pointed to the red zone was a good idea or not.

"I said that Wrecker of Engines is not totally accurate."

"Hey!" Morgan spun around at the sound of his hacker handle so carelessly dropping out of Tidwell's mouth. "Where did you get that name?"

"I rather thought it belonged to you these days."

"Yeah, it's mine." Morgan eyed Tidwell more closely than he ever had. The man just came with the building. Morgan still didn't know anything about him except that he made a good pot of tea and never mentioned having a first name. "It's...my mother—" He stopped, not wanted to explain he taken the name from the back of a photograph, a photograph taken at the Adventurers Club.

He felt an odd compulsion to tell Tidwell about his search for his mother's connection to this place, as well as his recent hacks into tong bank accounts, but all his childhood training revolted against that. His family didn't stay alive by giving away secrets. He compromised by saying, "I don't exactly have a Wrecker fan page with my picture on it."

"Of course not, sir. Such names must serve as a mask to protect the wearer."

"Yeah." Something about Tidwell's patient, waiting attitude made Morgan want to talk. It was an unusual sensation. "If anyone knows it is me, my head gets broken. I'm not exactly popular."

"But not a random vandal of other people's property."

"I have never hurt anyone who wasn't trying to kill somebody else."

Tidwell seemed unsurprised. "You are not the first to use the name in Cobalt City. But the man who wore the mask was a good man. That I know."

Morgan felt a tingle in his fingertips that had nothing to do with the dial he was still twisting under one hand. "You've heard the name before?"

"It has been several decades, but there was a friend of Professor Chandler who used that pseudonym. He was not unknown in the city during his heyday, but times change, and people forget."

"Is there anything here about him?"

"Not in this room. Perhaps in the library."

"The reading rooms upstairs? Lesser or greater?"

"Frankly, sir, I would suggest the Cobalt City Library. They have an extensive collection of material on all the city's heroes, both past and present, in the main building downtown."

Morgan nodded. He would have to check the library resources out. He thought about hacking into their systems, but somehow, spending more time with his computers upstairs strangely didn't appeal. He'd enjoyed his brief encounter with other teenagers at the aquarium. Possibly he could observe some more Americans at the library.

"Okay, I'll look at this downtown library. But maybe I can spend some time down here tonight." Morgan looked around the communications room again. It was impossibly fantastic. He resolved to figure out exactly what all the dials and buttons and levers did. Even with the few switches he had flipped, the place seemed to be more alive, almost humming with anticipation of wonders to be revealed.

"Very good, sir," Tidwell said with a faint smile as Morgan left the room.

Strangely, for once, Tidwell did not follow him into the elevator, and Morgan was able to pull the lever and push the buttons himself. He shot up to the main floor.

Shrugging his leather jacket over his black hoodie, Morgan ran down the back steps to the tiny carriage house that opened onto the alley where the Club's prosaic garbage cans and recycling dumpster sat. He rolled his new shiny red Vespa out of the stall that had once housed a horse. This brand-new bike wasn't as sweet and retro as his old ride, but it still blasted through the streets, especially after a few engine modifications.

He slammed his helmet over his head and took off down the alley with a neatly popped wheelie onto the main street.

In the communication room, Tidwell watched the lights continue to flicker and blink. With a whir of clockwork and the clack of type, a small white card dropped through a brassbound slot and into a black mesh metal tray.

"SOMETHING CHANGED," the card read. "LIGHTNING, MORE POWER. I HEARD HIM." A long pause, more clicking of keys, and a second card dropped on top of the first. "WILL HE BE MY FRIEND?"

"I hope so, miss, I truly do," murmured Tidwell, as he closed up the room.

CHAPTER 3: IN THE LIBRARY

"WELCOME TO THE LIBRARY," SAID THE YOUNG WOMAN, almost lost behind the tall wooden and marble counter.

Morgan spun around. He'd been looking straight up at the paintings depicting science, history, and superheroes splashed across the vaulted ceilings of the enormous entry. "Hello."

"How can we help you?" chirped the librarian. She didn't look that much older than him. Streaks of her hair were dyed pink, but there was something about the fuzzy sweater that marked her as a permanent employee of this monument to the printed page. Her nametag proclaimed she was Janet, junior librarian, and she wanted to help.

"I'm looking for information about the heroes who lived here," he said. "Old stuff. Like the twentieth century."

"The special exhibit!" Janet beamed at him. "It fills up the entire basement! Free tours on Mondays, Thursdays, and Fridays."

"It's Tuesday," Morgan pointed out.

"Yes." Janet's face fell. "We don't have a tour today."

"How about a self-guided tour?" Morgan suggested.

"Certainly. But could you sign the guestbook?" She pushed a large book across the marble counter at him. Most of the page was blank, and the last signature was dated several days ago.

"Sure." Morgan scribbled his name in English. It looked a little odd, and he realized he almost never wrote it out. For so many years, he had hidden behind so many other names that "Morgan Lee" had become the true alias, the name no one knew was his.

"Oh, thank you! If people don't sign, we don't have any record of how popular it is. And records are important. Especially when it comes to getting grants. And staying open."

"You should get a fan page. Or a blog. Or something. Where people can follow you online and leave notes."

"Yes, well—" Janet twisted one pink lock around her index finger. "Ms. Garnet isn't very interested in fan pages. Well...I did suggest it. But she said no. That we should keep things simple and use the guestbook until it was filled up. After all, it still has a lot of blank pages."

Morgan grinned and picked up the pen again. Below his name in English, he wrote the Chinese characters for one of his pseudonyms. "There. That's two lines filled and two lines closer to going digital."

"Oh. I don't know. I guess that's okay." Janet stared at both of his signatures and then gave him a shy half-smile. "Enjoy the exhibit. Just follow the stairs down instead of up."

On Lizzie's first day in Cobalt City, she went straight from the train station to the Inventor's Exhibition and Grand Science Fair. She hoped there might be a story there, something she could write up and sell to one of the city's newspapers, something that could prove she was more than a fifteen-year-old girl with a half dozen clips from her hometown newspaper about pie-eating contests, new bonnets, and the bank's improper foreclosures on three farms they wanted to sell to the railroad.

The last story drove her out of her hometown. The banker had told her widowed aunt that Lizzie's poking and prying might well jeopardize the loan on her aunt's boarding house.

Besides, Lizzie admitted to herself, she'd been dying to leave Aunt Emily's kind but often smothering protection and travel somewhere, anywhere. She'd thought about Boston or New York or Chicago, but none of them had the type of stories coming out of Cobalt City. And in 1896, when the world was bursting with new possibilities, the place for a young woman intent on making a career in journalism was obviously here, in a city where the very latest inventions, inventions never seen before, were being exhibited free to the public under the high glass roof built by the great inventor himself, the Mechanism Man.

Inside, Lizzie wandered past exhibitors extolling the virtues of their automatic tea-brewing machines or revolutionary egg coddlers. She stopped to gaze with wonder upon the ice cream emporium set up in the very center of the glass dome. Tiny tables with white marble tops and gilded legs circled a bandstand blasting oom-pah-pah enthusiasm from a collection of clockwork brass instruments, all driven by steam and Cobalt City ingenuity. Waiters in pink and white striped aprons carried frozen confections on silver trays to waiting gentlemen and ladies.

Lizzie fingered her coin purse. What little jingled inside needed to last until she found a job. So, with only one or two hungry glances back over her shoulder, she passed down the exhibition hall to the area where large signs proclaimed: "The Age of the Automobile."

An enormous, shiny, horseless carriage, all brass lamps and gleaming panels of metal and wood, was surrounded by a gaggle of gentlemen, some weighty with civic importance and broad from club luncheons, some lean and more poorly dressed. Lizzie noticed a number of the leaner ones had pencils and notepads in hand. She judged she was not the only eager writer seeking a story in the fair.

A quartet of judges, all dressed very fine indeed, examined the four-wheeled horseless carriage with ponderous care. The inventor, a solid little man in a checkered suit, bounced on his feet as he waited for their verdict.

"We look to you for assurances that it is harmless; that this vehicle will not suddenly shed its safety valve," one judge remarked to him. "That the populace need not worry about explosions of its engine or other dangers."

The creator of the car answered curtly, "The one thing my inventions do not do is explode."

"Well, it exhibits a certain superficial beauty," one graybeard remarked to another. "Those bright blue cushions, tulip wood, and polished metal lend it an air of luxury."

The inventor bared his teeth, but Lizzie could detect no genuine warmth in his smile. "Laypersons so often remark on such unremarkable things. A true scientist knows it is the motor that matters." He lifted a brass lattice that stretched across the front of the vehicle, disclosing bulbous cylinders and a tangle of pipes and wires.

"This engine will work as long as there's a single puff of steam in the boiler. It will carry you at forty miles, nay, sixty miles an hour without the slightest evidence of strain. It will do the work of ten horses or more!" His voice rose with excitement as he began a litany about explosion chambers, sparking plugs, and other motor technicalities.

"Why, with a tank of water, a modicum of coal to heat it, a pump, a radiator, a magnet, some geared wheels fitting together, and a lever or two, I have turned mere metal into a chariot fit for a king!" He leaned forward into the depths of the machine, his voice echoing oddly as he bent over the controls. "You move this lever, you press your foot lightly on this pedal, the engine transfers its power to the wheels, you move. It will take you away with speeds comparable to a locomotive, but a locomotive that you and you alone control. You can hurl yourself from place to place, never bound again to the pedestrian and plodding methods of transportation suffered in such cities as Boston, New York, or London."

An enormous blast of steam blew out of the boiler in the back of the car. One nervous young man yelled and jumped back as Lizzie pushed her way to the front of the crowd.

"Sir, are you truly sure this contraption is safe?" cried a tall judge with bushy side whiskers.

The startled inventor pulled his head out from under the hood of the car and hurried to the back, where his hands flew in a blur across a series of levers. "A mere moment to adjust the pressure," he yelled to the crowd, who were rapidly drawing away from his steaming automobile.

A second blast of steam erupted from the top of the boiler, and the automobile rocketed forward. The hapless inventor hung onto the back end of the car. The machine shot through the velvet rope surrounding it and barreled across the room.

With shrieks and shouts, the crowd dived out of the way as the horseless carriage sped down the length of the exhibition hall. It shattered the glass doors and burst out into the city, as Lizzie and the men of the press ran after it.

In the room where she was trapped, Lizzie still recalled that day with more vivid clarity than any other, and the exhilaration of running through the city after the steamcar, certain she could turn her adventure into a newspaper story.

Like the library entry upstairs, Morgan found the exhibit downstairs eerily empty. Not even another junior librarian to chirp at him.

The walls were lined with Cobalt City newspapers under glass, stretching from faded reproductions of colonial days and masked riders outwitting British redcoats to modern headlines about a flaming Ferris wheel. Open doorways and discreet signs pointed to themed collections within the exhibit. Morgan glanced in one room and spied a wax mannequin of Abraham Lincoln and something shiny in a corner. He passed it by. Too old.

Another room showed models of rocket ships and a disco ball. He shrugged. Too new, he guessed, to be connected to the Wrecker of Engines he was seeking.

Then he saw the mask through a doorway marked "After the War." Next to a newspaper proclaiming in giant type "The Wrecker Saves The City" was a man's hat and a porcelain mask. Morgan recognized the black lines filling the blank white face of the mask as I Ching symbols. He'd never been interested in the fortunetelling stuff, not like Mr. Wong, but he thought these symbols had something to do with justice.

Morgan walked through the door and was surrounded by mid-century mementoes of mad men and deadly dames. A jukebox gleamed in the corner, a thing of rainbow-glassed beauty, and an early pinball game depicted a guy in a fedora with two guns blazing straight at the players. Covering his face was the same mask as displayed in the case.

He leaned over the case and read the small, typed card that stated the Wrecker of Engines, a prominent hero during the Depression years, disappeared during World War II but returned to the city after the War.

After several "spectacular" adventures chronicled in the press, according to the index card below the mask, the Wrecker of Engines again vanished. However, his combination of detective work, disguises, and industrial sabotage inspired a series of "tough guy" heroes through the 1950s who thwarted (Morgan grinned to see "thwarted" in an official context) such villains as Deadly Mickey, Killer Kate, and the Black Alley Gang.

The card also noted that the mask on display was a copy, one of many sold during the 1950s when the popular radio show about the original masked hero transitioned into television.

"An interesting era for superheroes," said a woman behind him.

Morgan glanced over his shoulder. The lady in the doorway looked like an older, plumper version of Janet upstairs. Fuzzy sweater, sensible shoes, but no pink streaks in her hair. A pair of glasses hung from a chain around her neck.

"Hi," said Morgan.

"It's nice to see someone in the exhibit who isn't being dragged through by a teacher," she said with a smile. And then, with a shake of her head, "Unless I missed your group. In which case, I apologize to your teacher."

"No, I'm on my own." Remembering his disguise of the moment, he pulled the map out of his jacket pocket and waved it. "I am seeing the sights recommended on this map."

"Ah, it's a little early for tourist season. Are your parents upstairs?"

Morgan gave the shrug he'd perfected years ago when adults questioned him about his lack of visible parents. "They're working, new job, we just moved here," he said in a quick jumble of words. "They suggested the library... to be educational."

"Oh, yes, we have an amazing collection of historical documents and artifacts. Quite unappreciated, I think."

"Nice." He rather wished she'd leave, so he could take a closer look at the newspaper stories about the Wrecker.

"I'm Ms. Garnet," said the librarian.

"Oh, yes, Janet mentioned you upstairs. When she asked me to sign your guestbook."

Ms. Garnet looked pleased. "She usually forgets. Are you interested in any particular heroes?"

"I read about this Wrecker guy somewhere," said Morgan, as casually as he could. "Interesting."

"Not many people remember him. He actually became more popular after he disappeared. Many people in my generation think he was only a fictional character from the radio dramas and television shows our parents liked. I'm surprised anyone in your generation has even heard of him."

Morgan shrugged. He hadn't known about the radio or TV programs, but he could probably track down a copy or two. Almost everything was available somewhere on the web. But he wanted more than stories. "I'm researching the real guy. Not fiction."

"School project?"

Morgan nodded. "Yeah. I have a paper to write. My parents want me to keep up with my studies."

He had discovered long ago in Hong Kong, adults would give you all kinds of interesting information if you simply said you were doing homework. He wondered if the technique would work with Ms. Garnet. If she wasn't going to leave him alone, maybe he could learn something from her.

"Commendable. Are you enrolling in one of the summer programs here? There are a number of excellent accelerated programs if your parents want you to attend college. I am sure we have a brochure upstairs—it comes with a list of recommended reading suggestions."

Morgan gave a noncommittal shrug. "I haven't...we haven't made any plans yet. Like I said, my parents just moved here." In Hong Kong, he usually claimed he had private tutors, something not unheard of and fitting to his usual fictional background of being the only child of rich and forever-absent parents. Did they have private tutors here? Was that an American thing? "I'm finishing classes online."

"Home schooled?" Ms. Garnet gave a sympathetic nod. "Do tell your parents we have many resources available at the library that you can use."

"Thank you," said Morgan, reverting to the fairly formal English that he found impressed Americans, perhaps because he sounded like a character in a movie. "My mother will be pleased to learn I can use the library." If I ever find her again, he thought, as he always did when he said this lie. "But what do you have about the Wrecker of Engines?"

"There's not much known about the real hero." Ms. Garnet wandered over to the case and peered inside. She snagged her glasses and propped them on the end of her nose. "I found very little in the archives. They say the Wilde family has some mementoes."

"Wilde?"

"Katherine Wilde. Socialite. Constantly being rescued from various heists and kidnappings by Wild Kat and other members of the Protectorate. Personally, I think she puts herself in danger for the publicity…but that's an unkind thing to say about a rather generous benefactor. She came to the opening of our last heroes exhibition, along with Stardust and his family. Those were busy days." Ms. Garnet sighed. "It took nearly a year to set up our exhibit. And it was popular, at first. But it's simply not drawing people anymore. And we need more visitors downtown to keep the main library open."

"Don't people come to check out books?"

"Not since the Stevens Foundation grants made everything available online and set up free Wi-Fi through the city." Ms. Garnet sighed again. "It was incredibly generous. I'm very appreciative of all Starcom did to digitize our collection. But it does mean we have a large, drafty, and seriously underused building here. The mayor has been pushing us to do something with the space."

"That's tough," said Morgan, echoing a line he had heard a few days ago at a coffee shop. He planned to check out the library collection online as soon as he could politely get away from Ms. Garnet.

"But I do think our next exhibition will draw people in. Would you like to see it? I'd love to have a reaction from somebody…well…somebody who isn't Janet. She loves the library so much, she's a bit biased."

Not knowing how to say no, Morgan trailed after her to the end of the corridor. A sign outside a closed door proclaimed: "Victorian Villains: Science and Madness."

"Nice sign," said Morgan.

Ms. Garnet smiled. "I'm so glad you like it. We found these artifacts in the subbasement. Behind the furnace. I can't imagine how they came to be stored at the library, but, of course, they are something of a treasure."

She swung the door open to reveal a device that looked like a cross between a machine gun and a bronzed bicycle.

Intrigued, Morgan checked it out. A giant glass bulb pulsed with a faint green light directly above what looked like a two-handed trigger. Below that were a number of long gleaming tubes of glass, something like test tubes. One was filled with a murky purple substance.

"Nice," he said and meant it this time.

"You like machines." The librarian practically beamed at him.

"Where I live now has a collection of old devices like this. But these are different." He bent over to get a closer view.

"According to the blueprints," said Ms. Garnet, "it was called an Edison Eradicator."

"Like Thomas Edison?" asked Morgan. Then, "do you mind?" as he squatted down to see how the thing was put together.

"Go ahead. Take a closer look. Our Edison was a very distant cousin of Thomas and lived here in Cobalt City. His name was Sheffield Edison. The press rather unkindly dubbed him Edison Junior. He failed to win the blue ribbon at the 1896 Expo with his Snorting Wonder, some type of steam-driven car, and the local cartoonists created a number of lampoons of it driving away with Edison hanging onto the back and screaming. We have them all in our archives. I'm planning to frame and display them around the walls."

"So how does that make him a villain?" Morgan bent double over the Eradicator, seeing if he could trace the wires back to the machines around the wall. There was something odd about the array, almost the reverse of what he'd expect to find.

"From 1896 until he disappeared in 1898, Sheffield Edison became Cobalt City's most notorious science villain. They called him Steambolt Ed because he used a combination of electricity and steam-powered engines. His battles with the Steel Suffragette and, later, the Electric Girl occupied dozens of dime novels. Which we also have in our collection."

"Mmph." Morgan had wiggled his way underneath the Eradicator and wasn't listening too closely. From where he lay on his back, he could see something like a clockwork key projecting from the undercarriage of the Eradicator. He reached up and gave it a twist and was rewarded with the faintest sound of ticking.

Ms. Garnet's round face appeared upside down as she bent over to see what he was doing. "Did you find something?"

"Not really." Morgan slid back out. "But the whole thing is a bit odd. A combination of clockwork and currents. I wouldn't plug it into anything. It might short out the whole building."

"Oh, no. It has its own battery. Not that I suppose it works." She indicated a large wood and brass box sitting to one side of the Eradicator. "Orville, our janitor, found it a few weeks ago behind the furnace."

Morgan looked at the slots on the box and the various wires trailing from the Eradicator. "It looks simple, a positive and a negative and a ground wire." He sorted the three automatically as he spoke. "Stick the plugs in the right holes and it should work. But I'm not sure what it does. So plugging it in might not be the best idea."

"Sound advice. But it would be interesting to see if we could get it running. A working Sheffield Edison invention. I don't think even the Starcom Industries Science Museum has that. It might attract the press...and the public."

"It is rad." Morgan circled around the Eradicator again. It certainly reminded him of the gleaming communications room in the basement of the Adventurers Club. "Maybe you can carry it upstairs and set it up in the lobby or something."

Ms. Garnet looked shocked. "Oh no! Upstairs is for books and other paper ephemera. We only do exhibits down here, where there are fire doors and other protections. So important for a collection like ours."

"I'd love to see what this machine does." Morgan gave one last glance to the gleaming tubes, copper plates, and intriguing gauges. "But I'm looking for more on the Wrecker of Engines, the real one, not the radio show."

"Second floor, newspaper archives. Hubert can show you how to run the microfiche. Or—" Ms. Garnet sighed. "—you can use the online database. All you need is a library card. Janet can set up your application and issue your card on the way out."

"Thank you."

As he left the room, he noticed Ms. Garnet standing over the wires trailing from the Eradicator. She settled her glasses firmly on her nose and gave him a little wave as she bent closer to the Eradicator.

Morgan waved back and circled through the room with the Wrecker's mask one last time. But there wasn't much there. He decided to head upstairs to talk to Janet and secure a library card for further research.

The first year Lizzie lived in Cobalt City, the madhouse for females still existed. It stood just outside the city's boundaries, on a plot of land that fell under no clear jurisdiction, which meant the worse for the poor women incarcerated there.

Certain the place deserved to be shut down, and its terrible matron locked in prison for her cruelties, Lizzie intentionally had herself committed. The corrupt judge was known for sentencing many a poor girl to the erstwhile "asylum" that offered no comfort to anyone. As she told her editor, she knew the walls of the asylum hid a great, terrible story.

All her time in the madhouse, Lizzie found herself listening constantly for the clocktower bell, which marked the slow hours. Its clanging could be clearly heard in her little attic room. She marked the bell's strokes inside the tiny memorandum book she had smuggled into the madhouse and numbered the days inside its cover.

Now, once again, she waited in the darkness, but there was no friendly bell to mark the hours. But still, something stirred in her heart, a certainty brought by the lightning storm that her work was not done, that there was still a story to pursue, a villain to catch.

Down in the basement, Ms. Garnet ran her hands just a hairs-breadth above the Eradicator, careful not to smudge or mar its gleaming surface. She could see her own distorted reflection in its huge glass bulb, staring anxiously back at her. The previous night's dreams stirred in her memories, dreams that had been recurring every night since she began working on this new exhibit. Mocking laughter and shouts of derision echoed through her mind. The nightmares had been growing stronger since the night of the lightning storm.

She shook her head. This exhibit would work. Look how long that boy, the young Asian tourist, spent looking at Sheffield Edison's devices, she told herself.

But what she truly needed was more press, Ms. Garnet decided. Another big opening, like the last one for the superheroes exhibition. Patrons, a few celebrity types, something to attract attention.

She'd sent out invitations, but she hadn't heard back from many people. Perhaps she should make a few personal calls.

But first, she thought, she should plug in the Eradicator and see if it worked. Just a little test, to see what it did. It was amazing Orville had found the battery.

Lightning had struck the rod set up on the roof of the library and grounded itself along the ancient nineteenth-century wire that led into the lowest basement. Orville had followed it to a back room and discovered the battery there. He claimed it had felt hot when he picked it up.

Under her palm, it felt cool, almost cold. It needed to be connected, to unleash the power stored within, she decided.

Another part of her, a sensible and screaming part, protested.

Driven by the desires inspired by her dreams, Frances Garnet ignored that tiny voice of reason.

She reached down and finished plugging the wires into the Eradicator's battery. She went to the wall and flipped the switch that gave power to the whole array that surrounded it.

The purple mist in the long test tube swirled up and through unseen tubing, filling the giant glass bulb on the top of the Eradicator. Deep in the heart of it, sparks lit and then burned out, like tiny falling stars trapped in a glass universe.

Moved by a compulsion that seemed almost outside of herself, Frances Garnet slid the long necklace holding her glasses off her neck and looped it around the trigger of the Eradicator. Then she stepped in front of it.

Somewhere, somebody was screaming, "no, don't do it." It sounded almost like her own voice.

But Frances yanked on her necklace. The trigger snapped. A horrible hum began, and then, with a sizzle of spent electricity, a bolt of purple light shot from the nozzle of the Eradicator. It engulfed the head librarian.

She fell to the floor with a thud.

As the air cleared and the scent of lightning dissipated, Frances Garnet sat up. She clutched her aching head and moaned.

A rattle of footsteps sounded outside the door.

Janet peeked into the room. "Oh, Ms. Garnet, are you alright?" she asked, as she hurried across the room to help the head librarian to her feet.

"I think so." Ms. Garnet faltered. "What happened?"

"All the lights flickered and went out. Then the computer screens upstairs all went black and came back on with nonsense messages. Hubert went to check the fuses with Orville."

"How about the patrons?"

"There's nobody upstairs. The library is empty."

"Of course it is." Frances Garnet sighed and then felt unfamiliar anger sizzle through her. "But they won't ignore us for long. Our day is here again."

"Ms. Garnet?" quavered Janet. "Are you sure you're okay?"

"I am fine," she snapped in reply. "Come along. We have work to do. Important work. The first thing I need is a list."

"A list?"

"Of heroes. Don't stand there. We have much to do." Frances Garnet marched out of the room, leaving the humming, spinning, awakening machines behind her. Ideas zinged through her brain, and a new, strange resolution stiffened her spine. Soon, nobody would dare ignore Cobalt City's head librarian.

CHAPTER 4: MESSAGES RECEIVED AND SENT

HIS PHONE BUZZED IN HIS POCKET AS MORGAN LEFT THE library. A text showed on the screen: "Stop the thief."

Startled, he looked around. It seemed as quiet outside the library as inside. A few people waited at a bus stop. Morgan checked the phone again. The sender name was blanked out. But this time he was prepared. He ran his own personal tracer app, only to growl when it came up with his own name and number.

"Stop the thief!"

Intrigued now, Morgan settled down on the stone paw of a literary lion crouched outside the library entrance. "What thief?" he typed.

The screen stayed blank for several moments. Then the answer appeared: "The one who stole my life."

"Who are you?" Morgan texted back.

No response.

"Where are you?"

Another long pause. Then: "Lost. Alone."

"Let me help you." Morgan typed with his flying thumbs.

"Find Pharaoh's Ghost," came the almost instant response.

"Who?"

"Ask—" But then the text flickered and died. The screen came up with a standard message that the connection was lost.

Lizzie rode her bicycle down a shadowed street. All around her, buildings appeared and disappeared as she sped by. She wanted to stop. She wanted to get off and run up the stairs, pound on the doors, demand that someone, anyone, tell her where she was.

But she couldn't stop. The wheels whizzed round and round. If she looked back, if she dared to look back, she knew nothing would be there. Not the city she'd known, not the friends she'd loved, nothing but a blur of shadows in a darkness that wasn't night. The darkness that was something else.

So she gripped the handlebars as hard as she could and kept pedaling as fast as possible. With every thrust of her foot, with every turn of the wheel, she felt the memories flooding back into her head.

She remembered stepping off the train in the grand downtown station of Cobalt City. The porters shouting, the people hurrying by, and the steam whistles screaming impatiently about journeys about to begin. But the journey from a little town in Ohio to the bustling platform of this magical metropolis represented only the beginning of her story.

The next bit started the morning after the science fair, as she walked from newspaper office to newspaper office, then from magazine editor to magazine editor, at first offering her account of the spectacular accident that ended the exhibition, then offering to take on any work, to take any pay, to go unpaid if only they'd publish one small story, to give her a chance.

At every door, some office boy turned her away, told her the editor didn't have time to meet with a fifteen-year-old girl, not even a girl with a dozen clippings of previously published stories clutched in her gloved hand. Editors only had time to meet with the men: serious men, real newspaper men.

"There are more than two thousand newspaper women from New York to San Francisco," she declared. "Writing on everything from sweatshops to murder trials."

"Then you'd better hop back on the train, miss," said one particularly annoying young man. "Try your luck in one of those cities."

But she'd kept walking and she'd kept talking, until she had a hole in the sole of her shoe and only a dime left in her purse. Then she met Charlie Faversham, twelve-year-old copy boy and all-around dogsbody for the *Cobalt City Clarion*.

"You best come in," he said, setting aside his broom and leading her up the stairs that rattled with the roar of the presses laboring below, "and meet Mr. Black. He's the editor and he'll decide. But he's been saying he wants a women's page."

"I'm not writing about society teas and hats." Although at that moment, she would have cheerfully typed blackberry jam recipes for the cost of a night's lodging.

"No, he wants a women's page about the superheroes, the new ones, like the Steel Suffragette. What the ladies think about a lady fighting crime and so on."

"Ah," she said, hurrying up the stairs behind Charlie, "that I can write!"

Now Lizzie pedaled on, faster and faster, the stories of her past fluttering behind her, pages of newsprint blown away by the wind of her passage. But the story wasn't finished, and neither was she, not by a long shot.

So she sped on, never looking back, always looking forward, gathering the needed momentum to send another message out into the world.

Morgan stared up at the office tower housing Starcom's newest corporate headquarters in Cobalt City. It wasn't on his tourist map, but he couldn't resist taking a side trip to check it out.

Even in Hong Kong, home of every electronic gadget ever imagined, Starcom products held a special luster. He remembered spending hours just staring through the gleaming glass windows of the Starcom store, admiring the sleek simplicity of the displays. On glowing screens, Stardust flew like a blue comet across the sky.

In Morgan's head, this was, and would forever be, the true face of Cobalt City: the sparkling possibility of science married to the gritty heroics of men like Stardust and women like the Worm Queen.

Now he was here, right here. He cut the engine on the Vespa. He could go inside, introduce himself to Jaccob Stevens, tell him some of his ideas for making Starcom's amazing computers go even faster and do even more.

He drew a deep breath. He would rather fight gangsters across a rooftop or trail giant mutant rats into the sewer.

Stevens wouldn't take him seriously, Morgan thought. After all, he was new to the city, unknown, untested. A seventeen-year-old immigrant with no hope of impressing an American billionaire revered around the world.

Then he remembered his mother one day when she had come back from a battle. Her hands were bloody, and the bruises blossomed across her back as she slid out of the black clothing covered with mystical symbols that she wore as the Phantom Lady. He had watched through the open crack of his bedroom door as Mr. Wong bandaged her wounds and scolded her with the privilege of an old teacher and trusted friend.

"Why do you do this?" he had asked. "The boy's father is dead. No matter how many you capture, how many you defeat, nothing will raise him from his grave. Honor him by living for your son, not dying for his memory."

She raised one slender hand for silence. "How can I live without the courage to face my worst fears? How can I abandon those who need me? The fight cannot end here."

Then she turned and caught five-year-old Morgan staring through a crack in the door. Her arms flew wide and her smile wider as he ran into her embrace.

"You are my courage," she whispered.

"But I am afraid," he whispered back, for the sight of her injuries always terrified him with the reminder of her vulnerable humanity.

"There is nothing to fear, for you have the heart of the tiger, the heart of our ancestors, beating within you. The tiger will always carry you to victory. Listen to your heart, my son, and never be afraid."

Now Morgan stood outside the revolving doors of Starcom Tower and told himself she would not have hesitated to go inside. Her courage would carry him forward, past all his doubts, just as it always had.

A crowd of laughing, shoving, exuberant employees came tumbling out of the doors and swirled past Morgan. He caught their chatter about a softball tournament as they spilled across the sidewalk to a line of waiting buses.

One guy, a tall thin man only a few years older than himself, paused to admire the Vespa. "Sweet. Love your ride."

"It's okay." Morgan relaxed into a response. Talking about machines always came easy to him. "For a new model. I used to have a sixty-seven. That was a great machine."

"Oh, wow, I'd love to have a bike like that."

"Takes some work to keep the old ones running. I replaced the clutch completely. And the electrical system needed overhaul more than once. But when everything works—"

"Sweet machine," the other guy guessed.

Morgan nodded. Then he asked, "Where are you going?"

"Starcom summer picnic. The big boss pays for it every year. Harbor ride, softball tournament, too much to eat. Dancing tonight at the biggest club downtown."

"Nice," Morgan said, and meant it.

"Seriously. I'm glad I landed here. Couldn't believe I made it through the applications...the first day, I was afraid to walk through those doors. Thought I'd puke if I had to talk to the big dude. I mean, Jaccob Stevens. He's kind of a god."

Morgan laughed. "Guess so."

Somebody shouted from the steps of a bus, "Hey, Harry, are you coming? Move it, man, or the food will be gone before we get there."

Harry turned and waved at his friends. "Yeah, yeah. I'm there."

"So I was thinking of going in there—" Morgan nodded toward Starcom.

"Can't go inside today," Harry said over his shoulder as he walked away. "Place is closed for business, as they say. Everyone is partying today. Even the boss man is heading out of town."

"Thanks," Morgan shouted after him. "Maybe later."

The buses roared away, trailing verses of a boisterous song. Something about ninety-nine bottles.

Morgan took one last look at Starcom Tower. He would come back, and come back soon, he resolved.

His phone buzzed with his text notification.

Another mystery text, caller ID blanked out. "He is coming."

Morgan's thumbed a response: "Who?"

"The start of my story—" The message cut off, like a dropped connection.

Morgan swore and ran his usual trace. Nothing. This was becoming embarrassing. He was the hacker of hackers, the elite of the data crashers. How did this anonymous caller keep finding his number and, even more baffling, keep eluding his attempts to identify him or her?

An idea popped into his head. A modification to his current firewall. But he'd have to program it from his main computer. Then he could catch this caller.

As Morgan sped down the street, he failed to notice the resolute and plump figure of Cobalt City's head librarian as she marched down the sidewalk toward Starcom's headquarters.

Billionaire industrialist Jaccob Stevens dropped back into his office chair. Every muscle in his body ached. It was easier fighting villains than trying to pack Elizabeth and their two teens, and all the stuff he thought they needed, into the massive RV he'd purchased for their extended trip across America.

Still, with the kids' private school out for the summer, this trip would broaden their horizons, and he could show off some wilderness survival skills when they got to the national parks.

Of course, the RV was stuffed with the latest tech and complete Wi-Fi service bouncing off his own Starcom satellites. His wife had been a little snarky about Jaccob's "survival skills" and "roughing it" plans. But she quietly accepted the plans to send them off with a driver and a couple that doubled as summer tutors for the kids but were really live-in bodyguards. As a rich man, he wanted to buy all the protection possible, even if the kids weren't enthusiastic about the idea. Or even vacationing away from Cobalt City. Still, Elizabeth liked Jenny, one of the bodyguards, especially after she found out about Jenny's previous career as a racecar driver and her willingness to help teach young Chuck how to pass the driving test. Teaching their older son, Mike, had added gray hairs to both their heads.

And it would be nice to have some alone time with Elizabeth, he thought, time away from Cobalt City to be just a couple.

"Just remember," Elizabeth said, as she kissed him good-bye, "it's not a family vacation without you. Because it's not a family without you."

"Three weeks," he whispered, as the kids groaned and complained about them getting mushy. "Just need to work out the new StarPad."

"If you're not in Yellowstone on time, I'm flying back to get you."

"What about the brats?" he said with a wink at his kids.

"They can scare the bears or whatever you do in a national park," she answered firmly. "Just remember you're taking vacation. And a vacation means no suit. Leave it at home. Leave it all behind."

"I promise."

And he meant it, although he didn't tell Elizabeth about the spare suit already stashed under the floorboards of the RV.

Whether villains went after his family because he was the inventor of the world's coolest electronic gadgets or because he was the hero Stardust, the most amazing fighter of crime to ever don a bright blue suit, didn't matter. What mattered was, just because he was who he was, his family always needed protection.

However, this notion of keeping his family moving around the country this summer, surrounded by all the latest technology his considerable wealth could buy, was a brilliant idea, if he did say so himself. Now he could peacefully finish his project, and then take a wonderful, relaxing vacation teaching his kids how to hike, fish, and do whatever else it was that you did when you went camping. Jaccob Stevens made a mental note to look up "wilderness vacation ideas" online before he joined his family, if only so he could impress them with all his knowledge of things to do outdoors.

A reminder pinged on his smartphone's calendar. His afternoon appointment was due. Jaccob frowned a little. He hated to disappoint anyone, but there was simply no way he could fit another gala event into the summer. He had too much to do already.

The intercom for the outside entrance buzzed. Jaccob automatically checked the video screen. His expected visitor stood patiently in the elevator lobby.

He hit the sequence on the number pad necessary for opening the door and disarming the weapons hidden in the entry. He tracked her progress across the lobby and up the elevator to his office door. His staff was already gone for the annual Starcom softball tournament and summer picnic, so Jaccob went to the door to greet Ms. Garnet and escort her into his office.

"It's nice to see you again," he said with a flash of what one broadcaster had called his "billion-dollar" grin and his wife called his "sliding out of this one" smile.

Ms. Garnet sat on the very edge of her chair, clutching an enormous bag on her lap. He always wondered what women carried in totes the size of a small suitcase.

"Have you had time to consider my invitation?" she said.

"Yes, and as I said in my email, I can't make it work with my schedule. I'm sorry, but, of course, I could send another representative of Starcom. Maybe my Chief Operating Officer? She's very interested in books."

If it had been anyone other than Ms. Frances Garnet, Cobalt City's chief librarian, Jaccob would have said the woman growled.

"You must come to the library. I need you there. Your grasp of this century's technology exceeds everyone else in this city." Her voice was deeper and rougher than he had ever heard before.

Obviously his attendance at this fundraising gala meant a great deal, but he couldn't reschedule his life around the librarian's wishes. He felt a twinge of guilt—after all, he'd used the library's resources extensively in his college years, when he was first creating the gadgets and gizmos that would launch him to technical superstardom.

"Ms. Garnet, I'm so sorry to turn you down," Jaccob apologized. "But, of course, anything else we can do to help make your exhibition a success, just please ask. I'd be happy to make a personal contribution—"

She shook her head and reached into her oversized bag. Out came an enormous brass and steel gun. "You simply must be part of my collection."

Jaccob's eyes widened at the piece of antique super-weaponry. "Is that a Sheffield Edison Eradicator?" he asked in awe, completely distracted by the gleaming piece of nineteenth-century technology in her hand. "Are you putting it in the exhibit? That's quite the prize. The only one I've ever seen is in the Cobalt City police collection, and that doesn't work."

"This one works perfectly."

"It does?" He bounced out of his chair to get a closer look. Sheffield Edison's bizarre weapons were exceedingly rare, but every example he'd found was a fascinating mix of art and artifice. "How do you know?"

"Oh, I've used it many times today," she said quite calmly, as she shot him square in the chest. Ropes of yellow, blue, and green light twisted around him, binding his arms to his sides and gagging him.

As he toppled to the floor, Jaccob's last coherent thought was: "Who would suspect the librarian?"

"Another package has arrived," Tidwell announced on the house phone.

"Great! Where is it from?"

"Another box from Starcom Industries. Quite small this time."

"Oh, it's my mask. I don't suppose you want me to come down and get it?"

"Unnecessary, sir."

A few minutes later, the door of the elevator slid open, and Tidwell stepped out. On a silver platter, he carried a little box, the size and type jewelers used for rings.

"Fantastic." Morgan plucked it off the tray and carried it to the workbench he'd set up under the paintings of Solomon Cree. He cracked open the tiny box and unfolded the thin white cloth rolled up inside.

"What is it, sir?"

"Digital cloth. It will hit the market next year. You have to have a developer's license to get a sample, but that's not a problem."

"Because you have one?"

"Since I was ten." Morgan leaned over a keyboard and fed in the code he had purchased earlier from Starcom. His terminal began to transmit instructions to the material now lying flat upon his workbench. A discreet beep indicated the download was complete.

Morgan tapped two fingers on one corner of the digital cloth and watched it stiffen into a curved oval, resembling a blank white face. A second tap and I Ching symbols began to scroll across the surface, dissolving into Chinese characters and then mathematical symbols.

"Ah. The Wrecker's mask."

"A bit like it." Morgan recalled the smooth porcelain copy of the Wrecker's mask he'd seen at the library's exhibition. "I used paper masks sometimes in Hong Kong, but this will be better."

"To hide your face?"

"Or take somebody else's. Watch." Morgan tapped the cloth again, and it flushed into a flesh color, reforming under his fingers until it resembled another man, a man whose picture was easy to find online, Cobalt City's most public and flamboyant inventor, billionaire, and superhero.

Tidwell stared down at this copy of Jaccob Stevens' face and frowned. "A dangerous identity to borrow."

"Yeah, maybe," said Morgan, resetting the mask to a blank white. "But I can become anyone with it. Anyone whose portrait shows up enough online for me to recreate the face. But it's no full body suit. I have to stick to people close to my size. And it's not like I can talk or fool anyone up close."

"Then what is the use?"

"Trick a surveillance camera, hide in a crowd." Morgan ran his hand again across the smooth, silky surface of his new mask. A final tweak of his fingers and the material rolled up into a small ball. He pocketed it. He didn't have a use for it yet, but he could feel the excitement building somewhere deep inside. He'd been sitting quiet for too long, following Mr. Wong's orders. It was time to start again as a masked crimefighter.

The computer rang a note. Somebody had posted a query about the Wrecker of Engines in Hong Kong. Morgan swung around and checked it. Just the usual stuff.

"I keep thinking somebody knows I'm here," he said. "I think the tongs are trying to get a fix on my location."

"Why?

"I keep getting these junk calls, strange text messages. Perhaps they're testing my defenses."

"Or perhaps somebody is trying to contact you. Somebody who needs help."

"Nobody knows I'm here," Morgan pointed out. "Nobody but you and Mr. Wong. And neither of you know how to text."

Anna Lyta frowned at the empty lobby of the downtown library. There should be someone here to help her. She was tempted to summon up a directional worm to lead her to the research monograph she needed. But worms and books—or, rather, worms and paper—were a volatile mix at the best of times.

Besides, as she told herself often when faced with the petty annoyances of life lived in a city full of whimsical human beings, she needed to stop relying on her superpowers for ordinary tasks. Being able to summon "worms" or, more accurately, space aliens of unbelievable power, to do her bidding might make her the Worm Queen when it came to fighting crime, but those powers would never win her the Nobel Prize. For that, she needed to use her much-better-than-average intelligence and superb academic research skills.

Still, she felt slightly lucky that Dr. Fukunaga's monograph on the development of a new breed of moon moths from prehistoric pupae was housed in the Cobalt City Library. She'd been searching for almost a year for this paper, which was published once and only once in the 1960s. A copy here, almost under her nose, as it were, was an unbelievable find. This monograph documented a necessary link in the influence of alien DNA on genetic mutations among Earth's worms, a link that made all the difference to her own theories.

Anna checked the notification that had been texted to her phone. According to the catalog, the monograph was filed in the basement of this building.

With impatient steps, she crossed the lobby and took the stairs. A number of exhibits about Cobalt City's past decorated the walls. Anna glanced at them and moved on. Such things did not interest her.

At the end of the hallway, she found a room filled with a buzzing sound like a swarm of bees. The modulated noise came from an array of machines built out of well-polished wood, gleaming copper, and a fascinating array of glass tubes and cloth-covered cords.

At the end of the row of machines, Anna glimpsed a female figure. The back of the woman's fuzzy sweater was toward her. As she watched, the other woman ran her hands across the gleaming machines, patting them like old pets, then adjusting dials and tapping on gauges.

"Can you help me?" Anna asked. "I'm looking for the research monographs storage."

The woman turned and Anna recognized Cobalt City's head librarian from previous visits.

"Ah," Ms. Garnet said, adjusting her glasses, "thank you for coming. I thought my message would bring you here."

Anna blinked, suddenly slightly confused. It was an unusual sensation for her. "What message?"

Ms. Garnet smiled. "A library notification. Who would suspect anything wrong in that?"

The appearance of a gleaming brass gun in Ms. Garnet's hand startled Anna. It made a high-pitched electrical whine, something like a wasp's buzz, and looked far too dangerous for the librarian to safely handle. Anna had just started to warn Ms. Garnet that the piece in her hand was about to go off when ribbons of electrical blue and green light wrapped around her.

Endowed with certain psychic abilities, finely attuned by her years as the Worm Queen, Anna became aware of the oddest sensation as she dropped to the floor. It almost felt as if there were three people in the room: herself, Ms. Garnet, and somebody else.

As she passed into unconsciousness, Anna Lyta thought, "But how could something like this happen in the library?"

Morgan combed the web for more information on the man who had once used the name Wrecker of Engines. By far the best database was the one maintained by the Cobalt City Library. Not surprisingly, it also came with a small banner that stated: "Made possible by a grant from the Stevens Foundation."

In it, Morgan found the recent history of the Protectorate and the Mysterious Five, and older heroes too. There were rumors of Norse gods rampaging through discos, tales of Civil War spies outdone by robotic wonders, and allusions to the ever-changing but ever-familiar Huntsman who popped up in every era.

But he couldn't find much more than vague stories about the Wrecker of Engines, a man who disappeared from Cobalt City around 1950. A couple of short articles mentioned a possible connection to the Wilde family. Morgan looked them up. Rich, English, and represented in Cobalt City by Katherine Wilde. Pages of pictures came up of her, usually going in or out of some fancy event. A red-carpet type, as far as Morgan could tell. He found a website called "Kathy's Guys" that listed all the men who had supposedly dated her, as well as a lot of comments from guys and gals about who she should or shouldn't date. But nothing there about the Wrecker of Engines.

Bored with the gossip stuff and remembering the message from a few days earlier when he was leaving the library, Morgan typed in the name "Pharaoh's Ghost." The search came up with nineteenth-century theater posters showing a magician in a hood. Morgan frowned at the page. Why would somebody send him a text message telling him to find a long-dead stage magician?

"An interesting picture," said Tidwell from behind him. When he wanted to, the man could sneak into the room like a cat.

Morgan refrained from jumping in his seat, preferring to appear nonchalant. "It's nothing," he said, spinning around in his chair.

Tidwell was carrying a tray, and Morgan recognized the square cardboard box on it as his supper. They had pizza in Hong Kong, but it didn't taste anything like this deep-dish stuff he could order here.

"You know, you don't need to put my pizza on a tray to bring it up. In fact, you don't even need to bring it up. Just buzz me when it gets here, and I'll come down for it."

Tidwell sighed with an exhalation of breath that sounded as if it rose from the labyrinthine basements of the Adventurers Club. "Old habits. Most difficult to discard."

"Okay." Morgan popped open the box. "Would you like some pepperoni?"

Tidwell eyed it for a long moment and then shrugged. "What harm could it do to me?"

"Take a seat." Morgan was cheered to see the usually so formal Tidwell gingerly pick up a slice dripping with greasy cheese.

"Might I inquire as to what you are doing this evening?" Tidwell asked between hesitant nibbles at the pointy end of his slice.

"Checking to see who is checking on me." Morgan grinned

as he ran a series of inquiries through various search engines he'd designed to track worldwide chatter about the Wrecker of Engines. Anyone looking for his alter ego would generate an automatic alert to Morgan's monitoring software. "Wow, I'm worth double what I was last month," he said, as he pulled up the current bounty on his living body or detached dead head.

"That does not concern you, sir?"

"No. Right now, everyone's looking for a middle-aged guy from Shanghai."

"Rather than a young man of seventeen years living alone in Cobalt City."

"Absolutely." Morgan typed with one hand and stuffed pizza into his face with the other. He began to lay down trails, fabricate clues, manufacture new false photos, and parlay phony phone messages to various sellers of information.

Under a series of names, he began chatter that the Wrecker of Engines now resided in Moscow.

Tidwell finished his slice and cleaned away the debris of their midnight feast.

Morgan clicked over the final piece of his false trail and went to bed.

In the morning, armed with a cup of tea from the ever-obliging Tidwell, he began his monitoring program to check airline manifests. It showed several well-known assassins were flying to Russia. He alerted the Moscow mafia that the Hong Kong tongs were muscling into their territory.

Peering over his shoulder, Tidwell remarked, "It seems a violent confrontation is now inevitable."

"Not at all. Watch." He triggered a series of timed messages to alert Moscow's law enforcement. Because that sometimes wasn't enough, he also notified international media of the locations of new criminal activity. "In a few hours, both Moscow and Hong Kong will have more criminals behind bars."

"This internet does contain some inherent efficiencies," Tidwell admitted.

CHAPTER 5: DANGER IN THE STACKS

LIZZIE SAT ALONE IN A ROOM WITHOUT CEILING OR WALLS, although she was certain it was a room. Or a prison cell. Light glowed from an unknown source on the telegraph key in front of her.

On the wall that didn't exist but was in front of her, she could see a map of Cobalt City. Streets glimmered and shifted, reformed, and then dribbled off the edge of the paper like raindrops down a windowpane.

At the center of it all, a beetle crawled across shadowy streets and rooftops. Light glittered on its lapis lazuli wings. A lion roared and swatted at it with inky paws.

With a nod of resolve, she began to tap out her next message. She only hoped the boy living in the real city would understand.

Morgan leaned across the counter of the coffee shop, trying to catch the eye of the barista in the tight t-shirt. He wanted a refill. He wanted a date. He wanted something to do.

All his research into the Wrecker of Engines had led him to dead ends. A burned-out warehouse where the man supposedly once stopped a criminal takeover of Cobalt City. A shuttered bar where the owner claimed the Wrecker stacked the jukebox with his favorite tunes and rigged it so it only played what he wanted when he wanted. A block of gleaming offices built over the crater of a lab explosion blamed on the Wrecker. Half hero, half devil, nobody seemed to know anything more about the man. Except that, after all his adventures, he disappeared from Cobalt City into the chaos that was mid-century China.

A couple of newspapers were stacked on the counter. One was Cobalt City's remaining daily newspaper, a thin rag that seemed to consist mostly of stories bemoaning the city's lack of professional sports teams. The other was the free weekly full of advertisements for various clubs and shows. Earlier time spent in other coffee shops had taught Morgan that the weekly ran a police blotter column written by a woman named Nancy Phan.

Morgan skimmed down Phan's selections from various neighborhood police reports. Several missing persons, all of them quite different. A man named Wenders vanished from a downtown apartment building and nobody noticed anything until a leak from an overflowing bathtub flooded a neighbor below. A Rachel Czerny left a restaurant with friends, went back to leave a tip on the table, and then never returned. Inquiries inside and outside of the restaurant turned up no trace of her. A researcher in nematology, Anna Lyta, failed to appear at her laboratory job on a Monday morning, a break in routine that her assistants claimed was impossible. "She always came in early on Monday," said one. "She loved those worms."

He flipped the page and hit a gossip column. Rumors that the socialite Katherine Wilde had eloped to Tahiti with her latest beau were being fervently denied by her publicist, but as the reporter breathlessly pointed out, Wilde had recently skipped several prominent charity functions that she usually attended. Most unusually, she had not been at the Royal Enclosure in Ascot this season, although that may have been caused by the recent ban on wearing fascinators there. Wilde, stated the reporter, was well known for pushing the edges of Royal tolerance with her memorable Ascot outfits.

Morgan studied the grainy photo of the woman stepping out

of a limousine into a barrage of paparazzi at some Cobalt City charity event. He remembered Ms. Garnet talking about her, the woman who was always being kidnapped, and the vague mentions in a couple of old articles that her family was somehow connected to the Wrecker of Engines.

The barista waved a lazy hand at him and disappeared into the back to look for something. Morgan switched to the daily newspaper. The top headline screamed: "Stevens Needs a New Star."

"Jaccob Stevens abruptly disappeared earlier this month, supposedly for an extended vacation with his family. Is that the truth, or is he busy planning the next Starcom production?" the article began, then discussed how the tech savant and alter ego of the superhero Stardust was expected to unveil a new version of the StarPad soon, leading to long lines of eager fans camped out in front of Starcom's shiny new Parkside store.

"Or is Stevens finally ready to reveal what we've all been waiting for? Our own personal jetpacks so we can fly ourselves around Cobalt City too?" asked the writer. "He's been teasing us for years with rumors that this will be the century when personal flight becomes as easy and environmentally friendly as riding your bike to work."

Morgan studied the newspaper's sketch of a possible personal version of Stardust's jetpack with interest. He'd love to have something like that himself. It shouldn't be impossible—he could think of three or four hacks to existing tech that might give him what he wanted.

"Whenever Stevens reappears in Cobalt City, we're certain he will have multiple goodies to share with his eager fans and even more eager stockholders," ended the writer.

The barista returned and asked Morgan what he wanted. His head full of possible plans for single-manned flight, he grunted for a refill and settled down at a table by the window. He pulled out his own tablet from his backpack and began sketching something more elegant than the newspaper speculation. Of course, he didn't have a lab or a crew of assistants, not like Stevens, and the Vespa was still the sweetest ride in his universe. But, if he could get this right, it might be a way to introduce himself to Stevens.

As he was doodling, a message appeared on the screen.

"Pharaoh's Ghost."

Morgan swore. The tablet was hooked to the coffeeshop's Wi-Fi, but he rarely used it for more than drawing and, sometimes, a quick photo recon of his current location.

He responded to the IM program as he always did when these messages appeared: "Who are you?"

The question was ignored, and the next message said: "Go to the library."

"What?"

"Pharaoh's Ghost is there."

"Who is Pharaoh's Ghost?"

"A friend."

"Why should I look for this Ghost?"

"Need a friend."

Morgan wondered which of them needed a friend: the messenger sending the strange texts or himself? But, as always, the exchange ended without any warning, and the screen showed a frustrating blank.

"It's a conjuring act, in a theater," Lizzie protested to her editor. "I write about crime and the heroes who fight it. Mad women, burning buildings, the reappearance of pirates in the harbor. The nefarious deeds of Steambolt Ed. The Steel Suffragette's triumphs."

"And it's fine writing. Indeed, you've been doing wonderful work," said Mr. Black. "Quite the best of all my reporters. But Joe is sick, and we need a review."

"He was probably poisoned by that actress he called a graceless ostrich," Lizzie muttered. The *Clarion's* theater reviewer was rumored to dip his pen in acid before writing about any of the performances taking place on the city's busy stages.

Her editor snorted. "Quite possibly. And thankful we should all be that he's not reviewing this new magician then. The man makes people disappear. Or so the posters say. Here—" Mr. Black handed her two tickets. "Take Charlie with you. A lady should have an escort, and the boy has been dying to see this since the posters started appearing all over town."

With a suspicious look, Lizzie took the two tickets and tucked them in her purse next to the notebook, two pencils, and the electric stinger gun she always carried with her. "Do you need a review, or are you looking for an excuse to give Charlie a treat?"

Mr. Black grinned at her. "Who says it's only Charlie I want to reward? Time you took a night off, my girl, and enjoyed yourself."

That memory faded and she found herself alone, walking through the lobby of one of Cobalt City's many gilded theaters. She looked around automatically for Charlie, but, of course, he wasn't there. He would never be by her side again. Still, she didn't need the jubilant boy's comments buzzing in her ear. Inside herself, she could feel the excitement rising. The show was about to begin. She knew it.

Morgan found the library as empty on his second trip as his first. This time, not even the friendly Janet sat at the front desk.

He headed downstairs toward the villains' exhibit, thinking

he'd look at the Sheffield Edison inventions again, only to encounter Ms. Garnet heading up the stairs.

"Hi!" said Morgan.

She stared at him with the cold piercing gaze of a puma—or a librarian in a hurry. "What are you doing here?"

"I thought I'd look at the Eradicator again."

"There is no such thing."

"I saw it," Morgan said, startled by her vehement denial. Earlier, she'd seemed eager for his opinion. Adults, he decided, were never predictable. Must be something age did to them.

"You did not see anything." Her face hardened into lines of disapproval.

Morgan wondered what was wrong with her today—she'd seemed nice enough on his last visit—but then, people did just go strange every now and then. Maybe she'd broken the Eradicator or something and didn't want him to know.

Faced with the impossible barrier of a middle-aged woman he couldn't shove past or even really argue with, not without feeling like a bully or an jerk, Morgan retreated back up the stairs.

Ms. Garnet followed him. She frowned at seeing the empty front desk. "Janet should have been guarding the door."

"Maybe she's helping someone," Morgan suggested.

"No one is allowed inside."

"Uh, it's a library—"

"Sticky-fingered children, careless adults chattering on cell phones, teenagers!" Ms. Garnet's cheeks burned pink with outrage. "They should all be banned. They are not good for the books."

Morgan backed up a little more. He looked around for a distraction. Noticing the map showing the various collections upstairs, he asked as casually as he could, "Do you know where

I could find more information about someone called Pharaoh's Ghost?"

Ms. Garnet blinked, and her face softened. She ran a hand across her eyes. "I'm sorry. Did you need assistance?"

"Ah, yeah, I'm looking for something about Pharaoh's Ghost—"

She smiled. "The Victorian stage magician? We have a wonderful collection of theater posters and programs upstairs. Right next to the nineteenth-century newspapers. Hubert can help you with that."

"Thanks." Morgan started toward the elevator. Then he swung back and looked at Ms. Garnet.

She had moved behind the help desk and was fussing with some papers on it.

"Are you okay?" he asked.

She sighed and rubbed her forehead again. "A headache. It comes and goes." She looked around the desk and frowned slightly. "Where can Janet be? It is not like her to abandon her post."

"She's supposed to stay there and keep people out?" he asked, as casually as he could.

"Keep people out? What an absurd idea! We need more visitors. Why would we want people to stay away? A library needs patrons!"

The flush rose on Ms. Garnet's cheeks, and Morgan decided it was a good time to make a quick exit. He hit the "UP" button and jumped into the elevator as soon as the doors opened.

"Keep people out?" Ms. Garnet was still saying, as the doors closed. "How can we stay open if we keep people out?"

The stage was empty, but Lizzie could clearly see a large box sitting in the wings. It resembled a grandfather clock, but one without hands or numbers. Yet, she knew it was a clock because she could hear ticking, loud ticking, reverberating throughout the theater.

She'd heard that sound before, but where?

Memories of smoke and fire. Golddust Gertie, the Dynamite Queen, visited Cobalt City once, offering marriage and mayhem to Sheffield Edison.

On the night of the mad inventor's nuptials, as the Electric Girl, Lizzie had flown above the city in the marvelous green balloon borrowed from the circus, searching the streets with her amplified telescope and telegraphing the location of Steambolt Ed's auto-mobile as it raced through the darkened streets to rendezvous with his demon bride.

The ticking increased in urgency. Lizzie concentrated, and the wireless telegraph key appeared under her fingers. She began tapping her message, faster and faster, as the ticking clock grew louder.

On the third floor of the library, Morgan met Janet again. She was hanging over a desk, talking to a tall, skinny guy with oversized glasses.

"She's been acting strange again," Janet hissed at the guy. "I don't think she's going home at all. I think she's sleeping down there, in the basement, with the exhibits."

The guy spotted Morgan and nudged Janet. She looked over her shoulder at Morgan and smiled. "Oh, you're the one who signed our guest book twice!"

Morgan shrugged. "Guess so."

The glasses dude, the one whose name badge proclaimed him to be Hubert, research librarian, asked, "Can I help you?"

"I'm looking for Pharaoh's Ghost." Morgan gave another shrug, like a fellow sent on a homework quest, something not very important, but willing to do it. He'd spent a couple of days hanging around a bus stop near one of Cobalt City's high schools, watching the American teenagers, copying their moves. He thought he blended pretty well now.

"The stage magician?" Hubert typed a few words into a terminal.

"Guess so. Is there more than one Pharaoh's Ghost in Cobalt City?"

"It's complicated." Hubert shoved his glasses up his nose with one finger. "Like all the good names, it's been used more than once."

"Uh…good names?"

"Heroes," injected Janet and clapped her hands.

"And villains," added Hubert, with a frown at her. "It's the basis of my thesis—"

"Hubert is working on a master's degree in superhuman taxonomy."

"And before you ask, it has nothing to do with stuffing them or mounting their heads on plaques to hang from the wall," Hubert said in a rush of words that betrayed far too many people had asked him this question far too often.

"Uh, interesting, but about Pharaoh's Ghost—" Morgan replied.

But Hubert was rolling now, obviously excited to have a new audience. He swung around his computer terminal, which was filled with the glowing lines and boxes Morgan recognized as a relational database.

"My working hypothesis is that we can better define sub-classifications based upon the names selected by heroes and villains.

Especially the so-called epic designations that are re-used on a consistent basis. Does the name inform the man—"

"Or woman," pointed out Janet.

"Or does the man—I'm using it in the non-gendered sense, Janet—inform the name."

"So this is like the heroes database that Starcom underwrote."

Hubert sniffed. "That is like comparing a bookcase to a library. The Starcom database holds some interesting data, but the relationships here are thought out to the seventh or even seventeenth degree."

"Oh, is it like that game where you guess what movies two actors have in common?" Morgan asked with a smile. He recognized a mega nerd when he met one, and he'd always liked the species, although he worked hard not to resemble them. Hubert would get a lot further with Janet if he rode a Vespa and practiced martial arts, in Morgan's opinion.

Hubert's snort of derision at Morgan's description was not unexpected. "It's nothing like—"

"I had the same idea, the first time he explained it to me," Janet said.

"It is not like that! See, some names, such as the Huntsman, keep coming back. Over and over again. Every era."

"Family name?" Morgan suggested, thinking of how he'd taken the name of the Wrecker after he found the photograph left by his mother.

Hubert shook his head. "Not likely. All the heroes using that name are different. Some were even women. But they all have certain distinct characteristics and abilities, which probably led them to take the name. And, by association with that name, naturally to make connections to certain other heroes or villains."

"You mean like the Protectorate or the Mysterious Five." Morgan remembered those groups from earlier research.

"Exactly. So the more we can classify the superhero names, and comprehend the hierarchical structures implied by them, the better we can understand the abilities of the groups and the individuals within them. We can even extrapolate potential powers and, more importantly, how those powers may be enhanced or refined by those relationships."

"Like the 'Power of Three,'" beamed Janet.

Hubert sighed. "That is a television show. But, yes, some heroes work best in partnerships and teams that magnify certain aspects of their innate abilities. And some heroes actually may be drawn to Cobalt City when a team needs to be formed. You could say that the need for the partnership creates a vacuum that must be filled by a certain type of personality. So if you have only two, to use the 'Power of Three' analogy, then a third will appear shortly."

"Hubert's database puts all our records from the library into a searchable timeline that shows when different types of heroes appear...or disappear," Janet added.

"Fibraster tried something similar with the styles of capes and cowls and masks back in the 1980s, but that's very crude stuff. I heard he kept his records on handwritten cards in boxes." Hubert rolled his eyes. "However, my work will show that by creating faceted taxonomies of the known nomenclatures, we will be able to literally predict what type of new heroes...or villains...will appear next."

"You mean when the need is greatest, a King Arthur shows up," suggested Morgan, who was beginning to enjoy this discussion. From what he could see on the screen, Hubert's coding wasn't bad. He might have to take a more in-depth peek later.

"See, Hubert, I told you it was like *The Once and Future King*," Janet said. "I love that book!"

"So do I," said Morgan, who remembered his mother reading T. H. White to him once when he was sick.

Janet beamed at him.

Hubert grumbled something and swung his terminal around to tap some more letters into it. "You were asking about Pharaoh's Ghost?"

"Yeah."

"There was a stage magician who performed in Cobalt City in the 1890s. His specialty was making himself disappear into shadows on the stage. He was even suspected of being responsible for the Grand Vanishing."

"The Grand Vanishing?"

Hubert's face brightened. "I did an undergrad paper on it, based mostly on the newspapers in our collection here. In 1898, more than a dozen superheroes vanished within the space of a month. In less than thirty days, they were all gone. And then, and here's the strange part, and why I always notice it in my database, none of the names ever reappear again. The Steel Suffragette, Appleseed Angus, Iron Peacock, the Lady Detective, Six-Shooter and his dog Soupy, and the Electric Girl," Hubert recited. "All gone, like they were erased forever. And Sheffield Edison or Steambolt Ed. Although he's the only true villain who disappeared."

"Sheffield Edison. Wasn't he the guy who built the machines downstairs?" Morgan asked.

Hubert nodded, his eyes brightening behind his glasses. "One of the least understood villains of the nineteenth century, in my opinion. Everyone thinks he only did things with machines. But the guy was seriously ahead of his time, even in science as it existed here in Cobalt City. He was fascinated by the idea of bio-electricity, as well as steam power. Had this insane theory that he could wed the two together to build a perpetually powered city."

Morgan had a feeling that if he didn't drag the conversation back to where it started, he was going to end up hearing all of Hubert's undergraduate and graduate research. "So, Pharaoh's Ghost?" he asked when Hubert paused to draw breath. "Was he one of the ones that disappeared then?"

"No. He's not a superhero, at least not by true definition. He seems to have worked with some of them. Or maybe been a consulting detective. It was a popular occupation at that time. Anyway, he's a hard one to classify properly. Definitely not a sidekick or a minion. Fibraster once speculated that the same man used different names at different times...for centuries even...based on some buckle or amulet or something. He linked Pharaoh's Ghost to the Black Hand, who definitely was a sorcerer according to the accounts from the Vampire Wars."

"And you don't think that's possible?"

"Probably not. The name delineates the hero. Not the other way around. If someone kept changing their name, they'd keep changing their characteristics."

Morgan shrugged. "Maybe. Maybe not. It's rather like saying the name Hubert makes you who you are."

Hubert just leveled a stare at him. The light glimmered on his oversized glasses and gave the young man the look of a goggled alien.

Morgan shrugged again, admitting defeat on that point.

"Anyway," Hubert continued, "we do have an extensive collection of playbills from that era, including several for Pharaoh's Ghost. They're in the stacks, section B, east wing." He sketched out the route on a library map and handed it to Morgan. "But, really, the good stuff in that area are the Sheffield Edison articles. Nobody has ever done much with them. There are nine or ten volumes of newspaper clippings about him that he donated to the library. Think about that. The guy kept his own scrapbooks and made sure they were cataloged for posterity."

"Ah, well, maybe some other time," said Morgan.

"I've made my own undergrad research available online," Hubert said, not discouraged by Morgan's backing toward the nearest exit. "Feel free to access it. I'm here every day between eight and four, too, if you have questions."

With a wave of noncommittal acknowledgement, Morgan headed east through the empty rooms. Behind him, he could hear Janet resume her conversation with Hubert.

"I am worried sick about Ms. Garnet. She's not even interested in the new books. She barely glanced at the mysteries when they arrived last week," Janet said.

"It's probably nothing."

"No, I think she's in trouble."

"Oh, come on, she's the head librarian. She knows how to take care of herself."

Their voices faded away behind him as Morgan went deeper into the stacks. Shelves of books without dust jackets, just black or blue or brown spines, towered above him. All the librarians in Cobalt City were a little odd, he decided, but friendly. Maybe he should think about getting a part-time job here. He didn't need the money, but it would give him a base, a place to operate from, outside of the Club.

But he would have to do it under a fake name, he decided, because using Morgan Lee would mean that name on tax forms and government records. It might make him too visible to certain people looking for the Wrecker of Engines. And, since he had already told Janet and Hubert his real name, it might be easier to get a job elsewhere in the city.

Somewhere with girls who aren't librarians with pink-streaked hair, said a small voice in the back of his head, girls closer to his own age, girls who might be interested in a guy with a Vespa and wicked good computer skills.

As he argued amiably in his own head about the best places to make new friends and how to do it, Morgan found himself walking into the wing marked with the reference numbers cited on Hubert's map.

Nothing disturbed the eerie hush of the library, not even the street noises of the city penetrating this far into the stacks.

Then he rounded another corner and, inside the room marked B East, he found a bomb ticking quietly and discreetly towards destruction.

CHAPTER 6: THE CAT COMES BACK

MORGAN DROPPED TO HIS KNEES TO GET A CLOSER LOOK AT the bomb and its trigger. The thing looked almost like a cartoon contraption. First, there were the classic sticks of dynamite at the base. Part of his brain wondered who would use dynamite instead of a plastic explosive.

Then there was the clock detonator on the top. An actual clock, something incredibly old with a round face and hands moving around, with red and blue wires leading to a box that probably contained the fuse or a secondary smaller explosive. There was even a slowly turning key protruding from the back of the detonator. He checked it twice to make sure he was seeing it right.

Morgan drew a deep breath, settling his mind into the state of calm and calculation that made him the Wrecker of Engines. It might look like a bomb designed by Jules Verne, but there was enough TNT there to cause some serious damage. According to the clock face, he had about six minutes to defuse it.

Fishing out his Swiss Army knife, Morgan briefly reflected on whether it was better to cut the blue or the red wire first. Wrong cut, and he could trigger an explosion rather than prevent it.

His phone rang in his pocket. Morgan ignored it. Blue wire seemed the most likely target, he decided, snapping open the blade of his knife.

The ring of his phone switched to a louder, more insistent tune. Startled, Morgan pulled it out of his pocket. He didn't know his phone had the finale of the "1812 Overture" as a ringtone.

A message was flashing on and off in all caps: "STOP THE CLOCK!"

Morgan glanced back at the clock face as the big hand ticked one minute closer to twelve.

"STOP THE CLOCK!"

"Okay," Morgan muttered at his phone. "I hear you."

With the tip of his knife blade, he delicately and deliberately bent the minute hand. It quivered in place, straining to continue up the dial, then a grinding noise came from inside the clock. The slowly turning key stopped.

Morgan waited for a few more seconds. Nothing happened.

He glanced down at his phone. A new message appeared: "Red wire."

"I'm not sure," he said, even as he neatly snipped the red wire in two. Still no explosion. "Alright, so you know what this is."

He dismantled the bomb, making sure all the pieces were separated and could not accidentally go off.

Once he was certain the bomb posed no further threat, Morgan began to search for the information on Pharaoh's Ghost that Hubert had promised was here. He didn't believe in coincidences. Somebody wanted him here. Somebody wanted him or something in this room destroyed. He didn't think it was the same person (or else why send the messages on how to stop the bomb?). But something decidedly odd was going on.

Which made Morgan grin. He liked having a mystery to solve. Now he needed to find some clues.

The playbills were bound together in a volume marked 1897 to 1898. Several magic acts, including visits from Harry Kellar and Houdini, were included. But six programs trumpeted "A Mystery of the Pyramids Revealed: Man Vanishes into His Own Shadow." Each showed the drawing of a hooded and cloaked figure with the name Pharaoh's Ghost printed in elaborate curlicue type below the sketch.

On the back of the first program was a quotation from a newspaper, obviously drawn from a longer review:

"Whether he was a man or a ghost, no one in the audience could say. I sat on the very edge of my seat, my eyes never wavering from his shadowy figure, and while I judge myself to be more observant than most, and far more conversant than many with the tricks science can play upon our eyes and ears, I must confess myself confounded by his illusions. Most astonishing of all was the final act, and I dare you, dear readers, to explain it as anything other than magic most mysterious."

The picture that accompanied the quote showed Lizzie Blythe of the *Cobalt City Clarion*. She looked cute and younger than he expected, with a cluster of curls tumbling over her forehead and round, wide eyes that stared straight off the page at him.

Morgan leafed through the rest of the programs, but they all were very much the same. Pictures of Pharaoh's Ghost vanishing into his own shadow, a set list of illusions, a few advertisements for popular eating establishments, and the same review by Lizzie Blythe quoted on the back.

The final program, however, varied slightly. Instead of the quote from Lizzie Blythe, Morgan found a drawing of a scarab beetle, and below that were a series of hieroglyphs. The Wrecker of Engines immediately recognized these ancient symbols for numbers. It was a formula for calculating the height of a pyramid, only it didn't quite resemble the examples Morgan had seen before.

He pulled his tablet from his backpack and snapped a picture, determined to look into this later. But now he had a bigger problem. He needed to get the dynamite safely out of the library. He thought about finding one of the librarians and letting them know, but that would lead to police and questions about how he managed to dismantle the bomb.

Morgan opened his backpack and stuffed the now inert, but not yet harmless, dynamite into it. After a moment of consideration, he decided taking the main staircase wouldn't be the best idea. He didn't think they checked bags going out of the library, but his backpack now bulged, and he didn't want to attract attention.

He reached into his pocket and pulled out his Wrecker mask. He pulled up his hood and attached the mask carefully to the edges. With a tap of his fingers, the mask stiffened into a clean white oval. With his face covered, he breathed a little easier. He just needed to find an unobtrusive exit. A quick search behind the stacks led to a service elevator and a ground floor exit.

Back on his Vespa, he roared home to the Adventurers Club. Disposing of dynamite would be easy for Tidwell, he suspected.

The desk in the library's main lobby held a number of security screens tucked neatly under the counter. Frances Garnet frowned at the one that showed a slight young man with a bulky backpack exiting the library through the service door next to the janitor's office. There was something familiar about his figure. Through the headache pounding behind her eyes, she couldn't remember what.

Instead, she looked at the list she had written on a notepad usually used for jotting down directions for patrons. A series of names, terribly famous names, was printed out in a handwriting that oddly didn't look like her usual scribble, even though she was sure she had written out each one. Every name bore a careful checkmark beside it except for the last: Wild Kat.

Frances Garnet switched her attention to the computer database she'd just pulled up. The headache, and all her rational thought, melted away as she typed inquiries into the location of the feline superhero.

Katherine Wilde entered her penthouse apartment through the service elevator. She dropped her single suitcase with a clatter in the laundry room. Tomorrow, or maybe the next day, she'd call the maid service.

But for now, as she kicked off her high-heeled shoes, she just wanted to collapse into the silence of the empty apartment. Nobody knew she was back in Cobalt City, and for the moment, she wanted to keep it that way—at least as far as her public life went. She'd call her friends only, the ones who battled at her side when she was Wild Kat. She felt she had an obligation to let them know she was back.

Ever since the battle at the Dark Carnival, she knew Jaccob and the others worried about her. Even Anna looked up from her worms long enough to tell her that the dark circles under her eyes were classic symptoms of fatigue or possibly food allergies.

Since the battle with the carnival creeps, she felt like she'd been spinning faster than their possessed Ferris wheel, endlessly flung up and down. In her dreams, she still heard the whispers of the fortuneteller, his warning that she had already lost what she wanted most.

She'd run from that prediction for a long time now. But not even dancing on the beach under a Tahitian moon had solved that heartache. Instead, it just left her longing for home.

As the silence grew and stretched and wrapped all around her, Katherine fished her phone out of her tiny designer handbag. She spent a long time scrolling through the menu of contacts, rejecting each one out of hand, finally settling on Jaccob's private number, the one he always answered, no matter where he was or what superpowered suit he was wearing. She tapped to initiate the call and listened, in amazement, as it rang into his voicemail. Stardust never let her go to voicemail.

She tried a few more numbers. Each one led to recorded messages or, worse, dead silence. Even Anna's, and although Anna never liked voicemail, she usually let a worm forward her calls or send back an automated response.

Katherine tapped one polished fingernail against the screen of her phone. It was as if all the heroes of Cobalt City had simply disappeared. But that didn't make sense. If they were kidnapped by aliens, forced into an alternate dimension, or gathered in some high-tech retreat prior to battling for the city, they would have called her first. Let her know that she had to get home and help them.

Wouldn't they?

Sitting alone, in a dark and empty apartment, Katherine Wilde wondered if she had run too long, too far. If the heroes of Cobalt City no longer needed her.

Then she shook her head with a growl. Nonsense. As her nanny used to say, "Pull up your socks, girl. Go to it."

First, Katherine decided she needed a shower to clear away the grime of twenty-four hours of continuous travel. Then she needed to let her inner kitty out and start prowling through the city, looking for her friends.

After emerging from the elevator, Tidwell informed Morgan the dynamite was safely stored in the explosives room.

"You know, the strange thing is I'm not surprised we have an explosives room."

"It does prove useful at times. Did you know, sir, that those sticks were three parts nitroglycerin, one part diatomaceous earth, and a small amount of sodium carbonate? Classic Nobel's Blasting Powder."

"You're saying that dynamite was from the nineteenth century?" Morgan had loved science history when he was a kid, constantly driving his mother and Mr. Wong mad with his questions until Mr. Wong bought him an encyclopedia of great inventors of the world. He recognized the original recipe for dynamite immediately.

"Actually, the sticks appeared quite new, but homemade. And, frankly, a rather limited quantity of nitroglycerin. Inside a stone room, like the one in the library that you described, the blast would have been largely contained."

"Tough on the books or any patrons who walked in."

"Oh, I am certain it would have destroyed any nearby paper. Possibly it was meant to start a fire?"

"That doesn't make much sense. Who would want to burn down the library?"

Tidwell acknowledged this with a thoughtful nod. "It may have been meant only for what was in that room. The library has some powerful protections, state-of-the-art, much as this Club does. Civic leaders of our earlier eras knew how to build buildings that would last—and they also knew the city faced unusual threats from time to time."

"Didn't know you were such a student of architecture."

"It rather comes with the position."

"Maybe the bomb was aimed at me." Morgan remembered the explosion that had destroyed his home back in Hong Kong. That bomber hadn't been worried about other people. Only intercepting the tong's messages to their hitman had given Morgan enough time to trigger the building fire alarm and get everyone out before the bomb went off. "I went into that room because of those strange text messages. There's only one room in the library with information on that stage magician, Pharaoh's Ghost. Doubt many people are looking for that."

Tidwell looked distressed. "The messages might have been a coincidence. One should not assume they were meant to harm."

"Well, this time I've got them. They tapped into my tablet, and that's going to be easier to trace than those earlier ones." He wirelessly connected his tablet to his cloud array and started a series of backtracking programs, trying to find the origin of the message that had sent him to the library.

Nothing happened. Every query fizzled out, a dead end.

"They're good," Morgan said out loud.

"Sir?" asked Tidwell.

"Whoever is sending me messages. It's like a ghost. Nothing there." Morgan ran his hand through his hair, sending it straight up in spikes. He tapped a couple more keys. "Nothing. Just nothing. That's not possible. Everything leaves a trace."

Then he saw it, not the data he was expecting, but something else glowing in an inquiry. Somebody else had been tracking information about the Wilde family recently, with a few references to Wrecker of Engines. These inquiries seemed to originate from a public terminal at the downtown library. It ended with a search for Katherine Wilde's address in Cobalt City.

Morgan pulled up the same information—it wasn't well protected, he tsk-ed—and found she lived in a penthouse in the same neighborhood as the Adventurers Club.

"So what does she know?" he wondered out loud.

"Sir?" Tidwell inquired.

"Katherine Wilde. Somebody is looking for her," Morgan said, paying more attention to his screen than Tidwell.

"Ah, the Wilde family. I believe there is a book about them somewhere here."

"Why would we have a book about the Wildes?" Morgan spun around in his chair until he faced Tidwell.

The other man looked very thoughtful, almost puzzled. "There were a number of Wildes who belonged to the Adventurers Club. Big game hunters in the early years. Fond of stalking large and deadly prey in unusual corners of the world. Quite obsessed with big cats, especially man-eaters, as I recall. There is a saber tooth rug in the third drawing room that Cornelius Wilde donated to the Club. Apparently, his wife did not care for it."

"Isn't the saber tooth an extinct species?"

"Certainly, after Mr. Wilde shot it. It was on an expedition beneath the surface of the Earth, when the Steel Suffragette pursued the molemen. They were something of a problem in the 1890s for certain sections of the city."

Morgan checked Tidwell's expression. The caretaker seemed serious and quite earnest. Morgan wondered if he was joking. Still, this was Cobalt City.

"Katherine Wilde is out of town," he said, remembering the newspaper article about her elopement to Tahiti. "So what could be in her apartment?"

He ran a few inquiries. The security at the Wilde penthouse wasn't simply high end, it was insanely elaborate, which started him thinking about what the socialite might be hiding there. Could there be more to Katherine Wilde than the articles suggested? More than once in Hong Kong, he had met female criminals who masked their trade behind the guise of rich girls. He never forgot how the Jade Sisters nearly took him out in their quest for Genghis Khan's dagger.

He ran a few tests against Wilde's computer system and found her firewalls more than secure. They were so beautifully designed that he suspected they were a Starcom product.

So he started checking for secondary ways to find more information on her building. The quickest and most obvious was the famous architect who designed the tower where she lived. The security at the architect's office didn't rate more than a few minutes of typing "password" for a password and using the first name of the company's chief architect for a login. Morgan shook his head over the laxness of it all. Your security and privacy were only as good as all the people you gave your information to—when were the super-rich going to figure that out?

Morgan reviewed the digital blueprints he'd dug out of an intern's computer. Despite all the "do not copy" warnings on them, he found accidental copies still hanging out in the trash, which eliminated the need for more elaborate hacks into the firm's undoubtedly protected archives.

The easiest way into the apartment was the private elevator that came up from the garage, stopped once at the main lobby, and then went straight to her penthouse. Morgan also considered and rejected coming down from the roof to the large terrace that wrapped around the outside of the apartment. Since he didn't own a flying machine, he would still have to use the building elevators to get up to the roof. If he was going to hack that, he might as well use the direct route.

He considered all the ways to access her apartment without triggering her state-of-the-art alarm system. He could wreck it, but that wouldn't be fair to Wilde if she wasn't a criminal. She'd have to pay to have it repaired or replaced. Maybe he could find a way that didn't require breaking her security system, he thought.

He pulled the tablet out of his backpack and tapped into the building concierge's computer. A cleaning service was on call for

Wilde and had clearance for her penthouse whenever they came out. Which, he found after tracing some emails, gaining access to the service, and reading their calendar, seemed to be fairly often, but not on any regular schedule. Nor did they always send the same crew. Perfect, thought Morgan, switching back to the concierge's computer and adding an appointment for Katherine Wilde's apartment to be cleaned the next afternoon.

This housekeeping service had their uniforms cleaned at a commercial laundry. A couple of emailed instructions were sent, and the next day, Morgan roared up to the door on his Vespa.

"I'm here for a Sunshine Cleaning pick-up," he said, carrying his tablet to the counter.

"Yeah," said the tall girl behind the cash register. "The rush order?"

Morgan shrugged. "Guess so." He flipped the tablet toward her and held out a stylus. "Sign it there," he said, tapping the white square on the form he'd mocked up a few minutes earlier.

She signed with a finger and handed over the package containing a Sunshine coverall.

"Weird that they just wanted one back right away," she said.

Morgan stared blankly back at her, a perfect copy of a kid he had watched at the bus stop. "Wouldn't know. I just deliver stuff."

Two blocks later, he pulled into an alley and donned the Sunshine Cleaning uniform. He sauntered around the corner and buzzed the concierge sitting behind the long desk in the lobby of Wilde's apartment house.

Upon seeing Morgan's uniform, the concierge let him in. Then, checking his age and shaggy haircut, the man stopped him at the desk.

"Which apartment?" the concierge asked with a suspicious look.

"Penthouse. Wilde," Morgan said, pretending to check an order on his tablet.

"Don't you usually come in teams?" The concierge pulled up the calendar for the building and clicked something. Morgan guessed he was checking that a Sunshine Cleaning person had arrived at the time Morgan had programmed into the calendar.

"Flu. But it's not a big job. My instructions say dust the rooms and vacuum. We'll be back with a full team when Ms. Wilde requests it."

"You look younger than the usual crew."

"Summer job," Morgan replied, remembering conversations on a favorite American sitcom he had watched in Hong Kong when he was a kid. "Saving money for college."

"Alright," said the concierge, already bored with conversation. "Take the left elevator. It goes straight up. You've got the key code?"

"Oh, yes," Morgan said, because he'd already copied it off the concierge's computer that morning. "This should only take an hour. Maybe less."

The concierge waved at him and went back to playing a video game that squeaked and beeped on his phone.

The apartment was empty, as Morgan expected. But what he hadn't expected was the blinking red light of a silent alarm. He checked it. It appeared it had been turned off earlier in the day. Odd, for an apartment that was supposedly empty.

He slipped his smartphone out and ran his personal app for detecting bugs, cameras, and other surveillance gear. It showed a number of cameras stationed throughout the apartment, all looped back into a system recording visuals, but the system didn't broadcast them out. If someone was watching who was visiting the apartment, they were in this building. Most likely somewhere inside the penthouse, judging by the signals on his screen.

A message popped up on his screen. The sender, of course, was blanked out. "The cat came home," it said.

Morgan typed back: "Who?"

"The collector is looking for her."

Then the message disappeared. Morgan shook his head. A little less cryptic, a few more clues, would be nice. Oh, well, time to go hero mode.

He slipped out of the Sunshine Cleaning uniform and pulled up the hood of his black sweatshirt. He took his mask out of his pocket and, with a tap, set it to reflect the face of his favorite movie action hero. He knew the actor had an alibi, as he was currently filming in Australia, but the face should confuse anyone running facial recognition software.

The Wrecker of Engines moved cautiously out of the entryway into the oversized living room. The walls were decorated with art that Morgan registered as expensive museum-type stuff. The furniture was large, luxurious, and positioned to take full advantage of the city views visible through floor to ceiling windows.

Morgan popped in his earbuds and set the phone to reverse amplify. If anyone was in the apartment, he should be able to hear them, even if all they were doing was breathing. Then, he slipped on the electric gloves he had rigged earlier in his workshop at the Adventurers Club. He had gotten the idea from one of the books Tidwell had pointed out in the Club's library, a scribbled journal of various inventions created by a club member for his era's superheroes. The stuff was pretty crude—the journal ended around 1930—but the ideas were intriguing.

With a crook of his thumb, Morgan set the voltage on his gloves to low stun. A rap of the knuckles against any opponent would give them a jolt, not enough to harm, but certainly enough to knock them back.

Armed now, and ready for anything, Morgan slipped through the apartment. A den, a library with glass cases and memorabilia displayed prominently, a media room he would love to copy at the Adventurers Club, a kitchen (not so interesting but stuffed with the latest gear), and a long hallway that appeared to lead to bedrooms and bathrooms. Here, Morgan finally heard signs of life.

At the end of the hall, somebody was behind one of the closed doors. At least he thought it was somebody. The amplified breathing sounded more like that of a wild animal than that of a human. Morgan wondered if Katherine Wilde kept exotic pets or a guard dog. He crooked his thumbs again, upping the charge on his gloves, and slipped down the hallway, keeping close to the wall.

As he approached the final door, it burst open, and Morgan caught a flash of fur, fangs, and claws before a humanoid feline leaped on him and swatted him down the hall like a giant cat toy.

Spinning head over heels, Morgan turned his tumble into a cartwheel and then a running leap up the wall, pushed off from the ceiling, and dove into a flying kick followed by a swift strike with his stinging gloves at his opponent.

The catwoman roared, a growl like a combination of lion and tiger, and did her own running spin up and around him, raking with claws out.

Morgan ducked, weaved, and slid under her, with the sound of ripping sweatshirt nearly deafening him as the earbuds picked it up and played it back into his ringing head. He swiped out the earbuds and turned, kicking low and then trying a gut punch with the gloves to disable his attacker.

She bent double, and he thought he'd hit her, only to recognize a moment later that she'd dodged his attack and feinted to draw him closer. Both clawed hands landed on his shoulders and bore him down onto the carpet. Morgan fished up his earbuds and landed one in her ear. He amped the reverb on his phone with a flick of a finger.

With a howl, the feline female jerked back, swatting at the earbud wire and severing it with one claw.

Morgan used this momentary distraction to start a flat-out run for the living room and exit. He slapped his opponent in passing, giving her enough of an electric shock to knock her off her feet.

He knew it wasn't enough to take her down totally. As he heard her hunting howl behind him, he sailed through the kitchen, kicking over a serving cart and sending crockery spinning.

He sprinted through the media room and practically vaulted over the furniture in the living room, springing off the big leather couch and using one hand to flip over the oversized armchair facing it.

She was faster than he expected, making the dash over the debris in the kitchen in record time, streaking across the living room, and leaping over him. She did a one-eighty in the air, gracefully landing on her feet in the elevator alcove, cutting off his preferred route of escape.

Morgan backed up slightly, settling into a crouch that would allow him to strike in several directions easily, depending on how she decided to attack.

Instead, she cocked her head and stared at him. "You want to show me your real face?" she hissed, her sharp little canines giving her a slight lisp.

Morgan shook his head, tapping the edge of the mask so it went blank and then began to scroll characters from the I Ching.

"I've seen that before. But you're not the Wrecker of Engines."

"How do you know?" The mask's vocal distortion device

turned his normal light tenor into a deep rumbling bass. If Morgan hadn't been concentrating on how he was going to get out of Katherine Wilde's apartment alive and mostly intact, he would have been impressed with the way he sounded. As it was, he hoped conversation would distract the angry catwoman long enough for him to do something spectacular. Unfortunately, all his ideas for spectacular lacked practicality and even achievability.

He shoved his hands casually into the front pocket of his hoodie, fingering the smartphone still there. With one hand, he slid out the braille keyboard that let him type by touch while keeping his eyes on the murderous feline.

"The Wrecker of Engines, the real Wrecker, was a member of my family," she said.

Surprise made his fingers fumble on the keyboard, and he had to restart his sequence of code. To buy time, he argued, "Maybe I'm the real one, and he was just a story."

She shook her head. "Next you'll tell me I'm not Wild Kat."

Morgan swore to himself. Not only had he gotten caught breaking into Katherine Wilde's penthouse apartment, he'd tangled with one of Cobalt City's famed superheroes.

But it was her next question that really rocked him. "So, how did you know to come here to catch me, and what have you done with my friend Stardust?"

Figuring honesty couldn't hurt, even at this stage, Morgan responded, "I didn't expect anyone here. And I don't know anything about Stardust."

"Of course he doesn't," said a voice from behind him. "This boy is nothing. I'm the one who took your superheroes. I am the new master of this city."

Wild Kat's eyes widened as she stared over his shoulder, and Morgan grimaced at the use of "boy." In the mirrored elevator doors behind her, Morgan saw a shadowy, rotund shape wearing what looked like a big bowler hat and a pair of huge brass goggles. Then the figure in the mirror raised what looked like a giant handgun, and a belch of light twisted out of it.

Morgan went flat on the floor as ropes of light entangled the screaming Wild Kat. She fell unconscious on the floor.

"Now, what shall I do with you?" asked the voice behind him.

Morgan didn't wait for an answer. He finished the sequence on his smartphone and every appliance, monitor, light, and other gadget in the apartment sprang to noisy, distracting life. The blinds over the window snapped up and down, the TV in the media room screamed out the news. Best of all, the elevator doors slid wide open.

Morgan dove into the elevator, grabbing Wild Kat with one hand and pulling her into the car with him. He slapped the lobby button, and the doors slid shut as another blue rope of light hissed overhead. But the doors finished closing and cut off the mysterious attack.

In the main lobby, Morgan staggered out of the elevator, carrying the unconscious Wild Kat to the security desk. The rent-a-cop behind the counter sprang up, fumbling for his gun at his belt.

"Call the police," Morgan bellowed in his artificial Wrecker voice. "Call an ambulance. And shoot whoever comes out of that elevator next."

"Uh, yes, sir, uh, wait—" The security guard put one hand on Wild Kat to check her pulse, instinctively grabbed for his walkie-talkie with the other hand, and lost track of the gun he'd been about to draw.

Morgan nipped out the doors and sprinted for his Vespa. He heard the chop-chop of blades above him and looked up to see what appeared to be an antique helicopter belching steam and heading toward downtown. From below, it looked to be a single seater, with the heels of a pair of heavy boots clearly dangling on either side of something like a bicycle seat. The pilot leaned on the big stick that caused the whirlybird to bank steeply and disappear around the corner.

Morgan jumped on his Vespa and chased the fleeing villain through the canyons of downtown Cobalt City. As he roared down the center line, weaving around honking taxis and swerving to miss nervous drivers who slammed the brakes as he banked around them, the antique helicopter rose higher and higher.

He lost sight of it in the bright sun reflected off one of Cobalt City's tall glass office buildings.

Morgan wheeled into a dark alley. Behind him, he heard sirens screaming as Cobalt City's finest joined the manhunt. More ordinary chopper sounds washed across the sky, and Morgan spotted two police helicopters circling high above. By their criss-crossing search pattern, he guessed they'd lost track of the little steam-powered whirlybird and him.

Morgan pulled off his hoodie and mask. He stuffed both into the cargo box under the seat of the Vespa. He ran his hands through his hair until it spiked into its usual disarray.

Then, trying to look as normal as any teen out for a joy ride on a warm June evening, he pointed the Vespa toward the Adventurers Club. He needed more information, and he needed it fast.

In a private room on the unmarked thirteenth floor of St. Sebastian Hospital, the genetically altered woman known as Wild Kat pushed aside the tray with its dish of wobbly beef jelly and snarled at the unfortunate nurse who brought it. "I want my clothes and I want them now."

The nurse sniffed. "Now, ma'am, you know the rules. No superhero brought here unconscious can leave until a full scan is completed. First, we need to make sure you can safely return to your normal life." Her tone suggested "normal" was not her first choice to describe Wild Kat's activities, but she couldn't think of any polite way to say it. "Secondly, after the last few years, it was collectively decided that any member of Cobalt City's superhero community found unconscious would be checked for possession, outside mental control, and personality-altering drugs. We haven't finished those tests yet."

"I am completely fit," hissed Wild Kat, swinging her furred legs out of the hospital bed. "And I am completely me. I need to leave now. I must find out what happened to Stardust and the others."

"Please, ma'am, if you would return to the bed. I'll call the doctor about an early discharge, but rules—"

"Are delaying me!" snapped Wild Kat. "Whoever attacked me is a new threat to Cobalt City. And I'm not so sure about that boy who you say saved me—"

"We had a report that you were turned over to your security guards by a man...I don't know his age."

"I know that. Enhanced sense of smell. Male, young, most likely in his late teens. Given the way he fought, well trained and with better than normal physical control. But definitely human. Not a mutation. He relied on mechanical devices to increase his offensive and defensive power."

The nurse listened to Wild Kat's musings with mouth half open. "But, ma'am, how can you know all that?"

"Would you please stop calling me 'ma'am'? And fetch me some decent clothing to replace this stupid hospital gown. Otherwise, I will display my furry rump to the world as I stalk out of here."

With a resigned squeak, like a baffled mouse, the nurse pulled open the closet and removed the spare set of utilitarian and unisex clothes left there for superhero patients who refused to remain in the hospital.

Wild Kat slipped on the smallest pair of overalls and pulled the heavy flannel shirt over her shoulders. "It's no fashion statement," she said, glancing in the mirror, "but it'll do."

She considered the felted booties the nurse held out without comment but shook her head. "I may need all my claws out."

Wild Kat stalked through the hallways, ignoring the whispered and quite audible (for her) commentary following her down the hall. She'd only caught a glimpse of her second attacker, the one with the unusual electric gun, but something seemed familiar in the shape or perhaps the scent. She needed to go back to her apartment and look it over for clues.

The chandelier in the ceiling blazed with a hundred electric candles burning bright. And Lizzie knew every candle bore the name of a hero.

She looked at the walls of the empty theater. Murals covered every inch of plaster. Instead of the scenes from Shakespeare that Lizzie remembered from past visits in another time, outside the machine, each vignette depicted the friends and the city she had lost.

The Steel Suffragette raised her painted sword high, pointing at the dragon that threatened to swoop down and engulf her. The banner curling over her head read "Courage."

The next mural was unfinished, a city half painted, not yet frozen in a lost time like the others. High above Cobalt City flew a green balloon that Lizzie knew as well as she knew her electric bicycle.

A marvelous glass tower sparkled in the rays of the painted sun. The ink-stained lion prowled its base, but the lion looked odder than usual. Lizzie peered more closely at the shadowy outlines. The lion turned into a chimera, bearing a second head of a serpent and a poisonous sting hidden in the tufted end of its tail. The beast sought to climb the tower, pursuing a woman whose own face was hidden under the mask of a cat.

Lizzie nodded. She knew what message she needed to send.

Morgan decided he wasn't asleep. His eyes might be closed, his head propped against the hardwood of his desk, and his hand going numb on the keyboard under his chest. But he wasn't asleep after nearly twenty hours of coding. If he was asleep, he wouldn't hear the insistent buzzing of his phone under his cheek.

The buzzing grew louder, and Morgan shook himself upright. He grabbed the phone. A text message appeared.

"Got you!" he muttered and hit the key to trace the signal. No way his mysterious messenger would escape his web of backtracking viral trace and destruction. He owned the internet!

"Or not." Morgan sighed as twenty hours of coded traps, firewalls, traces, and bots dropped into what appeared to be the equivalent of a digital black hole, a null space defying all logic and reason.

He muttered a couple of words in Mandarin that Mr. Wong always said were "too damn rude" to say in Cantonese.

Then he read the message.

"Take the green balloon," it said. "The one on the roof."

Morgan wondered what type of green balloon would be stored on the roof of the Adventurers Club. He was willing to bet it wasn't a kid's toy.

Well, if he was going to go flying, he needed to gear up. He grabbed a cup of cooling tea, chugged it fast, and set his fingers to flying over the keyboard.

"Going to wreck and roll," he hummed to himself as the windows turned lighter and lighter with the coming day.

CHAPTER 7: WHO ARE YOU?

"I should go back to Katherine Wilde's apartment," Morgan told Tidwell.

"Do you think that wise, sir?" Tidwell was moving around the apartment with a Swiffer, polishing along the edges of the wooden floors. Morgan had pointed out that there were robots who could do the same job. Tidwell had reluctantly agreed to a Roomba for the public areas, but he insisted on cleaning the apartment himself.

"I hate to invade her space again, and she's got some dangerous friends," Morgan said, thinking about his encounter with Wild Kat. "But there has to be a clue there. I'm sure of it."

"How are you going to gain access?" Tidwell had stopped cleaning to look over Morgan's shoulder at the computer screen.

"Good question. Sunshine Cleaning won't work twice."

"Repair person? Miss Wilde will call one after the damage inflicted."

"Never work." Morgan was scanning the concierge's computer for Katherine Wilde's building. "New orders from the tenants' board. Nobody is to be allowed in, not without prior appointment, confirmed security check, and photo ID. I could fake it, but it would take too long."

"So how?" Tidwell put the Swiffer aside and produced a feather duster for the bookcases.

"Roof and then down through the elevator shaft." Morgan shifted the screen to schematics of Wilde's building. Once again, the architect firm's lax security proved beneficial.

"And how does sir plan to gain the rooftop of a fifty-story building?"

"Funny, but I received a message about that this morning."
Tidwell raised his eyebrows.

Morgan flashed his phone to show the latest untraceable text message. "Ask Tidwell for the balloon."

"If you tell me you don't know anything about this, I will be disappointed."

Tidwell sniffed. "A relic of a circus, later modified to suit one of our members. But it is still stored on the roof, along with the other necessary equipment."

Morgan grinned. "Wicked! I've never flown a balloon before."

"Technically, sir, it is a bicycle dirigible. And you will need to pedal to steer it."

Morgan resisted an urge to fist pump his excitement. "Lead on, Tidwell, lead on. I want to see this."

They took the less-than-secret stair leading from Morgan's room to the rooftop. There, in a small structure Morgan had earlier assumed housed the Club's HVAC system, Tidwell unearthed a series of boxes and a small bicycle with a propeller fastened on the back.

A quick glance informed Morgan how the dirigible's balloon fastened with a series of webbing straps to the bicycle.

Tidwell unspooled a slender hose from the rooftop shed. "Helium. We always kept a tank up here, for our guests who preferred to use the air currents rather than the streets."

"Did that happen often?"

"Most frequently in the earlier days. Although quite a few used other methods." Tidwell walked across the roof to raise a small flag on a pole. "Windsock." Glancing at some gauges at the base of the pole, Tidwell added, "Light steady breeze, south by southwest. Perfect launch conditions."

Morgan tightened the straps connecting the steering mechanism to the balloon and checked the rotation on the pedal propeller that ingeniously drove the direction of the balloon from the rear. "How fast can she go?"

"Pedaling at a constant rapid pace, and with a good tailwind, previous riders have clocked speeds as great as two full knots."

Morgan did the math in his head. He would certainly get there faster on the Vespa, but the Vespa wouldn't land him on the roof of Katherine Wilde's apartment building.

"Nothing with a combustible engine up here? Or solar powered? Like a jetpack?" If there was a jetpack in the attic or in the basement, he was taking it out for a test flight as soon as he could pry it out of Tidwell's guardianship.

"Of course not. Those remain quite rare, although there was one gentleman who flew in from California, back during the last world war. But he only stayed for a few hours and then went on."

The balloon filled with helium until it swelled above the tiny bicycle and its propeller. Morgan hopped on. The straps creaked, and the balloon bobbed above his head. He looked across the roof at Cobalt City lying before him. This was an adventure, he decided. This was being a true, take-to-the-clouds superhero.

"Wish me luck," he said, but he didn't need it. He knew this would work, that soon he would be flying high above Cobalt City. It might be the slowest flight ever recorded in the metropolitan skies, but he would fly. He pulled the Wrecker's mask out of his pocket and tapped it to the hardest setting, slipping it over his head so it protected his face.

Morgan adjusted the earbud wirelessly connected to the phone securely tucked in the front pocket of his hoodie. A quick tap on the smartphone, and a steady stream of aeronautical information began to sound in his ear. Wind speeds, low-flying aircraft warnings, and other data were relayed from his main servers in the Adventurers Club. Suddenly, for truly the first time in Cobalt City, he felt like the Wrecker he had been before his Hong Kong apartment blew up.

With a two-finger swipe on the smartphone in his pocket, the easiest route to Katherine Wilde's penthouse apartment began to be relayed by a friendly female voice. For luck, he screwed an old compass onto the handlebars. The needle gyrated for a few minutes and then settled into a steady heading of true north.

Morgan waved again at Tidwell, giving him the old "thumbs up" gesture so beloved of pilots in Mr. Wong's collection of Hollywood movies.

Silently, Tidwell handed him a motorcycle helmet.

Morgan settled it on his head and then began pedaling toward the roof's edge.

Faster and faster he went.

Tidwell strode to a wheel planted in the center of the roof and cranked it. Then he waved both his arms to the left.

Morgan spotted the break in the masonry lining the roof. A ramp lifted out of the roof, and with a grin, Morgan aimed the dirigible bicycle at it. A bump, a slightly stomach-churning lurch, and he floated out past the Adventurers Club, still pedaling madly through the empty air. Far below his sneakers, the cars and buses whizzed by. Distant traffic noises drifted up to him, the taxi horns squawking and the squeal of a brake too hastily applied.

But in the sky, he was alone, and the liberating silence flowed around him. He wanted to pedal forever, to sail past the city and out over the harbor, to go wherever the wind took him.

Then the compass needle spun a quarter turn to keep tracking north, the computer voice informed him of a needed modification to his current course, and Morgan adjusted to continue to Katherine Wilde's building.

Lizzie still sat alone in the theater, but she felt as if a crowd was joining her, waiting for the show to begin. The shadows were stirring. The memories were clearer in her head than they had been for decades.

She wondered what he looked like, the young man on the other end of her telegraph, the one who sent her that message: "I want to be your friend."

She wanted to speak with him, learn more about him, but even a few words took all the strength she had. Tidwell had warned her, if she tried too much, she risked losing herself within the machine.

Still, events were set in motion. Trouble was flowing into Cobalt City, an old evil resurrected, but there was a new possibility too. A real possibility of freedom, if only the Wrecker of Engines would truly prove to be a friend and find Pharaoh's Ghost.

Katherine Wilde let her anger drain away and her body settle back into human form. Walking out of the hospital in full fur and fangs satisfied the fury of the moment, but the long trek home across Cobalt City calmed her.

By the time she reached the gleaming doors of her apartment building, the face reflected in the glass looked normal. The overalls and her extraordinarily dirty bare feet earned her a few concerned glances in the lobby. She ruefully acknowledged that she should have taken that nurse's offer of pull-on booties.

"Ducking the paparazzi," she told Juan, the current building concierge. None of them lasted very long. Between attacks from villains who always seemed to follow her home, the frequent "visits" of Wild Kat, and the constant barrage of press inquiries about her largely fictional love life, the average concierge cracked quickly. "Let friends up, but keep the press out."

"Sure, Miss Wilde. Would you like your mail now? There's a few packages and letters."

"Just my dry cleaning."

Juan hurried into the walk-in closet behind his desk and fetched the plastic-wrapped clothing. "How was Tahiti?" He handed the slippery plastic bag to her.

"Not as hot as I hoped." Katherine immediately wondered if he had asked because he cared, just wanted to be polite, or was looking for a tidbit to sell to some celebrity blogger. Damn, she decided, she needed to be less cynical or grow a shell instead of fur.

Katherine thanked Juan for his services and let him hurry out from behind the desk to push the button of the elevator for her penthouse apartment.

Home, she sighed to herself as she stepped off the elevator.

Between the recent round-the-world flying and the hospital stay, Katherine Wilde felt a little like a human pinball, careening off whatever came next. Time to take control.

She decided to review the damage caused by her latest fight in her living space.

Losing her feline senses was not as effective for investigating the recent battle in her apartment, but she needed to stay Katherine in case people came knocking at her door. Or, rather, were announced by the chagrined Juan, who had repeatedly told her as they waited for the elevator that he didn't know how an obvious impostor had entered her apartment dressed in a stolen uniform from Sunshine Cleaning.

She walked through the apartment, noting absently the claw marks in the wall, the tumbled furniture. All she needed to fix the damage, to redecorate, was cash, and she never lacked that commodity.

She needed to change the place anyway, Katherine decided. It felt so last decade, so much a part of what she had been, not who she wanted to become.

She wandered from room to room, ending in the undisturbed den that some designer had called a library. But the shelves were largely bare except for relics of her family's fantastic past. An open fan, painted with scenes of flowering trees, sat next to a white porcelain mask. She found herself staring at the mask, her own features faintly reflected in its smooth surface as if the mask wore the woman examining it so closely. She stretched out a hand and ran a finger down the cold curve of the cheek, lingering for a moment on the ancient I Ching symbols etched into it.

The man was dead, Katherine told herself. Lost in China so long ago. Nothing more than a story told to an impressionable child enchanted by a porcelain mask resting on a shelf.

The mask the intruder wore had changed and mutated as she fought its wearer down the hallway. It was not this mask. The body taking her blows had been young and male. The current Wrecker of Engines was no ghost.

"But who is he?" she asked herself.

Then she heard the thump of the terrace doors opening.

Katherine hurried into the living room. A stout figure in a loud checkered suit and a pair of smoked glass goggles stood outlined by the setting sun.

"Here, kitty, kitty," they said.

Forgetting she was only Katherine and not Wild Kat, she snarled and launched herself forward.

Ribbons of light ensnared her. As she stumbled and fell, the figure framed in the doorway pushed back their goggles, revealing the soft and rounded features of Frances Garnet, Cobalt City's head librarian. Katherine knew now why her attacker had seemed familiar. She'd opened exhibits for this woman.

"Finally!" Ms. Garnet said. "A complete set of heroes. Soon the light of knowledge will illuminate the city. Soon they will see the true power of science, electrical science!" Then she cackled, a static "ha-ha" that echoed through the wrecked and empty apartment.

As the darkness rolled over Katherine, she thought, "Who knew a librarian had such an evil laugh?"

The electric candles in the theater's candelabra blazed brighter and brighter, flashing in a sequence Lizzie recognized as the old Adventurers Club beacon flash-code. Tidwell was sending her a message.

With increasing distress, she watched as the pattern of lights recounted the heroes already captured. Steambolt Ed moved so quickly in this new era.

The balloon was launched, but would it be swift enough?

Frowning with concentration, Lizzie turned to the walls, scanning the murals, as she reached deep into the electronic heart of the city. Messages, images, streams of information, whizzing past her faster than any telegraph. Oh, how Marconi, Bell, and Edison would have adored this age. She barely understood it, but electricity was electricity, and she drew the power to her, changing the information flowing through the city into moving pictures on the wall, images that made sense to her mind.

A glowing map unscrolled across the wall of the theater, complete with fanciful curlicues of the type she remembered from the maps they had printed in the *Clarion*. Two lines raced toward each other, one red, one blue, each representing an airborne vehicle. They were set on a collision course.

She struggled to summon the telegraph key, to send a warning, but she lacked the energy. Lizzie pounded the dusty velvet of the empty seat in front of her, falling naturally into the static rat-tap-tap of a distress call.

The wind gusted up from the street below Katherine Wilde's building, rocking the dirigible sideways. Morgan fought the steering and struggled to turn the balloon for a straight landing atop the skyscraper.

His audio channel picked up a chop-chop sound from below. Morgan scanned the empty air beneath him. There, on the terrace, he spotted the gleaming wings of the odd steam-powered helicopter.

Morgan stopped pedaling, swaying in the wind. As he hung motionless in mid-air, a stout figure dragged a body to the whirly-bird. Morgan tapped the hard shell of his mask, and the enhanced vision he had programmed into it sprang into action.

Now he clearly saw the same goggle-masked villain who attacked him earlier. They loaded an unconscious woman into a wooden crate fastened behind the seat.

Morgan angled the dirigible down, intent on blocking the mini helicopter now puffing out steam in preparation for taking flight.

The goggled pilot glanced up, the sun reflecting on brass and glass face gear so brilliantly that the villain's features remained indistinct and unidentifiable. The intruder below shook a gloved fist at Morgan and then reached into the tiny cockpit of the steam helicopter.

Morgan looked at the telescoping barrel of the weapon being aimed at him and swore in three different languages. He pushed the dirigible into as much of a dive as could be achieved with an elongated balloon. The effect matched the style of Cobalt City's overfed ducks flopping into a park pond.

But the maneuver slipped him sideways and down. A bolt of lightning sizzled harmlessly past.

The figure below leaped into the cockpit of the little helicopter. The machine shot straight up into the air and then sped away from the apartment building.

"I need a jetpack," Morgan muttered, as he pedaled valiantly in its wake. He one-handed his phone out of his hoodie pocket and snapped a picture of the fleeing steam copter. Then, he pushed the photo into a self-designed app that instantly placed it on the social media pages and digital feeds of every smartphone-carrying teen in Cobalt City. He typed the question: "See this? Tell me where. Win something."

Across the city, dozens of teens began texting back locations. The app built a map, a red line running from Katherine Wilde's apartment building to the downtown library.

Morgan smiled beneath his mask. Okay, so he might not have the fastest flying machine, but what did that matter? Data moved faster than physical objects. Nobody could outrun the Wrecker of Engines.

⚡

Above her head, the electric candles in the gilt and crystal chandelier began to wink out one by one. The lights illuminating the pictures of past heroes also faded.

Lizzie watched the darkness growing. She'd never been afraid of the dark, not when she was in pursuit of a story. She felt a weight, or remembered a weight, dangling from her wrist. Her old, beaded purse hung there, the metal clasp worn smooth from her constant snapping it open and closed.

She reached inside, and her questing fingers touched the rounded wood of her pencil, her notepad, and her little electrical lantern. Lizzie drew the latter out. It fit into the palm of her hand. One twist of the top would send out a blaze of white light, guaranteed to dazzle and temporarily blind any attacker. Wind the key in the base, and a revolving glass slide would spin fantastic shadows onto the walls, the "shades" she had once used to frighten criminals into confessions.

Compelled by instinct, she wound the key tight and then twisted the top. Shadows sprang in bright relief, chasing each other in fabulous flying machines across a black silhouette of a city.

A scarab flew up from the stage in front of her, light glittering on its phantom wings. It tried to land on the shadow buildings, but every attempt failed. It spiraled up in the air, wings beating furiously.

Lizzie concentrated. This time, the telegraph key appeared on the now hardwood armrest of her theater seat. With a nod of satisfaction, she began tapping out her next message.

Morgan landed with a thump on the roof of the downtown library. The mini chopper stood abandoned, both the pilot and kidnap victim long gone.

"Two knots, maximum speed." Morgan sighed. Antique technology like the personal dirigible might look amazing, but it definitely lacked speed and power.

He unwound his tired legs from the pedals and hopped onto the roof. A couple of twists of rope secured his balloon to a conveniently placed mooring hook. Morgan was pretty sure Cobalt City was the only place in the world where the central library had a helicopter landing pad and balloon mooring hooks on its roof. "Love this city," he said to the wind whistling through the mooring lines.

With a final pat of the dirigible's green side, Morgan began his investigation.

A steel-clad door hid a freight elevator leading down to the library. The elevator car was long gone, and Morgan decided recalling it might tip off someone below that he was on the roof.

He tried another door and discovered a broad, bare staircase. Stairs or elevator cables? Which would be faster? Morgan considered this for a moment and then grinned. Cables.

He pulled a set of gloves modified for grappling and rope climbing out of his hoodie. A couple of clicks of his shoes electronically magnetized the soles so he could brake easily on the slide down. Starcom's website really did have everything, and he was glad he'd been quick to order every piece of desired gear as soon as he had moved to Cobalt City.

With a leap perfected by years of parkour and martial arts training, Morgan vaulted from the door edge to the elevator cables, gripping them securely with his gloves.

The long slide down cleared his head and brought all his energy rushing back. This was Hong Kong again, pursuing the crooks, wrecking their plans, moving so fast that there wasn't time to regret his lonely life, the isolation of always hiding behind the computer and the mask.

Morgan landed with a light thump on the top of the elevator. He demagnetized his shoes.

He unscrewed a panel and slid into the empty elevator. He didn't know what was on the other side of the closed doors. If they had been monitoring the roof, then they might be waiting for him. This was the moment, the one his mother called "the heartbeat in your ears" and Mr. Wong labeled "the balance point between." Now was the moment between being here and being dead, if he guessed wrong.

Morgan punched the elevator "door open" button. As soon as the doors slid back, he rolled through, tumbling in a pattern meant to buy him a second or two if an attacker waited on the other side.

He thumped into a library desk in an empty room.

With a sigh, Morgan stood upright. There were times, and this was one of them, when he truly would have preferred to have found the room full of ninjas or tong gunmen.

Instead, he'd ended up in the upper floor lobby where Hubert worked. Only today, no Hubert and no Janet whispered over the desk. Morgan slid into Hubert's chair and, with a single tap on the keyboard, brought the graduate student's computer screen to life. It appeared Hubert had forgotten to close his database project.

Morgan scanned the glowing lines and boxes forming an octagon in the center of the screen and the names of superheroes. Of those he recognized, almost all of them were the heroes recently lambasted in the press for failing to make their usual appearances around Cobalt City.

Patterns connected each of the superheroes, straight lines, curved lines, even lines that connected the bottommost name to the topmost one. It didn't look much like the relationship screen Hubert had shown him before. But it did look familiar.

Morgan brought up a web browser and entered a general query about schematics for certain types of power configurations. Some eighteen million answers popped up. Morgan narrowed his search. Suddenly, he knew what he was looking at: a giant battery, one powered not by stored energy, but by constantly renewing living energy, the energy of superheroes.

Lizzie heard something, a noise that couldn't truly be there. A phantom orchestra tuning their instruments in the empty pit of the theater. Old ghosts stirring? Warnings of what would come?

Or was it a signal that the time was right to rescue an old ally?

She summoned the telegraph key with barely any conscious thought. The boy was in the library, she knew that as surely as she knew she was not. But there was power swirling there, the same strange current that had woken the machines in the Adventurers Club, and she was the Electric Girl, now in fact as well as name. She drew the current to her, harnessed its power, and used it to whip a message back out into the world.

Morgan's phone rang. In the silence of the library, it sounded as loud as a gunshot.

He bolted out of Hubert's seat, pulled the phone out of his pocket, and glared at the screen.

"Summon Pharaoh's Ghost," it commanded.

"Busy," he typed back. With his other hand, he flipped the screen view on Hubert's computer to the library security cameras to see if anyone had heard his smartphone ring. The hallways appeared empty. Whoever had entered the library from the roof, and wherever they had gone with Wild Kat, remained a mystery.

"Summon Pharaoh's Ghost!" The message actually flashed at him.

"Not now," he typed back. He turned to Hubert's computer and sent a copy of the schematic of the superhero battery to his own computer. Morgan knew this wasn't just another science exhibit to attract tourists. If the librarians were building this thing somewhere in the library, people were in real danger. Superpeople, the heart and soul of what made Cobalt City what it was.

His phone made a static sound not unlike Morse code. Or a giant raspberry being blown at him.

"Shut up," he muttered. He considered turning it off.

"SUMMON PHARAOH'S GHOST!" came the message.

"Shouting won't help," he said to it.

Then that photo he had taken the other day, the odd equation scribbled on the back of Pharaoh's Ghost's theater program, appeared on his screen.

Morgan started to snarl, but something about the equation triggered an old memory. He began calculating the numbers. He knew this formula. He'd studied it once.

Morgan checked Hubert's computer and found some software for creating computer-aided designs. Feeding the numbers appearing on the screen of his smartphone into Hubert's rendering program, Morgan created a three-dimensional model of a pyramid. The formula was, he now suspected, the ancient equation for a pharaoh's tomb.

In the real world, the thing would be enormous, Morgan realized, four or five times the height of the tallest skyscrapers in Hong Kong. Nothing like this could ever be built. And, without any prompting from himself, the calculations continued running in the program, extending the base of the pyramid ever wider and the tip ever higher. An endlessly, infinitely, expanding pyramid, one that seemed to contain a fifth dimension, if he was reading the formula correctly, a dimension outside time and space.

Morgan let the calculation continue to run, intrigued now and wondering when it would overwhelm the software or Hubert's rather limited system. Eventually, the thing had to stop.

But the pyramid continued to grow in virtual space, and Morgan felt a strange sense of vertigo as it whirled and tilted before his eyes, the perspective always changing on the screen. Now it shifted and a doorway, or the shadow of a doorway, appeared at the base of the pyramid, a door that grew and grew until it consumed the entire screen, turning it into a black pool of shadow.

Then a hand thrust out of the screen.

Startled, Morgan pushed back from the desk.

The gloved hand was followed by an arm, a shoulder, and a head shrouded in a hood. At last, a man cloaked in a robe edged with gold and fastened with a scarab clasp stepped into the room.

"A most unexpected manifestation," intoned the apparition.

Lizzie was sitting on the very edge of her seat. She was still alone in the theater. She missed the audience gasping beside her and the magician standing on the empty stage in front of her.

Leaning forward, she strained to see through the gloom. There was only a shadow, the shadow of a hooded man, a shadow without a body. The shadow turned and bowed to her. Then it disappeared.

Satisfied, Lizzie settled back into her seat. The show was finally ready to start.

"Who are you?" Morgan asked the man in front of him. Morgan saw the pale gleam of white hair beneath the man's hood, but his face, although unnaturally pale, was smooth and oddly ageless.

"What century is it?" the man asked in return.

"The twenty-first. Aren't you going to ask for the date?"

"Not necessary. In this century, I am now Doctor Shadow."

Morgan blinked and resisted the urge to ask: "Doctor who?" Instead, he asked, "Should I know you?"

The hooded man tilted his head to one side. "Not yet. I believe this is our first meeting."

"As far as I know." Morgan backed up a little and tried to settle casually into a stance that would allow for quick flight or fight if needed.

Doctor Shadow drew a deep breath. "I apologize if I seem more cryptic than necessary. I was traveling between dimensions when I found myself suddenly drawn into an old manifestation of my psychic energy. Quite a clever little trap, one requiring considerable knowledge of Egyptian mathematics, as well as magic. Besides binding my soul with my former persona, it has left me slightly out of sync with my current timeline."

"So you were stuck in that formula?" Morgan sighed. This was magic, he knew it by its feel, and he always hated it when magic came into one of his adventures. It made outcomes so unpredictable. "You couldn't get out until somebody started solving the equation?"

"Quite so. You destroyed the spell and freed me by manifesting the pyramid in that computer. I gather you are the city's newest Wrecker of Engines."

"How did you know that?" Morgan asked.

"You are wearing the Wrecker's mask, a rather clever updating of it. Nicely done." Doctor Shadow looked around the room. "The library, I presume?"

Morgan put his hand on his mask and collapsed it. He knew this man too, now that he'd recovered from the shock of seeing him manifest out of a computer screen. This was the magician from the posters with a new name. Possibly, this was an ally.

"I am the Wrecker of Engines." Pulling the mask off, he added, "I'm Morgan Lee."

"Nice to meet you. This century, I am using Doctor Shadow for my hero's name, but I have been the Pharaoh's Ghost and the Black Hand, among others. I met the last Wrecker briefly. An honorable man, but one who carried heavy burdens on his soul. I see shadows of him in you."

"I think he was my grandfather." Morgan waited for a reaction. Could this strange creature of magic tell him what he longed to know about his family history?

Doctor Shadow raised one hand and sketched some hiero-glyphs in the air. "I was right about the date, and the need for caution. I have no wish to drag time into a new pathway. It is still far too soon to fully reveal your family or destiny to you. I do beg your pardon, for I do owe you for my freedom, and I promise I will repay the favor five-fold in the future."

Morgan shook his head. Every mystic he had met in Hong Kong with Mr. Wong was a little off. This one was no exception, but he rather liked him. He wasn't sure why, not yet, but he felt they could be allies, perhaps even friends.

Doctor Shadow looked over his shoulder at the computer terminal. The rendering program had shut itself off, and the sche-matic of the superhero battery once again dominated Hubert's screen.

"Another device out of its time." Doctor Shadow pointed at the drawing. "How did you happen to find it? And me?"

"I've been receiving these messages. They told me to go look for Pharaoh's Ghost."

"An old name of mine, but one that amused me once. How are

you receiving messages? Visions? Dreams? Please do not tell me about a Ouija board. I dislike those things immensely."

"No," Morgan said with a laugh. "It's always a text. Usually on my phone."

Doctor Shadow's pale eyebrows rose. "A text?"

Morgan pulled out his phone and brought up the last series of messages. "Like this. But I can't trace the sender. Which is strange. Usually, I can do traces like that in my sleep—or at least while doing ten other things at the same time."

The hooded magician turned the phone over in his hands, frowning at the display of messages on the screen. "I suspect the reason you cannot trace these messages is that they do not manifest from our current plane of existence."

"Outside normal cell range?"

"Outside our dimension, if I am correct. But anchored within our dimension as well. There is something familiar about this—almost like one of my own spells. Have you been anywhere near a building called the Adventurers Club?"

"I live there."

"Ah, that explains a great deal. We should go there immediately."

"I came here for a reason. I followed Wild Kat here."

Doctor Shadow nodded. "A capable woman. I know her well. She can take care of herself."

Morgan shook his head. "No, she was unconscious, last time I saw her. And look, here, in the schematic." He pointed to the left side of the battery diagram. The box contained Wild Kat's name.

Doctor Shadow looked more closely at the drawing, reciting names out loud: "Wild Kat, Stardust, the Worm Queen."

Morgan nodded. He tapped his smartphone and pulled up the newsfeed from his own servers. "All gone missing, according to these reports."

"Now, we must go to the Adventurers Club."

Even as Morgan protested, Doctor Shadow propelled him back to the elevator. The master of mystical arts simply frowned at the doors, and they quickly slid open. A nod at the control panel, and the elevator shot back up to the roof.

On the roof, Doctor Shadow raised one eyebrow at the bicycle dirigible moored there. "Not quite what I expected."

"I make do with what I can find. Reuse, recycle, you know, like the posters around town."

"An admirable and somewhat remarkable attitude." Doctor Shadow gestured with one hand, and the mooring lines fell away from the bicycle. "Come, I will assist your flight so we may return quickly to the Club."

"What?"

Doctor Shadow floated off the roof, beckoning with a crook of his fingers. "Hurry. We have no time to lose."

Morgan mounted the bicycle and began pedaling madly for the roof's edge. The bicycle lifted off with a whoosh he had not experienced before. He glanced at Doctor Shadow.

The wizard nodded again at him and took off in a streak of purple light.

Morgan found himself pulled along behind, reaching speeds the dirigible should not be able to achieve.

"Magic," he sighed and turned his attention to his smartphone. In response to the last text command to summon Pharaoh's Ghost, he typed, "He's here. Now what?"

Lizzie was back on her bicycle, and she was flying down the street. Just around the bend was safety. She knew it. She could hear someone shouting for her.

Then her feet were on the stairs, and the door was standing open. Someone was beckoning to her. "Hurry, miss, hurry."

She ran without sound, fleeing up the stairs and down the long dark hallway. The elevator door clanged shut before she even realized she was on such a contraption. Then the doors slid back. She saw gleaming tubes lighting up the air around them, heard the buzzing in the wires and the clicking of the telegraph key.

Behind her, the darkness spread. She felt it, like claws clutching at her skirt, but she pulled away, speeding toward the bright electric light in front of her. She found safety there. But she had been hiding too long. Now she needed to make some noise, now she needed to shout to the world, "I am here! See me!"

CHAPTER 8: THE ELECTRIC GIRL IN THE MACHINE

THE ADVENTURERS CLUB WAS EMPTY WHEN THEY GOT THERE. Morgan tried raising Tidwell on the house phone, but he received no answer.

"There is a room down below," said Doctor Shadow. "Full of gadgets."

"Yeah, the communications room."

"We should look there."

Morgan led the way, finding it vaguely disturbing that Tidwell wasn't around to run the elevator.

When they reached the basement, Morgan felt the hair on his arms bristle. When he reached out to pull open the cage door of the elevator, a spark jumped from his fingertips to the metal. He pulled back his tingling hand. "What was that?"

Doctor Shadow smiled. "A manifestation of an unusually strong spirit. I thought she was lost, like the others. I went looking for her several times, but never caught a glimpse of her."

"Who?" Morgan asked.

"The Electric Girl," said Tidwell, stepping out of the doorway of the communications room.

Doctor Shadow stopped and sniffed slightly upon seeing Tidwell. "So you are still here?"

"Where would I go? This is my home."

"Rather more than that."

Morgan looked back and forth between the two men. In profile, they appeared very similar. "Brothers?"

Doctor Shadow frowned and shook his head.

Tidwell answered, "We are distantly related."

"Quite distantly, but we both served the same ancient masters of magic. I was a priest," returned Doctor Shadow.

"And I was a caretaker," responded Tidwell, "and so I remain."

Morgan felt his phone buzz in his pocket. He pulled it out. The message read, "I am here! See me!"

He turned the phone so Tidwell could read it. "Do you know who is sending these messages?"

Tidwell nodded. "Miss Lizzie. The Electric Girl. Much against my advice. Each message threatens her stability within the machine."

"How did you save her?" Doctor Shadow asked.

"Stored lightning in a bottle," Tidwell said. "As you can see."

Blue arcs of electricity leapt back and forth across the communications room. Every light bulb glowed with brilliant white light. The telegraph key sounded like a pair of castanets, clicking out a constant rhythm, as needles jumped from left to right and then right to left on every gauge.

"Wow." Morgan stayed in the doorway, not needing Tidwell's gesture of warning. Anyone stepping into that room would be fried by the electricity whizzing through the air.

"What happened to her?" Doctor Shadow asked.

"She found Steambolt Ed. When he attempted to add her to his battery, she turned his Eradicator upon him," said Tidwell.

"That is why I found no evidence of him when I discovered his lair," Doctor Shadow mused. "I assumed the villain fled."

"The Eradicator?" Morgan asked.

"The Electric Girl ambushed him with his own weapon," Tidwell continued. "Being both caught in the beam, neither was fully dissolved. So Miss Blythe came here for aid. Mrs. DeCamp knew her true identity and often assisted with her cases. Unfortunately, there was nothing we could do to halt the Eradicator's effects. I was able to preserve her soul, but only at a great cost. My powers were severely diminished while Miss Blythe became lost in these machines. For years, we were not even sure she was there."

"What woke her? I came back here in 1900, and the mansion was locked tight," Doctor Shadow said. "I seem to recall the newspapers talking about Mrs. DeCamp traveling the world."

"Mrs. DeCamp aided some fellow adventurers in Europe. The thwarting of the overthrow of a princess disinclined to be married off to a prince," Tidwell said. "But I remained here. You should have knocked. I always respond to a knock."

The mystical mage shrugged, his cloak rippling. "I was in a hurry that night. But since then?"

"The opening of the Adventurers Club in 1910 helped. The installation of the communications room resulted in some messages from the Electric Girl. That was Mrs. DeCamp's idea. She thought if we could collect scientists and adventurers in one place, we might find a way to reverse the Eradicator's effect. Professor Chandler's early experiments in reanimation were promising. Of course, after his accident—"

"Unfortunate, although one should expect nothing less from a Yeti," Doctor Shadow said.

Tidwell nodded. "But the recent movie here caused an influx of old influences mingled with new as well."

"Brought the building back to life? "Doctor Shadow inquired.

"Just so," Tidwell responded. "Then, this year, the lightning storms began."

"Lightning?" Morgan asked.

Both men (if they could be called men, as he was realizing neither was human) nodded in a ridiculously similar fashion.

"Another pantheon," Tidwell said. "Fond of storms."

Doctor Shadow murmured, "The Norse brood."

The bolts of electricity arcing across the room seemed to be diminishing with each discharge. The light bulbs were settling down to a softer glow.

"Exactly, a new manifestation in another neighborhood. But the byproduct—" Tidwell began.

"Electrical energy mixed with magic. That would cause some interesting activity in Sheffield Edison's contraptions, if they were operational." The mage stroked his goatee, lost in thought.

"Hey! There's something called an Eradicator at the library," said Morgan, remembering his tour of the library's basement displays.

Tidwell turned to him. "Miss Blythe has been uncommonly agitated about the library for the last few weeks. Of course she would sense the same machine that trapped her spirit. But I thought it was destroyed."

"With the villain gone from the city, as I thought, and our heroes lost, I began traveling again," Doctor Shadow said. "Before I left, I made certain arrangements to store Steambolt Ed's infernal devices. I put them in the basement of the library."

"The librarian plugged it in," Morgan added.

Doctor Shadow and Tidwell both turned on their heels to stare at Morgan. "What did you say about plugged in?" they asked in unison.

"The Eradicator at the library is on," Morgan responded. "Ms. Garnet was working on it when I visited. She's been acting strangely—for a librarian."

The telegraph key began to jump up and down excitedly.

"What is the Electric Girl saying?" Doctor Shadow asked.

"My Morse has grown quite rusty. Miss Blythe commonly uses the card system for me," Tidwell replied.

Morgan interjected, "I know. It's very clear."

"Her message?"

"Stop the thief. Stop him now. Before the heroes are gone completely."

----.

CHAPTER 9: SEWERS AND TRAPS

"SO YOU'RE SAYING THERE'S A PERSON TRAPPED INSIDE THESE machines?" Morgan pointed at the array lining the communications room.

"More correctly, a disembodied spirit," said Tidwell, "once known as Miss Elizabeth Blythe, the Electric Girl."

A light bulb in the center of the ceiling flicked on and off, like a wink from the spirit Morgan now knew had been texting him.

"A ghost?" he asked.

"Not exactly," said Doctor Shadow. "Rather a being without a body, one who has been transformed into electrical energy."

"That's what Steambolt Ed's machines do," Morgan said. "That's what that diagram was about."

"Essentially," said Doctor Shadow. "Except Steambolt Ed's device does nothing to preserve the personality or spirit of those trapped within. Last time he used it, he reduced the seven captured heroes to pure energy. Once his process was completed, nothing was left. Not even ash."

"So why is she still here?" Morgan asked.

"Because the Club's devices provided a convenient vessel to hold what was left of her essence before it became too widely scattered," Tidwell said. "My duty lies in preservation of the places I serve, not necessarily the people dwelling within them. I made something of an exception for Miss Blythe. Or, rather, I enabled her to become part of this building. Which, in turn, allowed me to take care of what was left of her."

"I have always said the limits imposed upon you were quite ridiculous," said Doctor Shadow.

Tidwell gave the faintest of shrugs. "I find my boundaries somewhat comforting. I know my place in the world. Can you say the same?"

Morgan waved off the impending argument between the two ancient adults. "So, Sheffield Edison is back and, if that sketch in the library is correct, rebuilding his superhero battery with the help of the librarians."

"Once that battery is switched on, my friends will be gone forever," said Doctor Shadow. "Just like the last Great Disappearance."

"So we need to know where he has built this battery," Morgan said. "And shut it down."

"We have to find him, as well," said Doctor Shadow. "As long as he is free, he poses a grave threat to the city."

"He needed eight to complete the circuit," said Tidwell. "Last time, the Electric Girl stopped him by escaping his array. The lack of an eighth body in the machine caused him to be trapped within his own device."

"The schematics I saw looked smaller than that," Morgan said.

Doctor Strange nodded. "If he is drawing on the technology of today, he could reduce his battery."

"So how many has he captured? And where is he holding them?" Morgan asked.

But before anyone could answer, the telegraph key began to click up and down.

"What is she saying?" Doctor Shadow asked.

"Take me out of here," Morgan translated. He wondered what it was like, to be trapped inside a box, to be nothing more than a current flowing through a machine. He had often felt lonely and isolated in his life, but he was here, in the world, and the Electric Girl had been lost for more than a century.

Doctor Shadow sighed. "I fear the extraction of her essence would merely result in her rapid dispersal."

"What?" Morgan asked.

"In short, she would become a true ghost," Doctor Shadow said. "Some faint energy might still haunt this place, but no more than that."

"Can you do nothing?" Tidwell asked.

"A modification of an old spell, an ectoplasmic expansion, might strengthen her ability to communicate," Doctor Shadow mused. "It would allow her to communicate more often and with greater duration than her current methods."

"You mean you could boost her signal?" Morgan asked.

"A crude way of putting it," said Doctor Shadow, "but yes."

Morgan nodded. "Do it." Then, turning to Tidwell, he asked, "You said she's in the building. In the currents running through the wires?"

Tidwell nodded.

Morgan smiled. "I've got an idea." He sprinted to the elevator. As he waited for the doors to open, he turned to Tidwell. "Do you have any photographs of her? Of the Electric Girl?"

"Quite a few. You will find them in the lesser reading room, in a binder marked E. G."

Lizzie felt a tingle that started somewhere at the top of her head and spread through her body, a zing of energy that was almost, but not quite, like the power of the lightning bolt that had energized her earlier. She looked around her room. Sunshine was streaming through the windows, and the walls were covered with brightly colored clippings from newspapers and magazines.

She marveled at the unnaturally crisp photographs printed on glossy pieces of paper, pictures of people whose names she had once heard whispered in the messages that streamed through the city: Stardust, Wild Kat, the Worm Queen, and others.

On her once blank and empty desk was a black square of glass. At first, she thought it was a mirror, but when she touched it, the picture it showed was no reflection. She saw a room at the top of the Adventurers Club, lined with brilliantly painted pictures and, even more intriguing, more squares of glass like the one she held in her hands.

At the center of the room was a slender young man of her own age with Eurasian features. He was dressed in the garments of a field worker or miner, denim trousers and a loose shirt made of some type of knitted fabric that looked like an undergarment. On the front were the words: "Geeks rule the world." Lizzie raised her eyebrows at this phrase and wondered if it meant to say Greeks.

In the room she was watching, the young man grinned directly at her and waved his hand.

Surprised, Lizzie nearly dropped the dark glass pane in her hand. But words appeared on its surface, scrolling rapidly across it.

"Hello," it said. "My name is Morgan. I am your friend. Can you see me? I can see you."

And Lizzie Blythe, the Electric Girl trapped for more than a century inside the Adventurers Club, felt tears of joy streak down her cheeks and drop like falling stars. With tentative fingers, she traced back a response to the strange young man on the other side of this odd magic mirror.

"I see you. I see the world. Thank you."

Morgan fed the pictures of the Electric Girl into his scanner. With every faded photograph of the young heroine, the virtual avatar of her spirit grew more rounded, more real, on his screens.

At midnight, she winked and waved a hand at him.

"It's almost like you're in the room," he typed into the message system he'd set up with the help of Doctor Shadow earlier in the evening. The ancient mage had then departed to search the libraries of the Adventurers Club for further information on Steambolt Ed's creations.

Tidwell said that Mrs. DeCamp had bought up almost everything she could find on the villain, which is what made information about him so scarce elsewhere in the city. Not even the downtown library had as much material as the Adventurers Club, Tidwell claimed.

"I feel as if I could almost walk out the door and be back in the city," Lizzie responded to Morgan's last message.

"Maybe someday," he typed, hoping he wasn't lying. Surely there was a way to undo what Sheffield Edison had done.

"I can't wait," Lizzie wrote back. "I want to sit down in an ice cream parlor and have a sundae."

"Ice cream parlor?"

"Are there none left in Cobalt City? There used to be one on every corner."

"Now it is coffee," Morgan typed.

"That is not the same," came the response.

"I'll find you an ice cream parlor," he promised.

After the shock of being able to hold a real conversation faded, Lizzie told her friend they needed to remove the Eradicator from the library.

"Why?" typed Morgan.

"Because he has taken three," she responded. "And once he has four, he will use it to complete his battery. Without the Eradicator, he can do nothing."

"How does she know? That he has kidnapped three?" Doctor Shadow inquired when Morgan tracked him down in the Club's greater reading room. The hooded and cloaked mystic was hovering near the top shelf of a bookcase filled with ancient texts donated to the Club by various members. A stack of newspaper clippings and bound volumes of old magazines were piled on the floor, apparently all he could find about Steambolt Ed.

Morgan shrugged. "She's monitoring information through the internet." He recalled the earlier texts from Lizzie, when she had easily avoided his traps and tricks. "I don't think firewalls mean much to her."

"Most probably the captured heroes are Stardust, Wild Kat, and Worm Queen," Doctor Shadow said. "Based on the information the Electric Girl and you gathered."

"There were more names on the schematic. Seems like Ms. Garnet or Steambolt Ed made a list of possible victims." Morgan leaned against the bookcase. "What have you found?"

"Nothing useful," admitted the magician, as he gently floated back to the ground. "I have better copies of most of these spells in my own collection. Mrs. DeCamp and later residents did amass a great deal of information. But none of it applies to our current problem."

"Found anything on how to remove Lizzie completely from the machines?" Morgan said.

The mage shook his head. "Nothing we have not tried already."

Morgan considered the issue. If nothing else, he meant to come up with a way to give her greater mobility and awareness of the outside world. He had found some articles about a robot named Lumien—and while he didn't think Lizzie wanted to be an eight-foot-tall battlebot, he thought the tech might be modifiable to give her a real body and the ability to interact more fully with others.

Tidwell arrived in the reading room with a cup of something that steamed and smelled herbal for Doctor Shadow, as well as a pot of tea and sandwiches for Morgan.

"I think the removal and disabling of Steambolt Ed's equipment would be wise. Miss Blythe says something has manifested in the library that cannot be good for the books or the patrons," Tidwell said.

"Okay," said Morgan. "I'll go."

"It is midnight," Tidwell pointed out.

"Means nobody will be there, including the staff, and I won't have to worry about anyone getting hurt," Morgan said.

"How are you going to get in? Through the roof?" Doctor Shadow asked.

Morgan shook his head. "I'd love to fly the dirigible again, but the Eradicator is in the basement. It would be faster to go through the main level." He patted the pocket of his hoodie. "I've got stuff."

"Do you need my assistance?" Doctor Shadow settled into a chair with his mug and a book propped open on his knee.

"No. It's just pulling the plug on the Eradicator," Morgan replied.

His phone buzzed, the indicator of a text from Lizzie. "Don't unplug it. Wreck it. Or Steambolt Ed will use it again."

"Okay," Morgan typed back. Then he asked aloud, "How can she hear me? I'm not feeding audio back to my system."

"I lend her my knowledge of what is happening inside the Club," Tidwell said. "Unfortunately, my awareness does not extend beyond the walls."

"So she can't really see what's happening outside the Club?" Morgan thought about security cameras throughout the city. Could he create a web of "eyes" for Lizzie to allow her more awareness of the world?

"Not exactly. Although she certainly seems very aware of certain events. Miss Blythe even has commented more than once about that motorized two-wheeler you ride," Tidwell said.

"The Vespa? It is a sweetheart." Morgan grinned, realizing Lizzie had already figured out how to hack into the local security cameras. There was one scanning the alley outside of the garage where he stored the Vespa. "She should have seen the scooter I had in Hong Kong."

"Want a red one, like yours," said the message that popped up on his phone.

Soon Lizzie would ride with him, Morgan decided. If Doctor Shadow could figure out the magic, he could figure out the electrical part.

⚡

At the downtown library, Morgan slid through the janitor's door. The alarm on the outside had been easy to silence and the keypad even simpler to short circuit. The door lock snapped open with a satisfying click.

The hall lights were still on, but dimmed, probably left that way by the night cleaning crew.

Morgan headed toward the lobby, intent on taking the stairs to the lower level and exhibit room containing the Eradicator. But as he entered the lobby, he spotted Sheffield Edison's contraption in the middle of the floor. It appeared to be disassembled. Or perhaps it was partially assembled. Had Ms. Garnet decided to move it to the main floor after all?

Morgan shrugged. Didn't matter. The new location just made it easier for him to tote the Eradicator out of the library.

His first inkling that this break-in wasn't going smoothly was the three masked minions who rushed him as soon as he touched the Eradicator.

Leaping to the top of the check-out desk, Francis Garnet let out a bellow of outrage. She was dressed in a checked tweed suit and loud yellow tie. It was the first time Morgan had ever seen the head librarian in pants.

A bowler hat squashed down her cloud of fluffy hair. Her reading glasses had been replaced by a glittering monocle. She removed the unlit stogie from her mouth and growled at the henchmen and henchwoman gathered around her.

"Get him!" she yelled, pointing at Morgan.

CHAPTER 10: POWER OF HEROES

MORGAN CARTWHEELED AWAY FROM THE MASKED MINIONS. Two swung pipe wrenches at him, and the third tried to hit him with a spanner. All were a bit greasy and dirty. Morgan suspected they had been working on the Eradicator before he arrived. The library lobby was now cluttered with stacks of parts and bits from the Sheffield Edison machines previously stored in the basement.

Dropping into a crouch, Morgan used a spinning kick to knock two of the minions to the ground.

One of them squeaked and bounced as she dropped her wrench.

Swearing under his breath, Morgan snatched at her black mask. It came off to reveal Janet, the junior librarian.

"Janet!" he hissed at her. "It's me!"

She swung a roundhouse punch at his jaw.

He snapped his head back so she missed. Then with a tap as gentle as he could make it, he dropped her to the ground.

A very tall skinny minion, with big glasses pushing his mask out of shape, charged him.

"Hubert, I presume." Morgan sighed. He used as careful a kick as possible to trip the research librarian and send him sliding across the slick marble floor.

Hubert crashed into the half-assembled Eradicator in the center of the lobby.

"Not good," breathed Morgan.

With a scream, Janet landed on his back. She thumped him on top of his head with her spanner. The reinforced lining in the hood absorbed most of the shock, but it still stung.

Morgan dropped and rolled again, doing a controlled slide toward the basement stairs.

"No, you don't!" Frances Garnet leaped down from the check-out counter, brogues narrowly missing Morgan's quickly curled fingers.

Morgan chopped the side of her knee and, with a muttered apology, dropped the head librarian to the ground in a rattle of monocle, stogie, keys, and plastic library staff card. Morgan grabbed the keys and card as he dived for the stairs.

The burliest of the minions grunted and hauled himself up, grabbing at Morgan as he cartwheeled past. Morgan dived out and under the man's grasp, knocking him back to the ground in passing. A whiff of Lysol made him suspect he had just dropped the library's janitor.

As Morgan raced down the stairs, he heard bumps and thumps as the others tripped over the janitor on their way toward the basement.

Morgan sprinted around the corner, opening every door as he ran. With luck, his pursuers would slow down to check the empty rooms behind him. A final door revealed another staircase leading down into a basement below the basement.

Rather than running down the metal stairs and alerting his followers, Morgan closed the door gently behind him and used Ms. Garnet's keys to lock the door.

The room was horribly warm. A deep rumble, like the snore of a sleeping giant, shook the darkness. Morgan switched his smartphone to flashlight mode. The beam showed the giant boiler furnace that supplied the steam to heat the library.

Stacked like cordwood on the basement floor were four tubes made of brass and glass. They looked like a cross between a test tube and a coffin. With a slightly sick feeling to his stomach, Morgan peered inside one. The face of Wild Kat was clearly visible under the glass. To his relief, a slight condensation on the inside of the glass made it clear she was still breathing.

Morgan ran his hands along the tube. It appeared seamless, with no discernible latch or lock. He found evidence of airholes at the very top of the tube, but the openings were too small to do him any good.

The screen changed on his phone. Lizzie stared up at him. Then the message appeared: "You found them!"

"Yes," he typed back. "But what do I do with them?"

The tube was too heavy for him to carry even Wild Kat away. If he could even find a way out of the furnace room. Morgan quickly checked the other tubes. One was empty, one held another woman, and the third contained a man he recognized. Jaccob Stevens, the founder of Starcom, was literally at Morgan's feet.

Above him, somebody was slamming a wrench against the door.

Morgan typed: "Exit needed. Urgently."

Lizzie flashed a map of the subterranean levels of the library on his screen, including a grate leading to the Cobalt City sewers.

With a glance of regret at the three tubes containing superheroes lying around him, Morgan bolted for the grate. A few quick twists with his screwdriver removed the covering, and he was down the hole. He hesitated on the ladder leading into the smelly murk below.

Lizzie flashed another message at him: "Go!"

Hooking an arm and a leg through the ladder, he typed back: "Wait. Need to hear them." Reaching over his head, he maneuvered the grate back into place and then killed the light from his phone, stashing it in his hoodie pocket. A tap on his mask turned it from white to black. With the dark gray hoodie covering the rest of his head, he hoped he would be invisible to anyone glancing through the grate. He eased a few more rungs down the ladder for better concealment.

The door to the furnace room crashed open. Boots clattered down the stairs. From somewhere above, Morgan heard Frances Garnet shout: "Is he there?"

Janet, standing on the grate over Morgan's head, shouted back. "Nobody's here. The door was locked. He must have kept going."

"When the others get back, have them haul this lot upstairs," Frances Garnet instructed her. "It will take me hours to repair the damage he did. But then I will open the doors and let Cobalt City see their heroes vanish before their eyes. They never gave me the credit I deserved the last time."

"We should make it a meet-up," Janet enthused, as she pushed a mechanized dolly under the tube containing the unconscious body of Wild Kat. With the push of a button and a puff of steam, the device rolled with a bang across the grate toward the stairs.

"A what?" asked the head librarian over her shoulder as she stomped out of the room.

"A gathering. I can use the library's accounts and send messages to all our patrons. Come see the heroes check out for the very last time." And then Janet loosed an evil giggle.

Morgan headed down the ladder. He needed assistance quickly. It would take all their resources to stop these librarians.

"Steambolt Ed is obviously possessing Francis Garnet," Doctor Shadow said when Morgan told him about the fight at the library.

Morgan winced as Tidwell applied ice to the bruise on top of his head. Janet swung a mean wrench. "Ms. Garnet has become one mean librarian. And something is wrong with all of them."

"And it appears he is once again using innocents as his minions," Tidwell said. "I recall similar behavior the first time he appeared in Cobalt City. A form of electro-hypnosis aided by one of his diabolical machines."

"Which are all set up in working order at the library," Morgan added.

Doctor Shadow nodded. "It is unfortunate Ms. Garnet switched them on."

"It was regrettable you left them there," Tidwell said.

Doctor Shadow frowned at him. Obviously ancient mages didn't take criticism well.

"So how did Ed escape into the world, but you can't free Lizzie?" Morgan asked.

"Electricity," texted Lizzie.

"Electricity?" Morgan asked out loud.

"Possibly." Doctor Shadow fingered the amulet that hung around his neck. "A transference of spirit via conductivity of a galvanized source, especially if the energy of the Norse gods was flowing through the city. It would create—"

"A true shock to the system?" asked Tidwell.

Doctor Shadow made a small moue of disapproval. "A flippant response unworthy of you."

"I have learned to tell jokes," Tidwell said. "The professor rather encouraged it."

Morgan ignored them, texting back and forth with Lizzie. "She says he moved in the current between the machine and Ms. Garnet."

"An arc of electricity allowed him to enter her body and steal her mind? As I suggested a moment ago," Doctor Shadow mused. "After all, what is the mind but a series of electrical impulses?"

"But what about Ms. Garnet? Is she still there too?"

"I suspect she is," Doctor Shadow said. "It is difficult, almost impossible, to fully erase a consciousness from a healthy mind. And, from all you have told me about the head librarian and her behavior over the last few weeks, she seems to have resisted this possession for long periods of time."

"So her blackouts and the headaches were Ed taking over?" Morgan asked.

Lizzie flashed a "yes" on the screen.

"And she was responsible for kidnapping the superheroes?" Tidwell asked.

"But not of her own free will," said Doctor Shadow. "They are all under the control of Steambolt Ed."

"Well, she or, really, Steambolt Ed, will turn the Eradicator on the heroes today to complete his battery," Morgan said. "In front of the public."

"But you said you only saw four tubes," said Doctor Shadow. "Last time, his battery used eight tubes, and seven were destroyed in its charging."

Tidwell nodded. "The only reason he did not complete the battery was that Miss Blythe escaped."

Lizzie beeped another message. An announcement had appeared on the library's website, inviting the public to come downtown for a "Stupendous Display of Astonishing Technology" at noon.

"That's it," said Morgan. "We have to stop him. Do we call the cops?"

"That might lead to shooting or worse," Doctor Shadow concluded. "As Steambolt Ed holds my friends hostage, we should avoid an outright confrontation."

"If the Eradicator is switched on and the battery begins charging," Tidwell added, "then they will all be lost forever."

"Exactly," said Doctor Shadow.

"So," said Morgan, "we need to make sure it doesn't work first. Then we rescue the heroes."

"What were you thinking?" Doctor Shadow asked.

"We'll need a distraction," Morgan said.

"I can help," Lizzie texted.

Morgan nodded and texted back, "I think we can transfer you to the library's computer once we are inside the building. I can create a worm for you to ride into their system."

"Ugh, worms." But then her face reappeared on his screen with a smile and wink.

"Inside that computer, you can lure them to another floor. All the building controls run off that system," he typed.

"I will wreak havoc!" Lizzie's face appeared on his screen, wearing a wide smile.

"No, that's my job," he responded. "Just lead them out of the lobby."

"And my part in this assault?" Doctor Shadow asked.

"Keep the people away from the library and transfer the heroes out as soon as I can shut off the Eradicator."

"That should not be difficult. You will need to open the main doors for me. Like most of our municipal buildings, the library is protected against magical intrusion. I cannot simply materialize in the lobby."

"No problem."

"Anything else?" Tidwell asked. "I wish I could be of more assistance."

Morgan shook his head. "You kept Lizzie alive all these years. You're definitely the man."

Tidwell looked pleased, then sighed as he stared down at Morgan's feet.

"What's wrong?" Morgan asked.

"I should not have brought you clean shoes or mopped the hallway," Tidwell said.

"No," Morgan agreed. "Because I'm going wading in the sewers again."

"I will be with you." The Electric Girl appeared on the screen of his phone in her former superhero regalia. She wore a cap and mask with a tweed coat that covered from neck to ankle.

"Appreciated," Morgan texted back. "But this phone does not give you a sense of smell. You definitely have the easy ride on this one."

Morgan climbed cautiously up the ladder from the sewer into the library's furnace room. Lifting the grate only an inch, he peered into the gloom. A single light bulb illuminated the bare concrete floor. The brass tubes containing the heroes were gone.

He slid himself over the edge of the hole and settled the grate as silently as possible. Tiptoeing to the stairs, he paused and listened.

His phone beeped.

Morgan jumped and hit the silent button.

The Electric Girl's masked face appeared on the screen, then the message: "Is the way clear?"

"Yes," Morgan typed back, as he waited for the thumping of his heart to subside.

He slid up the stairs with the catlike tread Mr. Wong had made him practice nightly on the fire escapes of Hong Kong. The door was a broken shambles from Janet's earlier assault. He checked the corridor. Also empty.

Like a shadow conjured up by the Doctor, he eased along the walls until he reached the stairs leading into the lobby. He checked his phone. The library Wi-Fi system appeared on the screen. He began his worm program. A couple of firewalls popped up, probably Hubert's invention, but Morgan overrode them with ease. A final confirmation screen popped open.

"Are you sure you can do this?" he typed to Lizzie. "Once I hit send, you'll transfer to the library's system."

"Hit send," she responded.

"Remember," Morgan typed, "if you get into trouble, let me know, and I'll send a message to Tidwell. He can retrieve you through the Club's system once we establish this link."

"Hit send," the message flashed. "Don't dally. There are people to save." Her face appeared briefly on the screen, a quick flash of a smiling but determined young woman in her checkered cap and black mask over her eyes. "The Electric Girl is ready."

"Ride the dragon," Morgan texted back, Mr. Wong's cheerful advice to him whenever he went out the door to trap another crook.

The Electric Girl whirled away into the shadows, riding the back of a wyrm, a beast of lightning, with wings of fire and eyes like shooting stars.

Beneath her mask, she smiled to see the walls surrounding the library's defenses fall beneath and then behind her. She raised one hand and felt bolts of pure energy zing through the air, ringing alarm bells, locking and unlocking doors, and lighting the electric lights from the top to the bottom of the Cobalt City Library.

She whooped upon the back of the wyrm and dived deeper into the electronic maelstrom of her creation. So joyous was her ride that she did not see the glittering net until it dropped out of the darkness. She fell into blackness as the wyrm dissolved into a shower of sparks and faded away.

Every fire alarm was blaring, every speaker was crackling with noise, and lights blazed on and off in the lobby.

From his hiding place at the top of the basement stairs, Morgan could hear Steambolt Ed's screams of frustration.

Morgan peeked around the door. Steambolt Ed, or rather Ms. Garnet, assaulted the main control panel with slaps and curses. The villain's back was turned to the lobby and the Eradicator.

The Wrecker of Engines sprinted for the Eradicator. Cables trailed from it to what he had once identified as the battery box and then to outlets in the wall. Other cords looped between the brass tubes containing the heroes, knotting them together in a diabolical diamond shape. Morgan pulled cords out, reversed them, and plugged them back in. He heard a satisfying sizzle and pop.

"Stop!" Hubert charged him, the skinny taxonomist obviously in the grip of a hypnosis-induced berserker rage. Or perhaps he was just upset that computer screens all around them were bursting into flame and then melting into puddles of foul-smelling plastic.

"Capture him," yelled Frances Garnet from across the room. "He is the one we want! Put him in the machine."

Morgan glanced behind him. One gleaming brass tube stood open and waiting for him, the fourth coffin of technology hooked to the diabolical battery. It looked ready to transform him into electrical energy.

The masked minions formed a semicircle around him, swinging their weapons and forcing Morgan back. He feinted to the left, only to have his escape route blocked by Janet. She'd snatched a giant pair of scissors from a lobby desk and stabbed like a fencer, attempting to skewer Morgan on the points.

Slipping on his electrified gloves, Morgan dashed to the right, twisting at the last possible minute to avoid a lethal blow from Hubert. The librarian smashed his wrench down onto a ruined keyboard. Morgan darted forward, hooking one foot across Hubert's ankle at the last possible moment, sending the raging library assistant crashing into Janet.

The janitor sprang forward to cut off Morgan's escape, swinging a metal toolbox. A lucky blow caught Morgan on the shoulder, staggering him back.

Morgan clapped one gloved hand on the toolbox, sending a mild electrical shock through the metal. His attacker yelped and dropped his weapon with a crash on the library's marble floor.

"Put him in the tube!" Frances Garnet yelled again. All traces of the gentle librarian were gone from her face. The look of fury exactly matched the line drawings of the villain Steambolt Ed that adorned the exhibition downstairs.

Morgan leaped backward, twisting in mid-air and kicking off the top of the tube. As he somersaulted over it, he clapped both gloved hands firmly on the wires connecting all four tubes. The Wrecker of Engines sent a controlled pulse of power through the wires and was rewarded by the smell of melting rubber and fried connections.

Steambolt Ed shrieked in fury.

The library's automatic sprinkler system kicked into action. Water cascaded from the ceiling, drenching the lobby and all the fighters.

Mindful of the danger when electricity and water combined, the Wrecker of Engines raced in his rubber-soled sneakers to the giant main doors of the library. Lizzie had done it, the electronic locks were sprung, and Morgan crashed through them.

On the other side, Doctor Shadow waited. With a nod to Morgan, he lifted his hands and began his incantations. Inside the library, Hubert and Janet yelled as bolts of electricity shot through the air.

Morgan turned back to the library's lobby. Steambolt Ed had retreated to the far side of the main desk. The computer screen there smoked slightly but appeared intact. The villain raised his stolen face to Morgan and grinned, a smile of pure evil such as had never before contorted the features of Ms. Frances Garnet, head librarian. Steambolt Ed pushed a key-board button.

Morgan started towards the doors, intent on seeing what Steambolt Ed was trying to do. But the wind of Doctor Shadow's magic engulfed him. The tornado of a spell spun him outdoors and then, in a blink of an eye, he found himself seated once again in the reading room of the Adventurers Club.

"A successful outing?" Tidwell inquired, as he handed Morgan a towel to dry his hair.

"Quite," Doctor Shadow said, appearing before them with a pop of displaced air. "I have sent our kidnapped friends to proper care at the Starcom clinic. They will be able to release them from the tubes and restore them to consciousness without any compromise to their identities. Stardust has excellent systems in place for just such occurrences."

"But the Eradicator?" asked Tidwell.

"Damaged by our young friend's quick actions," said Doctor Shadow. "Now I can return to my research."

Morgan tapped his phone, bringing up Lizzie's picture. He typed into the message box: "We did it."

No response. Morgan tapped the send button again. Still no response. He ran a search deep into the system. All signs of the Electric Girl were erased.

"Tidwell," Morgan asked, as worry started to knot his stomach with dread, "is Lizzie back in the communications room?"

The caretaker of the Adventurers Club frowned. "I do not believe so." He strode into the hallway and picked up the black house phone. He jiggled the switchhook and then listened again. "Miss Blythe is not there."

Doctor Shadow levitated, making mystical passes with his hands. "I cannot feel her essence within the building."

Morgan stared at the static screen of his phone. Nothing was there. Nothing. The Electric Girl, Lizzie Blythe, was gone.

CHAPTER 11: FINDING LIZZIE

"I KNOW WHERE SHE IS," SAID MORGAN.

"Of course you do. I am sure Miss Blythe can be rescued shortly." But there was a hollow note in Tidwell's voice and lines of worry creased the caretaker's normally smooth brow.

Doctor Shadow watched without comment, hovering a few inches above the floor, a mystical wind causing the edges of his cape to flutter and strange shadows to scurry across the walls of the Adventurers Club. He rotated toward Morgan. "Where do we go next?"

"The library," Morgan said. "But first I need to figure out how they caught her."

"Can you trace her through the communications room?" Tidwell suggested.

Morgan shook his head. "No, I need my stuff upstairs."

"Computers were never my forte," Doctor Shadow said, as they rode to the top floor in the elevator, "but I am happy to assist you in any manner I can."

"Wait." Morgan slid down into his chair in his den and began banging on his keyboard. "I need to see what he did to her." He watched the records of the past hour cascade across his screens. He found the hidden firewall that had destroyed his worm and cut the link from his server in the Adventurers Club to the library's mainframe. It was so sophisticated, it could only have come from the enslaved Hubert.

"We have an hour, maybe less." Rolling his chair to his workbench, he began to grab bits and pieces, slapping wires together with rapid speed. "We need to get Lizzie out quickly. This program forced her back into the energy store for Steambolt Ed's Eradicator. But the damage I did to it will start draining her out. It will tear her apart, literally."

"Do you have a plan?" Doctor Shadow asked.

"Yes." Morgan grabbed his hastily assembled device off the table and stuffed it into his backpack. "But I've got to be there, at the library, to make it work. I wish I could fly. Getting across the city in time is the big problem. Could use a jetpack now."

"I have never needed a jetpack. Flight is a simple matter," Doctor Shadow said with an upward curl of his thin lips. He steepled his hands together and barked out a string of sharp commands in an unknown tongue. His cloak unfurled. It spread like a cloud of ink through the room, wrapping around Morgan.

Together, he and Doctor Shadow began to spin faster and faster. Tidwell and the walls of the Adventurers Club faded away. The brilliant lights of Cobalt City's skyscrapers glittered below their feet while the stars and the moon spun above their heads.

With the lightest bump, Morgan and Doctor Shadow landed on the front steps of the library.

"As I said earlier," Doctor Shadow reminded him. "The building is warded against magical intrusion."

"Doesn't matter," said Morgan, running lightly up the steps. "I can get us in!"

"How?"

"I've got a library card!" Morgan pulled out the library staff card he had stolen from Frances Garnet. He swiped it through the electronic lock outside the library door. As he hoped, the red light turned green. He grabbed the giant brass handle. With a twist and a tug, he pulled the heavy oak door open.

Inside, the lights were dimmed. The alarms were off. The librarians obviously had control of the building's systems again.

"The library is closed!" The shout rang out from the gallery overhanging the entrance.

Morgan glanced up and then dove to one side as Janet let loose a bolt of energy from the brass and steel contraption that she pumped enthusiastically for a second shot at him.

"No talking!" she yelled. "No running! Shhh!"

Morgan cartwheeled over the rubble left behind by their last fight. The water still standing in puddles on the slick marble floor made it easy to slide quickly to one side. He vaulted over Janet's old desk, grabbing the visitors' book to shield his face from her second shot. The smell of burned paper filled the room.

Janet screamed when she saw the flames shooting from the book. "That's a fine for you, Wrecker," she yelled, as she let loose another bolt that sizzled across her desk and set a stack of bookmarks alight.

Morgan rolled under the desk for cover. He fumbled with the computer's cable, pulling it out of the outlet set in the floor. The plug popped free, and Morgan pulled out his own device, a crude box with one large red button on top. He hadn't had much time to cobble it together, and he'd been forced to use the spare parts on his workbench. But he thought the old-fashioned red button looked right and proper as he plugged the device in. He slapped the button and sent a pulse of pure power into the library's system.

Another blast from Janet's strange gun kept him pinned under the desk.

"We need to stop her," he shouted at his companion.

"With pleasure." Doctor Shadow flew up from the main lobby like a giant bat until he was hovering directly in front of Janet.

The young librarian swung her weapon to face him, but Doctor Shadow waved one hand to the right, letting loose a blast of mystical energy that tumbled it and Janet out of sight. He floated easily over the rail of the balcony and called down to Morgan, "I will render her unconscious for now."

"Do what you need to." Morgan scrambled out from under the desk and raced toward the stairs leading to the basement and the remainder of Steambolt Ed's reassembled inventions. "I'll find Lizzie."

The basement lights were dim. Morgan ran past the mementoes of past heroes, including the gleaming white mask of his ancestor.

The door to the villains' exhibit was shut. Morgan burst through it.

Steambolt Ed had completely taken over the mind of Frances Garnet. Her now-uncovered hair writhed around her head in an aureole of static energy. Her gentle, soft features were drawn into a terrible grimace of frustration and fury. She stood over the wet and dented remnants of the Eradicator, obviously dragged downstairs from the lobby. She hooked one cable directly to a brass and wood calculating machine. Sparks flew along the connection to the Eradicator.

"What have you done to my beautiful inventions?" she snarled.

"Alternating current, spiked the internal power source, fried the wires," Morgan panted. "I told you before, you really shouldn't turn old machines on."

Already tubes were starting to pop. Smoke curled out of many panels as needles swung wildly from left to right and back again on various gauges. Lizzie didn't have long. The equipment holding her spirit was literally melting down in front of him.

He pulled out his phone and typed a frantic text: "Are you here?"

The screen stayed blank, and his heart practically stopped

beating. The device he had triggered upstairs should have created a hole in Hubert's firewall and let the Wi-Fi link be reestablished. The signal wouldn't be strong, but it should be enough. If Lizzie was still in the machines. If she still existed.

With a snarl of fury, Steambolt Ed began to haul the battered Edison Eradicator around on its wheels.

Morgan didn't move. On the screen of his phone, a one-word answer formed with agonizing slowness, one letter after another: "Y-e-s."

Steambolt Ed cranked the starter. The muzzle of the Eradicator was aimed straight at Morgan's heart.

Morgan tapped frantically on the screen. "Jump, jump here."

The crackling energy of the Eradicator began to burn in the glass bulb at the top of the gun.

"I can stop him," Lizzie's text flickered into view. "Turn it off."

"No!" Morgan yelled out loud, as his thumbs copied the message into his smartphone. "No time. Jump!"

He started to shift, to get out of the line of fire, but the signal on his phone dropped away. Morgan swayed back into the one spot where he still could get a connection with Lizzie. He typed: "I will not leave you. You are my friend."

Behind Steambolt Ed, a spray of sparks shot out from a calculating machine, landing on the checkered jacket and causing it to smoke. The villain just snarled and continued to crank up the power of the Eradicator.

"Please run," Lizzie texted.

"No," he sent back, even as the whine of the Eradicator escalated to earsplitting decibels.

From the door, the deep throbbing tones of Doctor Shadow's most magical voice rang out. "For once, do as you are told, Electric Girl. Let us save you!"

With a snap of his fingers, Doctor Shadow spun the Eradicator, with a screaming Steambolt Ed still clutching the handle. The burst of power jetting from its nozzle struck one of the copper and wood calculating machines. It faded from view, transformed into a sparkling shower of motes that were sucked back into the Eradicator.

"Come on, Lizzie, jump," Morgan yelled and typed at the same time.

The screen on his smartphone glowed with a warm expanding light. It grew from a tiny dot far away to fill the screen with Lizzie Blythe's grinning face. She winked up at Morgan.

"Alright!" Morgan pumped the hand holding the smart phone into the air. "She's safe!"

"Excellent." Doctor Shadow let loose another spell against the Eradicator.

Steambolt Ed howled in fury as the handles slicked with ice. Another patch of ice formed under her sensible shoes, sending her tumbling to the floor.

"Sleep, sleep," commanded Doctor Shadow.

The gentle snores of Frances Garnet, head librarian, filled the room.

Morgan clicked the switch on the Eradicator. A glowing ball of energy began to form in the glass bulb on the top.

"Are you certain about this?" asked Stardust.

"Pretty much," he said. "Thanks for the tools. And the schematics from your collection."

"Hey, any time," said the man in the gleaming battle armor. "And if you want to come work in the Starcom Industries labs, just give me a call. I'm always looking for new talent."

"If I ever need a paycheck," said the Wrecker of Engines, "I'll call."

"Sometimes a job is about more than salary," Stardust said thoughtfully. "You'd make friends at the labs. There's a softball league. We play every Friday. We try to be like a family. Family is important to a hero."

"Yes, I know." Morgan liked Stardust. It was impossible not to like the cheery guy under all the amazing gear. But he didn't see himself committing his life to a cubicle, even if that cubicle was located in a big laboratory filled with like-minded geeks who got out once a week for a softball game.

"From what you've told us, you may well be family, and you're always welcome in my home," added Wild Kat. Her claws, fangs, and other assets still made Morgan a bit nervous, but she'd also given him a handwritten journal from the Wilde collection as a thank you for rescuing her.

In the journal were a series of entries written by the man Morgan thought was his grandfather. Also, unfolding from the cracked leather cover was a map showing a route to a mystical empire hidden beyond the western deserts separating China from Central Asia. Morgan stared for a long time at the route traced in dried brown ink and the tiny notations next to it about latitude and longitude. He thought this might be the ancient road his old teacher, Mr. Wong, was now traveling.

But right now, he had more pressing problems.

"Ah, I see we are ready for the next phase of this interesting endeavor." Doctor Shadow entered the laboratory. He waved a hand, and a group of orderlies wheeled in the sleeping form of Frances Garnet. Janet, Hubert, and the janitor were recovering at the downtown hospital. The remainder of the Cobalt City Library staff had been found bound and unconscious in the staff break room by the cops.

"Shall I wake him first?" Doctor Shadow inquired.

"Yes." Morgan nodded. "I have questions for Steambolt Ed before he's gone for good."

Doctor Shadow waved one hand in a circular motion over the head librarian's head.

Her eyes snapped open. "So, you've captured me again, Pharaoh's Ghost. Well, you will rue this day."

"Unlikely," responded Doctor Shadow. "You have come to the end of your stolen time here. But if you answer my young friend's questions, you may earn some leniency from me."

Steambolt Ed twisted her head to look straight at Morgan. "You want the girl, that Electric Girl? Let me keep this body, and I'll tell you how I did it. How I escaped from the machine. How she can take a body of her own."

"No," said Morgan with more resolve than he thought he had. He and Lizzie had texted back and forth about this for days, a long battle that Lizzie finally won. "She doesn't want that. She isn't a thief, like you. But I want to know if there is any other way we can get her out of the machine? Turn her back into what she was."

"You want to turn your friend into a real girl?" snarled Steambolt Ed. Then, in accents closer to Frances Garnet, the trapped villain added, "What do you think I am, the Blue Fairy?"

Doctor Shadow fingered his chin and frowned. "Hmm, the Collodi spell. Why did I not try that before?"

"I think you have about five minutes to start talking," Stardust said, watching the energy grow in the Eradicator's large glass bulb. "Then it's zap, off to dreamland, buddy."

"There is no way to restore the physical form," Steambolt Ed confessed. "Don't you think I tried? Do you think I wanted to rule this century in this impossible body, always craving chocolates and books to read?"

"Then you have no answers for me." Morgan turned to Stardust and added sadly, "It was worth asking before we ejected him from Ms. Garnet."

Doctor Shadow continued to mutter in the corner, "Blue dust...not impossible...a real girl...interesting notion."

"Wait," Steambolt Ed begged. "Don't you want to know where your mother is? I delved into your history to make sure you were the right hero to complete my battery. I learned things, things you will want to hear."

Wild Kat stepped forward with a snarl. "Tell me now. Morgan and his mother are now part of my family. And I do not bargain with villains."

A message from Lizzie popped up on Morgan's phone. "He's lying. I searched the library's databases. There is nothing there. I am sorry."

In the days since she was freed from the machines at the library, the Electric Girl had flown through the cloud of data binding all of Cobalt City together. Morgan knew that if any information about his mother's mysterious disappearance or current whereabouts existed in the library, Lizzie would have found it.

So he texted back, "Thank you. Are you still sure?"

"Yes," came the answer. "Give Steambolt Ed my message. I won't take my life back at the expense of another's mind."

Morgan leaned close to the bound villain on the gurney. "I've got a message for you from Lizzie. She says it is her story, and she will write her own ending. You didn't win then. You haven't won now. Put that in your pipe and smoke it."

Steambolt Ed let out a howl of misery through Francis Garnet's mouth as the energy ball at the top of the Eradicator began to whirl counterclockwise. A stream of sparkling motes rose from the head librarian's body. The spirit of Steambolt Ed was sucked down the nozzle of the rebuilt Eradicator. The light in the glass bulb changed from gentle blue to a deep purple, with little red sparks spitting out in all directions.

"A troubled soul." Doctor Shadow carefully removed the glass bulb from the top of the Eradicator and placed it into a soft leather bag that he stowed under his cloak. "And best that it be imprisoned."

On the gurney, Frances Garnet groaned.

Stardust leaned over her. "Ms. Garnet, how are you?"

With the help of a lab technician, Cobalt City's head librarian sat up. "I feel awful. What a headache. I just had the most horrible nightmare, that the books came alive and tried to devour the patrons."

"Not quite," said Stardust, "but there's been a few accidents at the library. A small electrical fire or two."

"Oh no!" cried Ms. Garnet.

"On the other hand, you did make the nightly news. Rather spectacularly," said Stardust. "And there's been a record number of overdue books returned today from patrons who don't want to upset you or the other librarians. Also, several thousand people signed up on your webpage to form a new 'Fans of the Library' group. They want to know when you're hosting a live meet-up and demonstrating some of Sheffield Edison's inventions. And what books you have about him."

"But we don't have a Fans page, do we?" the puzzled librarian asked.

"Apparently your staff set one up recently to invite everyone to come to a science demonstration," said Stardust. "A good idea, I think, and of course, I'd be happy to pay for the clean-up of the lobby, the rebooting of the Sheffield Edison calculating machines, and anything else you think you need. It's the least I can do for the Cobalt City Library."

"He just wants to play with the shiny stuff," muttered Wild Kat to Morgan with a smile. "But I'll send a check to Ms. Garnet as well. I own an excellent ad agency too. Time they did pro bono work for the library and publicized it. It would make a terrific tourist attraction."

"She's been worried about the mayor shutting them down," Morgan recalled.

"Not if he wants campaign contributions from Cobalt City's wealthiest inventor and most charming socialite," said Wild Kat with a wink at Stardust. "I'm sure we can convince him that extended hours are in everyone's best interest."

"Yes, and you should ask Janet and Hubert for some ideas about new ways to help people...and superheroes...at the library," said Morgan, flipping the switches to power off the Eradicator. "But I wish we could help Lizzie."

"Patience," Doctor Shadow said, as he joined them. "I will have an answer for you tomorrow. I will meet you at the Adventurers Club."

Tidwell examined the glowing glass bulb carefully packed in the padded wooden box. "So he is not permanently erased?"

The ancient magician shrugged. "There may come a time when Sheffield Edison can be restored to a physical form without harming others. I think it best that you take charge of him. Leaving this soul downtown in the Cobalt City Library seems to have been most unsatisfactory."

"Rather, you never know when he will be checked out." Then Tidwell gave a small snort, almost a laugh, at his joke.

Doctor Shadow tutted under his breath. "You have changed in the last century or so."

"I try," said Tidwell.

Morgan glanced up from the flurry of messages he was exchanging with Lizzie. "But don't you want to try your spell on Steambolt Ed first? To make sure?"

Doctor Shadow shook his head. "We lack the essential ingredients for this villain. Besides, the spell I am about to attempt is rarely successful, even with all the right elements in place. If the soul is selfish or resists the magic in any way—"

"She is stubborn," warned Tidwell.

"But never ungenerous and never unintelligent. She risked her life many times for her friends, both in her own century and this one," Doctor Shadow said.

"And she does know we're trying to free her, not imprison her," Morgan added.

A small "yes!" popped up on his phone's screen.

"Very true," said Tidwell. "Well, we can only hope."

They had assembled all the items that Doctor Shadow requested in the greater reading room of the Adventurers Club. There was a stack of clothing produced by Tidwell on the long oak table at the center of the room. Small black boots with buttons up the ankles, a tweed skirt and long coat in the same material, a high-collared white cotton blouse, and a jaunty cap with a feather fastened to it by a silver pin.

"Did she not wear a mask?" asked Doctor Shadow.

"Quite right." Tidwell produced a narrow black band embroidered with streaks of lighting on either side of the eyeholes. He placed it below the cap.

Morgan walked up to the table with his smartphone. "Where do I put it?"

"Over her heart. Or, rather, where her heart should be," Doctor Shadow instructed. "That seems appropriately symbolic."

Morgan set it down on the left side of the jacket.

"Very good. Now let us proceed." Doctor Shadow flung a sparkling handful of blue, shimmering dust in an arc across the clothes laid out for the spirit trapped inside Morgan's smartphone.

"Electric Girl," he intoned.

"Miss Elizabeth Blythe," Tidwell announced to the room.

"Lizzie," Morgan said, as his thumbs tapped her name into the air before him.

"We have named you three times, spirit," Doctor Shadow recited in English and then repeated the phrase again in another older, darker language. "Come forth. Return to the world as you once were. Come back to us."

"Come back," repeated Tidwell.

"Come on, Lizzie, come on, you can do it," Morgan whispered in encouragement. Then, in the Cantonese of his childhood, he invited his friend to return to Cobalt City.

The air began to darken in the room even as Morgan's smartphone glowed brighter and brighter. Finally, it flashed so bright that Morgan flung up a hand to shield his eyes.

Then he heard it, a laugh like a peal of jubilant bells.

"Well, it took you all long enough." Lizzie Blythe swung herself into an upright position on the reading room table. She kicked out her feet and laughed again to see her skirt and petticoats go flying up.

"Lizzie!" Morgan grabbed her around the waist and swung her round and round the room while she laughed and shouted and clutched at his shoulders. As they twirled around the room, a trail of sparks, like fireworks, exploded in the air.

They came to a dizzying stop in front of Doctor Shadow and Tidwell. The two smiled at them with nearly identical cat-like curls of the lip.

"Very nicely done," Tidwell said to Doctor Shadow.

"Thank you." Doctor Shadow inclined his head to Tidwell.

Lizzie just shook her beaming face at both of them and then grabbed Tidwell in a bear hug that nearly pulled the slender man over.

"Really, miss," Tidwell said, as he straightened his tie and jacket. "Even in this century, a bit more decorum, please."

"Oh, no, not me!" Lizzie tossed her cap and mask into the air. Her hair tumbled down in a cascade of auburn curls. "I'm going to kick up my heels from one end of Cobalt City to the next." She flung up her hands, and the lights flickered on and off in the room.

The assembled group all blinked, including Lizzie.

"Well," she said. "Some things have changed."

Morgan grabbed her hand and felt a slight shock run through him, not unlike the discharge from his electric fighting gloves. "That's quite a charge. We need to measure that. But you could use it too. Do some interesting damage to computers."

"A Wrecker of Engines and an Electric Girl," murmured Tidwell.

"A powerful partnership," responded Doctor Shadow. "Perhaps one that is needed now."

Morgan glanced over his shoulder at them. "I bet Hubert would say it was predictable. According to that database of his."

"Quite possibly," said Doctor Shadow. "We need to contemplate how this will be managed."

Lizzie snatched her cap off the floor and jammed it back on her head. "Tomorrow. Tomorrow I'll be serious and hard-working and figure out how I want to live my life in this century."

Then she turned to Morgan. "But first, I want a ride on that amazing red bike of yours."

He just grinned at her. He couldn't stop grinning. For the first time in years, Morgan felt unconditionally happy. "Wherever you want to go."

"Someplace with ice cream," Lizzie said, as they walked out the door. "Someplace with buckets and buckets of ice cream. I haven't tasted anything for more than a century."

"Bet I can find that." Morgan pulled another phone out of his hoodie pocket and tapped a command with one finger.

"Bet you can," replied the Electric Girl, hanging onto his arm.

EPILOGUE

COBALT CITY 2019

PAPER DRAGONS,
ELECTRIC WINGS

LIZZIE HUMMED ALONG WITH THE SONG AUDIBLE ONLY TO her, all about paper wings, paper kisses, and a broken paper heart under a paper moon. It seemed appropriate for sorting through the books left behind by the students in odd spots around the library. Lizzie loved this Saturday morning job, roaming up and down the aisles, pushing her book cart before her, collecting the books abandoned everywhere except the shelves marked "leave books here for reshelving."

College students did not seem keen to read instructions. Lizzie smiled and shook her head at the neatly labeled but clearly bare shelf. Perhaps they believed hiding the books in various corners would make them more accessible next time, she thought, as she crawled under one study carrel desk to retrieve a stack of economic textbooks, a play about the women of Russian fairy tales, and an unopened package of Kit Kats. Food was not allowed in the library. Lizzie felt no guilt about confiscating the Kit Kats to share later in the librarian's lounge. She dropped the marvelous candy treat into the pocket of her velvet vest.

Lizzie's other college student job was serving coffee in the Student Union. She loved that job, too, but the student manager, Hank, complained to the staff supervisor about working with her.

"It's the way she makes coffee. It's weird. Look, I don't mind her always being dressed in her steampunk cosplay outfits," she'd overheard him say to Iris Gunderson, the head of Food Service. "The customers think it's cute. Some of the other baristas started wearing their costumes to work too. One day we had a Stardust, Wrecker of Engines, and Lady Vengeance serving during her shift."

Lizzie smiled when she heard that. The Stardust and Lady Vengeance had been a couple of fans in their own fantastic interpretations of the superhero outfits. But the Wrecker of Engines had been real. Morgan Lee wanted to see what it was like working as a barista. Training for some undercover Wrecker op, according to him. She liked to think he wanted to spend more time with her before he left Cobalt City again for wherever he needed to go next. Being a hacker superhero led him to strange places far away, so different from her own journey from nowhere real to being grounded in this city.

Miss Gunderson, the gentle-voiced African American woman who always tried to find the best spot for her student employees, said in reply to Hank's complaint: "I think Lizzie is trying hard to fit in. This is her first time working in food service, according to her file. If you're not happy with her work, it's up to you, Hank, to show her how to make the coffee properly."

"The coffee is excellent," Hank admitted. "Nobody can pull the combinations out of that machine like Lizzie. The other day, she got it to serve a Banana Split Chai Latte."

"But isn't that a good thing?" asked Iris, sounding a little puzzled. "I thought the students liked ordering custom drinks."

"Oh, they do," admitted Hank. "And there's at least one fraternity running a bet on who can stump her. So far nobody has won."

"Then what's the problem?"

"Have you seen how she makes the drinks?" he asked, sounding frantic to Lizzie. Of course, her view of Hank's waving arms, as well as his agitated complaints, were relayed by the tiny camera she'd left on the cash register so she could keep an eye on the register when she wasn't working. She felt some qualms about spying on her boss, but she'd promised Miss Gunderson she would look into the recent thefts in the Student Union. Small amounts had been disappearing from various registers. The thief always took only one-dollar bills. Nobody could figure out how the thief did it. The camera was there for that. All the workers had been informed about the camera. If Hank had forgotten she could see and hear through it, that was his problem, she decided.

"What's wrong with how Lizzie is running the coffee machine?" asked Miss Gunderson.

"She doesn't touch it!" Hank flapped his hand at the automatic espresso machine. "She just lines up the cups, glances at it, and then the drinks start pouring out."

Miss Gunderson shook her head. "Still not sure what the problem is. I thought we put in these machines because the shot pour was automatic. Little training required, standardization of quality, and quick service. Push the button and achieve the perfect espresso drink."

"I know!" said Hank. "I went to that training seminar for these machines this summer. They were very clear that customizing espresso shots on the fly wasn't possible. But Lizzie does it. Without touching any button at all!"

Miss Gunderson sighed. "Now, Hank, we've talked about Cobalt City University. Some of our students, especially our local students, have certain skills. We want to honor that. Not everyone has to push the button the same way."

"But she doesn't push anything—" muttered Hank as he turned away. "She just looks at it. Sometimes she doesn't even do that. And where is she getting banana flavoring for the chai? We don't stock banana flavoring."

Later that day, Miss Gunderson and Lizzie discussed how to make Hank a little less stressed. At least that was how Miss Gunderson put it. Lizzie would have called it "to stop him from having the vapors again." But she understood that "hysteria" and "vapors" were words that had fallen out of favor in the last century. Time shifting was never easy. At least that's what her friend Tidwell said, and he'd lived enough centuries to see several languages change and the meaning of so many words go from deadly to friendly to forgotten. "Some words, thank all the household gods, are just not used anymore, which improves the language immensely."

Lizzie agreed. Nothing was perfect in this particular year. But she'd seen worse. Smelled it too. That was the one thing she always noticed walking across the campus. The stench of coal smoke, horse dung, and rotten garbage wafting up from open sewers was a thing of the past, her past, and she didn't regret the disappearance of those odors.

She certainly welcomed the sight of thousands of women strolling around the campus, taking classes, teaching classes, and working in all parts of the University. All those women, assuming they could receive an education, forge a career, and lead the way for others. It definitely wasn't perfect. Lizzie was flabbergasted and disappointed by the fact that American politicians were still predominantly men. She had assumed when women won the vote, they would have used their power to at least balance out the halls of government on all levels. Still, she often thought, if only the Lady Detective or the Steel Suffragette had lived to see how much had changed. They would have been astounded to meet Miss Gunderson, in charge of so many employees, and so proud of her too.

So when Miss Gunderson asked Lizzie if she had any ideas to help Hank out, Lizzie suggested shifting to a library job for Saturday mornings, and rearranging her remaining schedule at the coffee stand so she was there when Hank was in class or at home.

"That's kind of you," said Miss Gunderson. "But Hank must learn to handle differences. I'm not sure if this is the best solution. I'd rather figure out a way to have you work together."

"Hank suffered an encounter with the worms," Lizzie reminded her. "I think it's that, more than me, but he probably would do better without any reminders."

"Oh, yes," Miss Gunderson said. "I'd forgotten about the worms."

The worms had arrived on campus from another dimension, a common problem in Cobalt City. Lizzie and her friends had fought the wrigglers through the tunnels under the University. The wily other-dimensional creatures had flowed up through the manhole covers to engulf a number of students. Luckily, nobody had been seriously hurt, but several, including Hank, still tended to flinch when they encountered an earthworm on a sidewalk after the rain.

"I could work the last shift on Sunday through Thursday nights," said Lizzie. "That's when Mark manages the stand."

"Oh, would you?" said Miss Gunderson. "He's such a sweet boy. I don't know why people don't want to be on the late-night shift with him."

Mark Obiyashi usually took the 10 p.m. to 2 a.m. shifts, the ones that closed the stand for the night. The issue for his co-workers and customers was that by midnight, the ghosts tended to gather. Mark did his best to discourage them, but his grandfather was a persistent spook. The old ghost had a tendency to rattle the little plastic spoons and other items on the self-help table when he was feeling particularly lonely. Lizzie knew Mark's grandfather found her own energy a bit disturbing—apparently, he had once told his grandson she gave him the "prickles" whenever she was nearby. If she was there, the ghost tended to behave. Besides, her "contestants" would follow her to a new time slot. The "Stump Lizzie" coffee movement ran its own social media feed, with people posting pictures of Lizzie's drink concoctions.

So Lizzie assured Miss Gunderson. "I don't mind those hours, especially if it will give me Saturday mornings at the library. I've known Mark since my first year. We have many friends in common."

Mark sometimes yearned after Gizi, who used to live in the same dorm as Lizzie. This year, Lizzie had moved back to the Adventurers Club. As much as she liked all her new friends at the University, there were times when she just didn't want to pick her way through all the challenges that came with being a century or more older than everyone around her. It wasn't just missing more than a hundred years of history—she was also woefully behind on this generation's popular entertainment. At least when she was at the Club, streaming some movie with Tidwell, nobody said, "I can't believe you've never seen this."

The song changed on her playlist. The music was now slower and sadder. Lizzie rounded the corner of the aisle. A student was hunched in a study carrel, wedged into the window nook. The ivy outside crisscrossed the glass, casting shifting shadows on the carrel. Or perhaps the shadows entered the library with the young man sitting there. Recognizing the purple hoodie and ripped black jeans outfit, Lizzie called out, "Hello, Mark."

As always, it took Mark Obiyashi a minute to turn his head and acknowledge Lizzie with a half-hearted wave of his hand. "Hey," he said in his soft voice.

Lizzie smiled broadly. At least he'd heard her on the first try. There were so many voices trying to claim Mark's attention, he often missed simple greetings. Lizzie understood the problem. She had spent more than a century learning how to control, filter, and even ignore the distractions. The music in her ears faded away as she approached Mark. For the moment, she was intent on being present in one physical place rather than splashed across all of Cobalt City's electric networks.

"What are you doing here?" she asked Mark.

"Assignment." He pointed at the pile on the carrel's desk. A laptop, a couple of small notebooks, a multitude of pens, a blinking phone, and a crumpled print-out of a class assignment were piled next to his canvas messenger bag. Mark probably had upended it on the desk to find what he wanted. She'd seen him do that before. Parked under the desk was his beloved skateboard with its multiple ghost stickers.

"You've got a message." Lizzie nodded at the phone flashing in the center of the pile.

"Gizi," responded Mark, withdrawing even further into his hoodie. Lizzie could only see the tip of his nose and the edge of his chin. "Sending emojis."

"That's good?" Their friend Gizi loved the language of pictures, and she combined the colorful little icons in creative ways. Figuring out what she meant... that could be a challenge at times.

"It's a heart on fire."

"Passionate love?" Lizzie responded.

"Or burning a past love and moving on. We were texting about our favorite boba tea."

"New favorite drink?" Lizzie asked, settling into this game of guessing what Gizi meant.

"Or she's over me." Mark slumped more. "Because I like tiger milk."

"What's Gizi's favorite?"

"Lychee snow. She's a wild girl." Mark eyed his phone. "I guess I should send something back. Or I could work on this assignment." He poked at the paper crumpled on the desk.

"What is it?

"I need to write about dragons." Mark heaved a sigh of the student taxed with a dull assignment, although Lizzie thought dragons sounded better than many of the subjects Mark regularly researched. "How different cultures see the dragons differently. It's an anthropology thing. I'm supposed to present something about the Nordic dragons, and my partner will respond with the Asian dragons." Then, in a tone of ultimate gloom, he added, "We have to give our research to the class using a slide deck."

Lizzie shuddered. She adored the power of computers, enjoyed access to many streaming services, and couldn't imagine ever living again without a phone in her pocket. But this century's insistence on placing bits of information on slides and forcing all the eyeballs in a room or in an online gathering to focus on those slides—that was a barbaric development. The only thing worse was being asked to create one of those instruments of tedious torture. It was the only part of being a combined history and communications student that she loathed.

"So who's your partner on this?" she asked.

"Hello," said a deep voice behind Lizzie. She spun around to see a tall young man dressed in sharp contrast to Mark. If a white t-shirt could be said to be crisp, then this one was the ultimate in crispness, tucked with precision into dark blue jeans with knife-edge creases running from knee to ankle. The whole outfit, from top to bottom, appeared to be molded to the broad shoulders, muscled chest, narrow waist, and long legs of the young man facing her. Gizi would have responded with a heart bursting into flame, thought Lizzie. As it was, she fought to keep from flushing as he smiled at her.

"Oh, hey, Chao," said Mark, "this is Lizzie. We...uh...work together."

"Konglong Chao." Mark's study partner reached out a warm, dry hand and shook Lizzie's hand with a formality that startled her. She'd grown used to waves, elbow bumps, hugs across her shoulders, and other casual greetings since returning to Cobalt City. This gesture felt like something from her past.

"Are you a student here too?" Chao asked. "I thought college students were older in the United States."

Lizzie knew her small size made her appear very young to many people. As did the fact that she'd been essentially frozen at seventeen for so many long years in a virtual space beyond the physical realm. Others thought she would start aging now that she was a part of the physical world again. But Lizzie herself wasn't sure. She still felt the same as the day she was transformed into electricity by Steambolt Edison.

"I'm a student," she assured Chao. "Almost done with my degree too. Communications and history. At least that's my undergrad. I'm thinking about staying and going for a master's in library science." With the help of unlimited wealth from the Wrecker of Engines, Lizzie didn't need to worry about student loans. The timeless quality of a university life appealed to the young woman jolted out of her century. There were more than a few Cobalt City superheroes who used the alter ego of a harmless perpetual student to hide their true identity.

"An interesting combination of scholarly pursuits for a young woman," Chao replied. Mark had withdrawn more deeply into his carrel, poking at his phone and muttering at each emoji or gif he brought up. "Perhaps not as useful as others."

Lizzie drew a deep breath and recited all of Miss Gunderson's maxims about tolerance in the face of Chao's dismissive tone about her studies. Perhaps he thought she should be a math major. "And what's your major?"

"Myself, I am studying wealth. How to turn the power of money into an even grander supremacy of influence."

"Business major?" The flames inside died even more. She was sure, someday, she would meet a business major who loved books and didn't spend all their time talking about their plans for an internship at one of Cobalt City's international banks. She just hadn't met that individual yet. On the other hand, most business majors were uncommonly good at making slide decks, so perhaps this was the right study partner for Mark.

"I am not a business major," Chao said, reviving Lizzie's interest. "Perhaps in time. But I am beginning with anthropology. I believe it is important to understand what makes humans...ah...human. Once that is understood, then matters can be better arranged."

He strolled to another study carrel. Unlike Mark's pile, Chao's computer, notebook, single pen, and slim leather briefcase were all lined up in a precise diamond shape. "North, south, east, west." Chao tapped each item once as he leaned over his desk.

Looking over his shoulder, Lizzie noticed the center of the diamond was filled with small paper dragons. "Oh, those are charming. Did you cut those?"

Each tiny dragon was cut from colored paper. Predominantly green-colored paper, although some were brown, blue, yellow, or red.

Chao inclined his head. "Yes. It is an interesting art form. To balance both positive and negative space, turning an everyday object of insignificant value and available in multitudes into a creature exclusively its own being." He handed her one of the green and white dragons.

Lizzie balanced the tiny dragon on her palm. It was completely flat, not three dimensional like the origami creations some of her friends made. The green and white pattern printed on the dragon seemed familiar, but she was more intrigued by the shape created by Chao's art. The miniscule cuts in the paper delicately outlined the head, horns, and whiskers on one end, four legs ending in sharp talons, and a spiraling snake-like body that concluded with a tufted tail.

"The nine aspects of my paper dragon." Chao's finger hovered over her hand as he outlined his tiny creation from snout to tail. "From head to shoulder, from shoulder to breast, from breast to tail, the antlers of a stag, the head of a camel, the ears of an ox, the eyes of a demon, the teeth of a carp, the neck of a snake, the belly of a turtle, the claws of an eagle, and the tail of a tiger."

Even as he spoke, Lizzie felt a warm glow grow in her palm, a heat not unlike when she gathered energy to herself. But this didn't spark or sizzle like her own power. Instead, something nipped her hand with a sharp sting.

"Ow." A minute line of blood trailed across the tip of her thumb. She carefully tipped the fragile paper dragon into her other hand. She sucked on her thumb to stop the bleeding. "A paper cut. How did I do that? I hate when that happens." She groped in her vest pocket, trying to fish out a tissue. "I don't want to bleed on your creature. Or any of the books!" She extended her other hand to Chao, intent on giving him back the tiny dragon.

"Fascinating." Chao looked at the little green and white dragon that wobbled in the slight breeze caused by the movement of Lizzie's hand. "I thought only the demonic power of the ghost child could give them extra life. But you also seem to possess an abundance of energy, enough to spark at least a flight of dragons."

Lizzie blinked as the green dragon in her hand floated up in the air, suspended between herself and Chao. As the dragon flew in a slow loop-the-loop, she glimpsed a familiar eye floating in the center of a glowing triangle on its side. Suddenly she realized what the green and white markings of the dragon were.

"That's a one-dollar bill." As the dragon flew higher into the air, she added, "Or it used to be."

Chao looked pleased. "My first attempts to harness the energy of this world into my dragons came through the magical potency given by humans to this worthless paper. I favored the most powerful denomination to lend it extra demonic force. I heard on your newscasts the daily discussion of the worth of the American dollar in comparison to others. In classes, too, I often heard the professors speak of the might of the American dollar and its influence for good and evil."

Lizzie backed away from Chao. "I don't think that's exactly what they meant. The power isn't actually in the money."

"No," said Chao, advancing on her. "I realized that when my little creatures failed to flourish. Simply making them out of money gave them the briefest spark of life. But then I found the remarkable Ghost House in Mark Obiyashi."

Mark, who was muttering at his phone, poked his head around the side of his study carrel at the sound of his name. "Oh, hey, Chao, sorry, I'll boot up my computer and get my information into our slides. Lizzie, how would you respond to a phone with an arrow emoji? Does Gizi want me to call her?"

"Mark!" Lizzie exclaimed, backing away from the dozens of tiny paper dragons rising out of Chao's study carrel. "Mark! We should leave now."

"What?" He stood up, looking past the desks to his study partner. "What's happening?"

A swarm of paper dragons now flew around Chao's head and shoulders. He pointed his hand toward Lizzie and Mark, like a man casting a ball or a spell at them. Where he pointed, the paper dragons flew. The green and white dollar dragons were particularly aggressive, darting forward to nip at Lizzie, but also easily distracted into fights with other dragons. Lizzie thought she saw a pair of dollar dragons attack a larger Euro banknote dragon. A sprightly renminbi dragon zipped under the trio to fly at Mark.

"Lizzie?" Mark swatted the Chinese people's money dragon away from his face. He swore as it bit at his wrist, trying for the veins there. "Ow! Stop that." He grabbed the determined dragon with his other hand, crumpling it into a small ball of paper, and throwing it away. "Lizzie, what are these things?"

"Run!" Lizzie grabbed his hand and pulled him into the stacks. The dragons flew after them.

Mark tugged back. "Wait." He lunged for his messenger bag and skateboard. "I'm not leaving these to get stolen."

"Run!" Lizzie repeated, grabbing a book off a nearby shelf to swat away a few more dollar dragons.

Chao growled something between language and an animal's cry. He snatched his slender briefcase off the carrel desk and opened it. Another swarm of tiny currency dragons flew out of the case, coming straight at Mark and Lizzie.

Lizzie hooked one hand in Mark's collar and pulled him after her. Mark hopped on his skateboard and zipped around a corner. From old practice and countless fights with other villains, Lizzie swung herself up and around Mark to tandem ride his board. She locked her hands into his belt loops to hold herself on.

"What's attacking us?" Mark asked, as they barreled around the corner and down the central hallway of the library.

"Money!" hissed Lizzie into Mark's ear. "Why did you pick him for a partner?"

"I didn't pick him. Chao picked me." Mark dodged as a Canadian dollar dragon swooped ahead of the rest and then dive bombed them like an angry Yukon mosquito. "And he said he was studying anthropology. The history of mankind's—"

Lizzie gave him a glare.

"The history of humanity," Mark corrected himself, as they spun around another corner. "Our use of money to move...oh, damn." They reached the end of the bookcases and barreled into the graduate reading room. Long oak tables were centered in the middle of a faux Gothic hall. Green glass shaded lamps were set on top of the tables at intervals of a few feet. It was here students could examine materials brought up from the archives, under the watchful eye of a librarian stationed at the end of the hall.

Lizzie and Mark simultaneously rolled off the skateboard and slid under a long group study table. Luckily, being Saturday morning, this particular section of the library was empty of students. As long as they stayed in the humanities, Lizzie knew, there was little chance of running into innocent bystanders. While there might be some math and science types in another section of the library, no self-respecting literature student was going to appear before noon on a weekend. In fact, most students wouldn't make it to the library until the last possible moment on Sunday night. Too many parties and D&D gatherings on Friday and Saturday nights.

"What was Chao studying?" Lizzie asked, as they slithered under the table, swatting at the more aggressive dollar dragons that flew down to the floor. The bulk of the flock, for want of a better word, seemed to be content to fly up to the ceiling and spiral in the warm drafts created by the library's antiquated heating system.

"How money transfers power from one person to the next. He was a bit obsessed with it. Also cutting out those dragons. He kept doing that in the back of the classroom during all the lectures last week."

"Did you think that was odd?"

"Nah, there's at least two women crocheting in the front of the room, another crafting chainmail at her desk, and then there's the guy who keeps making these creepy dolls."

"Creepy dolls guy?

"Yeah, I was keeping an eye on him. Dolls can go wrong in so many ways."

More paper dragons flew into the room, filling the space between their hiding spot and the door where they had just entered. Luckily the tiny beasts seemed fairly mindless away from Chao. Two Japanese yen dragons turned on a fluttering Peruvian Nuevo Sol. The latter sank beneath their superior fighting powers.

"Seriously, why did you pick Chao?" Lizzie asked.

"Because he liked to do slide presentations. He said so."

"And that didn't tell you he was evil?"

"It was either Chao or the creepy doll guy. Besides, he just transferred into the class. He told me this was his first time in Cobalt City. I was trying to be nice to the new guy."

"That's the price of being a hero." Then a dollar dragon spotted them and dived under the table. The nasty little creature got off a few nips and shreds of its paper claws before they managed to crush it beneath Mark's messenger bag.

Lizzie and Mark crawled to the far end of the study table. Lizzie eyed an empty expanse of the marble floor that formed the lobby. There was a librarian's desk to one side of the massive oak doors, but whoever was supposed to be there must have left. Probably fetching a reference from the basement. Or confiscated Kit Kats from the breakroom.

"We should stop the dragons here, before they escape into the quad."

"Yeah." Mark fussed with his skateboard. "Better than having another worm incident. Oh, did you know worm is another word for dragon in some cultures?"

"Yes." Lizzie poked her head out from under the table to locate the flying swarm of dragons.

"Do you think everything we're learning in college is useless?"

"Not everything." Lizzie ducked back under cover.

Mark rolled over on his back, flat on his board, his head pointed to the opening at the end of the table.

"Tell me when you want a push."

He grunted. As Lizzie watched, Mark's face began to blur and distend, as he became the superhero Ghost House. He looked at her with darkened eyes that reflected the void with tiny sparks of electric blue in their depths. Milky ectoplasm coiled off him like oily smoke. His clothes twitched and rippled as if being plucked by invisible hands. "Ready," Mark said, in a voice that held the echoes of whispers beyond the veil.

Used to his transformation, Lizzie did not flinch. But an involuntary shudder shook her body as she laid hands on Mark's legs. Close contact translated to her senses as a feeling of frost or the chill she would receive by walking near the freezer section of the supermarket. She tried not to think about dead meat.

Gizi once told her that Mark's kisses felt as warm as anyone's. But Gizi probably never kissed him when he looked like this.

"Go!" said Mark, now fully transformed into the superhero Ghost House.

Lizzie shoved, giving the skateboard just an extra flash of her own power, so Mark shot into the center of the lobby in a shower of sparks arcing off the metal axles. A few of the bolder dragons, diving at Mark, caught fire or were crushed under his skateboard wheels. Others became entangled in the nets of ectoplasmic energy he wove around them. Mark flipped up and landed feet first on his skateboard's tail. With the tail of the board on the marble floor, he ran up the rest, spreading his arms wide as he threw off blast after blast of ghostly energy.

Lizzie rolled to the side and sprang from under the table just behind the flock of paper dragons intent on swarming Mark. From the corner of her eye, she saw her own reflection in the long windows lining the reading hall. She was completely manifesting the Electric Girl, her clothing now transformed to her white shirtwaist, long tweed coat, and divided skirt. This was the uniform of her days as the intrepid girl reporter of nineteenth-century Cobalt City. Her hair coiled off her shoulders into the practical braided bun of her past, and her beloved "newsies" cap appeared atop her head. The feather that had once decorated her hat was now as bright as flame, glowing white with the heat of her power.

Lizzie plunged her hands into the swarm of dragons, intent on overwhelming them with jolts of pure electricity. The little creatures clawed and bit, but Lizzie now bled sparks that set their fragile bodies aflame. Little wisps of ash drifted to the floor.

"No!" A roar shook the room.

Lizzie spun around and saw Chao enter the hall. With one smooth leap, he vaulted to the top of the oak reading table and ran down its length. As he ran, he transformed, his body elongating like a snake, his hands outstretched like "the claws of an eagle," Lizzie breathed. And, yes, his nose now appeared very camel-like as the stag horns sprouted from his head.

Chao launched himself directly at Mark. But Lizzie manifested her own wings, shooting like a shower of fireworks from her shoulders, cyan feathers burning with the power of the city. She launched herself at Chao, knocking him away from Mark with a sizzle of electric power.

They rolled across the marble floor, banging against the solid oak furniture and then twisting up to the vaulted ceiling to race across the wooden beams and down again into the diminishing flock of dragons. As Chao swooped and twisted, biting and clawing at Lizzie, she continued to counterpunch. Concentrating on stunning rather than harming, she was hampered by Chao's manifestation of his scales. One blow to his stomach rang off a belly as hard as a turtle. She spun away, shaking her hand and wondering if she had broken any bones.

Chao opened his mouth and roared again, loud enough to rattle the library's windows in their frames. He sprang for Lizzie.

With a push of her electric wings, Lizzie flew over Chao's head and then twisted in mid-air. She reached down with one burning hand and latched onto his bull's ear.

Chao yelled in pain. Lizzie twisted harder, forcing him down to the floor. As he subsided, the last of the paper dragons collapsed in Mark's ectoplasm net.

"I yield! Yield!" Chao was now almost human, all but the twitching ear that Lizzie still pinched in her burning fingers.

Now reduced to his human self, Mark walked up to them. "Not cool, feeding your study partner to your dragons."

Chao bowed his head even further. "I beg your humble pardon. I only meant to find a way to bring greater order to humanity."

Lizzie let her wings fold back into her being. She released Chao's ear, which transformed from its furry bovine shape to a more human look.

"Various people have tried that throughout history," she said. "Imposing order, especially supernatural or superpowered order, never ends well."

"But this world is so messy," Chao complained as he sat up. "It needs order." He rolled away from them. "And the King in Yellow commands!" With a shout, he summoned his remaining paper dragons to him. "Kill!" he cried, pointing at Lizzie and Mark.

"Now really," said a voice from the far end of the hall. "What are you kids doing?" It was the Saturday morning librarian, almost obscured by a huge stack of books in her arms. She thumped the reference books down on her desk.

Distracted by the returning librarian, Chao glanced away. Lizzie let loose the lightning bolt she'd been restraining between her hands. It arced through the air, attracted to Chao like he was a giant lighting rod. As the energy passed through the dragon, he burst into smoke and ash. For a moment, Lizzie glanced a world behind him, a swirling cosmos of chaos that reminded her of her own electrical prison.

Then with a sizzle, the dragon and his paper children were gone.

The librarian glanced up from her desk. "What was that? Are those lights shorting again? The janitor was supposed to fix that."

"Just a light bulb popping," said Lizzie, as Mark grabbed his skateboard and messenger bag from under the table. He stomped one weakly wiggling dollar dragon with relish.

"Those lights need to be replaced someday," said the librarian, turning back to her books. "Oh, did you need help finding something?"

"No, no, we're done here." Lizzie pulled Mark toward the outer door.

The librarian gave a look of disapproval at Mark's skateboard. "No using that in here."

"Of course not," said Mark, as if he hadn't already zipped through several reference sections on his wheels.

Other than a few small piles of ash from disintegrated dragons, the hall looked much as it had before their fight. Cobalt City had learned to build strong, to withstand the clash of titans within its borders.

"Everyone complains about money," said Lizzie to Mark as they left the library. "I guess I understand why Chao thought it would be a good thing to use in his spell. Money is an evil force, and all that."

"Necessary evil. Hard to go back to a barter only system. But order just makes everyone miserable. And anarchy doesn't work either. Everything to the strong and nothing to the weak. He obviously didn't listen to any of the lectures."

Lizzie shrugged. "His loss. That's what college is for. To debate these things. To learn."

Mark's phone beeped again.

"Gizi?"

"Yep. I know this one." Mark flashed her an emoji of a hungry face surrounded by a fork and knife. "She wants a snack break."

"Tell her to come to the coffee stand. I'll make her something special to go with the muffin."

"Won't Hank be there?" Mark asked, as they walked across the campus.

"Yes," said Lizzie with a twinkle in her eye. "Time to open up his mind a little. I think I'll make a double banana chai latte with whipped cream and a cherry on top."

"Does the machine do that?"

"It will after I get through with it," said Lizzie.

If Lizzie Blythe had stayed on her train and disembarked in New York or any other major city in nineteenth-century America, she would have found numerous other young women pounding the pavement in search of a good story. The most famous of these was Nellie Bly.

Born Elizabeth Jane Cochran, Nellie Bly arrived in New York in 1887. She'd already worked as a reporter in Philadelphia and as a foreign correspondent in Mexico. Fast talking her way into Joseph Pulitzer's offices, she first became a celebrity for having herself committed to an insane asylum and exposing the injustices there. In 1888, Nellie literally became a worldwide sensation when she set off to break the fictional record of Jules Verne's Phileas Fogg and prove that a woman could go round the world in less than eighty days.

Nellie made it in seventy-two days, and her feat inspired board games, glassware, and trading cards, all of which I have collected, so Lizzie's look owes a bit to Nellie!

Although Nellie is sometimes mistakenly called the first American female reporter, that title probably belongs to Anne Royall, the "literary wild-cat from the backwoods" who supposedly secured the first presidential interview in the 1820s. Sadly, the tale of her sitting on President Adams' clothes while he was skinny dipping in the Potomac seems to be a later fiction.

Nellie wasn't even the first major woman reporter in New York—Margaret Fuller and Jenny June (Jane Cunningham

Croly), among others, preceded her and had careers worthy of a book or two. But Nellie's exploits, which inspired a variety of other "stunt girls" to be hired by the more sensational newspapers, earned her a lasting place in the history of journalism.

By the start of the twentieth century, there were at least two thousand women reporters writing about every imaginable topic for newspapers across the country.

ACKNOWLEDGMENTS

Cobalt City was invented by Nathan Crowder, who then generously invited a number of other writers to create stories in his world. So a big thank you to Nate, Dawn Vogel (who also edited this book and fixed my very confused timeline), Jeremy Zimmerman, Erik Scott de Bie, and Amanda Cherry for saying on a regular basis: "I have an idea for an anthology!" or "Let's meet for a writing session." Online or in person, these writers rock, and you should check out their Cobalt City stories too.

ABOUT THE AUTHOR

Rosemary Jones writes stories, inspired by all the books that she's checked out of libraries since she was four years old. She still remembers the wonderful public and school librarians who helped her find hundreds and hundreds of good tales—and she's finally forgiven Mrs. M. for handing her John Steinbeck's *Red Pony* when she was nine and telling her that it was a nice horse story like the *Black Stallion* books. Today, she is a card-carrying Friend of the Library and the published author of several novels set in Ed Greenwood's Forgotten Realms with Wizards of the Coast and Arkham Horror with Aconyte, a series of nonfiction books about collectible children's literature, and multiple stories in science fiction, fantasy, and superhero anthologies. To find out what she's currently writing or where she's lurking on social media, check www.rosemaryjones.com.

ABOUT THE ARTIST

Janay Nowlin created the drawings on the cover and in the print version's text using scratchboard. The art was then digitally scanned and manipulated. A graduate of Central's Creative Academy and University of Washington's UX/Visual Interface Design Certificate, Janay works with nonprofits and businesses. More of her illustrations can be seen at janaynowlin.com.